FLEET FEAT

C.P. JAMES

BY C.P. JAMES

The Reassembly Series

Rocket Repo
Trawler Trash
Ship Show
Xeno Xoo
Fleet Feat
Dark Dodgers

The Cytocorp Saga

Dome Six
Into the Burn
Out of the Seam

*If our story doesn't change us,
then we weren't the hero.*

Vinci Books

vinci-books.com

Published by Vinci Books Ltd in 2025

1

Copyright © C.P. James 2023

The author has asserted their moral right to be identified as the author of this work in accordance with the Copyright, Designs and Patents Act 1988.
This work is a work of fiction. Names, characters, places and incidents are the product of the author's imagination or are used fictitiously. Any resemblance to actual persons, living or dead, places and incidents is entirely coincidental.
All rights reserved. No part of this publication may be copied, reproduced, distributed, stored in any retrieval system, or transmitted in any form or by any means, including photocopying, recording, or other electronic or mechanical methods, nor used as a source for any form of machine learning including AI datasets, without the prior written permission of the publisher. The publisher and the author have made every effort to obtain permissions for any third party material used in this book and to comply with copyright law. Any queries in this respect should be brought to the attention of the publisher and any omissions will be corrected in future editions.
A CIP catalogue record for this book is available from the British Library.
Paperback ISBN: 9781036701345

Printed and bound in Great Britain by Clays Ltd, Elcograf S.p.A.

CHAPTER 1
CLONE COLLEGE

He knew he shouldn't, but Geddy Starheart, captain of the New Alliance battle cruiser *Stalwart*, had a favorite clone trainee. Ninety-Two. To be fair to the other two hundred and seventy-seven, their differences weren't that great. And why would they be? They'd been grown in the same lab under the Myadan Xoo, fed the same food, infused with the same sex pheromone, and shown the same uninterrupted stream of graphic Tatiana Semenov-themed content. But the longer they trained, the more daylight opened between them.

Was it wrong to admire a younger, fitter, better-looking, better-trained copy of himself with a positive attitude? Maybe. As far as he knew, Geddy was the only person in the galaxy, and maybe in the history of the universe to be in this situation. There wasn't exactly a playbook.

He liked to sit in one of the ridiculously comfortable chairs on the handling platform, a raised semicircular structure at the front of the hangar and watch the clones train. A lap around the perimeter was precisely a kilometer, and Oz generally made them do ten in the morning and three after training on the simulators. A series of beefy tubular ribs followed the contours of the ceiling and ran down its entire length. Their purpose wasn't only structural, either — each one also served as a duct for re-pressurizing the hangar once the colossal double doors closed. The whole operation took less than five minutes.

The *Stalwart* was one of six heavily armed battle cruisers in the New Alliance fleet, a repository of unused ships jointly designed and built by member planets toward the end of the Ring War eighty years earlier. The conflict in which nearly half the galaxy had been embroiled still influenced politics and economies, generally to their detriment.

Like the *Armstrong*, the gunship Geddy now flew most everywhere, the *Stalwart* was a muscular ship, with a wide beam and conspicuous armaments that encircled her like a belt of badassery. She wasn't fully tukrium-clad like the smaller ships, but to compensate, her Gundrun-designed shields were extremely tough. According to Commander Verveik, leader of both the old and fledgling New Alliance, no weapons of the era could've touched her.

Unfortunately, this was a new era, and their foe, the Zelnads, had technology they didn't even know about, let alone understand.

Aside from the Zelnads' display of power over Gundrun and a mishmash of small arms sold to collectors by the late Sammo Yann, they had precious little intel on their enemy. That needed to change before it no longer mattered. All they knew for certain about the Zelnads was their hunger for tukrium and their abiding desire to destroy Sagacea and end their experiment with civilization. Everything else was designed to hurry along the so-called Reset. Not unlike the cloning operation itself.

The clones were coming around again, so Geddy got up

and leaned over the back of the platform, which looked down on the track. Ninety-Two was out in front as usual.

"Lookin' good, boys. Pick up the pace, Ninety-Two!"

"You heard the Captain!" he barked. "Move it!"

— Why run them so damn much? They're friggin' pilots. They sit, tap little floating screens, and work the controls. Zero cardio.

— *I think it helps keep their minds off you-know-who.*

Eli, his Sagacean companion, was probably right. The clones were developed by the Zelnads and conditioned to have a powerful attraction to his ex, Tatiana, who had also been cloned. Had him and the crew not intervened in their Myadan operation, they would've been distributed throughout the galaxy two-by-two. Their accelerated reproduction would have produced some of the worst humans to ever live, according to the Nads, accelerating the galaxy's decline.

"You should do PT with us sometimes," came Oz's buttery voice from behind him.

He spun around and smiled as his eyes roamed over her lithe body. Training with the clones had chiseled her into a warrior goddess. And boy, did her New Alliance uniform fit. The dark gray coveralls were accented with royal blue piping that tapered from neck to waist, forming a narrow V that her exquisite bosom was trying to turn into a U.

"Are you calling me fat?"

"Of course not. You're just comfortable to lay on."

Indeed, the Alliance food recombinators made it hard to eat healthy. They produced better chips than fruit, and it was starting to show.

Her big yellow eyes darted quickly about the hangar to make sure no one was watching, and she leaned in for a kiss.

When she pulled back, he gave his head a slow shake. "What could a girl like you possibly want with a guy like me?"

— *Y'know, I've been wondering the same thing.*

— You're still here?

— *My transfer didn't come through yet.*

"What's he saying?" Oz asked. "Wait, lemme guess ... did he have the same question?"

He wrinkled his nose incredulously. "How'd you know that?"

"Because I'm an empathic Temerurian woman. Also, your face goes blank for a second when you're listening to him."

"Really? I have a tell?"

"You have a tell." She kissed him again. "Remind me not to play uguinok with you."

"Can I help you with something?"

"No, but you're gonna want to see this."

They each took a chair, and Oz powered up the traffic control panel. She swiped past a few screens and expanded a window that bore the frozen image of Perrel Galway, head of the Intergalactic Justice Commission, and a chyron that read, "IJC Breaks Silence on Myadan Incident."

An electric jolt ran through Geddy. The IJC regularly broadcast its court proceedings, as it had when they were determining the clones' official status, but it almost never offered public commentary. The fallout over the cloning operation under the Myadan Xoo, however, had only intensified during the past two weeks. The pressure to make a statement had apparently reached critical mass.

Oz started the playback. The dark-skinned Eicrean's expression was as grave as his tone.

"As of this morning, the IJC has finished phase one of its investigation into the so-called Myadan Incident. Based on our initial review of the evidence, we have concluded that the operation discovered beneath the Xoo violated myriad intergalactic laws."

"Oh, you don't say," Geddy said with a roll of his eyes.

Galway continued, "Furthermore, a team of scientists from

the University of Tathe on Ornea have evaluated the technology in use at the facility and determined that it exceeds the capacity of all known worlds.

"Taken together with the available evidence and eyewitness accounts, the IJC now believes the so-called Zelnad Nation was responsible for the illegal cloning operation on Myadan."

Geddy sucked in a breath, his jaw hanging open as joy and vindication coursed through him. "Holy shit!"

Oz stopped the playback and smirked, turning to face him. "I've watched it four times. Gives me a lady boner every time."

Geddy cocked an eyebrow. Was that an invitation?

The IJC was the last official intergalactic organization that remained after the collapse of the old Alliance. Not all habitable worlds were members, but the ones that mattered were. A public accusation would carry weight. Heading into the summit, that was very good news.

Unfortunately, most of the galaxy still believed the Nads were a well-meaning technocult. They certainly didn't know they were ancient aliens preparing to take the universe off life support.

Even so, it counted as a big win.

"Whaddya bet Verveik nudged things in the right direction?" Geddy asked.

"He must've. The timing is too perfect."

"You think it'll help the summit?" she asked.

"Can't hurt."

The sudden sound of Denk's voice over the PA gave Geddy a start.

"Captain Starheart and First Officer Nargonis, you're needed on the bridge. Code ... um ... NOW."

The last few words chased across the flight deck loudly enough for Ninety-Two to pause his sim and look up. Geddy gave Oz the same confused expression. The *Stalwart* was parked over the gas giant Sulrinda, not far from the Karrea Ion Storm where thousands of other New Alliance ships were hidden. Nobody was supposed to know they were there.

Well, almost nobody.

The elevator doors opened directly into the bridge. Geddy stepped out to find Denk and Doc standing before the active front screen wearing uneasy looks. Dozens of ships filled it from edge to edge.

"What the hell …?" Geddy muttered.

Denk hurried over as fast as his stubby legs would carry him. He didn't appear panicked, exactly. None of the ships, or even all of them at once, posed any real threat to the *Stalwart*, but he was a bit amped up about it. Doc's emotional amplitude remained flat as ever.

"They just came through fargates! Two or three at a time in different spots!"

Geddy's pace quickened as he approached Doc, studying the ships to determine their origin. He already had an inkling about that. "Are the shields up?"

"Of course, Captain," Doc said. "I do not believe they are aggressive, but it is a fluid situation."

"Sadly, not my preferred kind of fluids." Geddy gave Oz a wink, and she smacked her forehead with her palm.

— *I will give you partial credit for that one.*
— Why partial?
— *This may not be a laughing matter.*
— Actually, I'm pretty sure it is.

"It's a strange lot," continued Denk. "Single-seat fighters, frigates, even a couple light cargo ships. From all over, too. I dunno what to make of 'em."

Geddy squinted at the screen and noted the readout. Makes

and models were all over the map. A handful had UNKNOWN where their transponder data should be. Denk was right — it was a mishmash, but he'd overlooked several important clues. The missing registry was telling, as were the armaments, most of which were aftermarket. Many were as old as the *Fizmo* and just as cobbled together.

Now he knew exactly what this was. In most other circumstances, he'd have been worried that this was some kind of a ballsy shakedown. Now, it brought a smile to his lips.

"If it's an army, it's not much of one," Oz said.

"The same could be said for us," Geddy noted. "Doc was wrong about them being aggressive. They absolutely are. And that's exactly what we need."

"What do you mean?" Denk asked.

A self-satisfied smile opened across Geddy's face. He hoped this would happen but couldn't let himself believe it really would.

"They're pirates, Mr. Junt. Mercs, smugglers, thieves … terrible people. And our new recruits."

CHAPTER 2
ARRR WE FRIENDS?

With the forward half of the *Stalwart's* flight deck cordoned off for pilot training, a pressure curtain activated to seal it before they opened the colossal hangar doors. Until he'd gotten to know the big ship better, Geddy could scarcely believe that a force field could be powerful enough to do that. Now, he had no qualms about standing right next to it as the doors parted and the first of the ships eased through.

The whole crew had gathered to receive the first batch of Geddy's "unsavories." Verveik was working to bring entire governments into the Alliance, but there was another world of fighters out there. People who operated outside the law whose loyalty went to the highest bidder.

"They fight Zelnads with us?" asked the giant lizard, Voprot, in a remarkably complete-ish sentence. He'd been practicing a lot because there wasn't a whole lot else for him to do. Geddy felt badly for him, but he was simply out of his element here. And he missed his girl, Iondra, who was still dealing with the Myadan situation.

"They fight for whoever pays best," Geddy replied. "Right now, that's us."

He'd made the case to Verveik that they couldn't just stand around with their dicks in their hands while diplomacy took its sweet time. The New Alliance needed a Plan B, he said, and Verveik couldn't disagree.

The pirate Queen Tymeri had snatched Oz from his hands back on Verdithea with the intent of extorting money from her royal Temerurian family, which easily could've resulted in her death. But the Nads screwed her over, and he'd taken advantage of her desperation, offering a million-credit advance on a promise of ten million later if she proved her loyalty to the Alliance and agreed, unequivocally, to come when called upon.

She was the perfect choice to put the word out, much to Oz's dismay. But damned if she hadn't held up her end of the bargain so far.

"Is Tymeri with this bunch?" Oz asked, her voice tinged with anger.

"I don't think so," Geddy replied, looking sidelong at her. "You still don't trust her."

Oz's lips formed a line as she shook her head.

"Are we training them to be pilots?" asked Ninety-Two, who had a habit of standing at attention even when he didn't have to. Unless that's what good posture looked like.

"I don't think too many of these guys will see the inside of a Chimera," Geddy noted. "I mean, the cleaning bills alone …"

"You should talk," Oz said.

"Whaddya mean?" Geddy raised his arm to sniff under it. The B.O. was significant. "Yikes. I guess you're right."

"Where's your other uniform?"

"In my closet. This one's softer."

"Because you wear it all the time! How often do you clean it?" Oz asked.

"Clean it?"

"The hyperclean unit in your quarters?"

"Hyperclean unit?"

She took a deep breath to calm her irritation. "Next to the sink? It folds out of the wall?"

This was news to him. "Huh. I thought that was a Murphy bed or something."

Her eyes narrowed as though he'd spoken a language their implants didn't recognize. "A Murphy bed. Like for surprise guests from out of town? What's the matter with you? Also, it's the size of a lunch tray."

"Fair point."

She closed her eyes and took a deep, cleansing breath.

The first ship was Gethenian, teardrop-shaped with one antimatter cannon perched on top and a couple welded-on missile pods in the belly, half empty. A four-by-three array of old Degarret 6D engines stuck grotesquely out the back.

An automated system of lights in the deck directed the ships where to land. One by one, they came through the doors and settled into position. He counted fifty-eight in all, which filled maybe a third of the hangar.

Denk activated the re-pressurization sequence, and the big doors slid shut. Massive fans in the ceiling flooded the hangar with air, a process that took a fraction of the time it took the much smaller *For Sale Make Offer*, which was currently tucked into a corner of the repair bay with the *Penetrator*, his and Eli's sadly naked ship still inside.

"I sure hope you're right about this," Oz cautioned.

"That makes two of us."

"How do we know there aren't any Nads among them?"

"Doc's got the Zelnad detector, and I've got Eli. If they're here, we'll find them."

The hangar finished re-pressurizing, and the orange scrim of the pressure shield dissipated.

Across the group of ships came the sound of hatches hissing open and the whir of creaky motors extending ramps and ladders. Rough characters of all shapes and sizes emerged from their ships like wasps from a nest, stretching and having hushed conversations as they took in their surroundings. At least half carried weapons.

Denk eyed them nervously but drew himself up to his full height — even with Geddy's navel — and pulled his shoulders back as though to brandish the shiny Alliance insignia on his left breast.

"You okay, Lieutenant?" Geddy asked.

"Yeah, it's just ... our last encounter with pirates was pretty scary."

The *Fizmo* was attacked outside Temeruria by a band of pirates that nearly punched their way into the ship. The Star Guard blasted them to bits, thankfully, but they later learned that the ship was one of Tymeri's. As far as Geddy was concerned, that made them even.

"Relax — these guys are on our side."

"We hope," Oz chimed in.

A hulking Gethenian from the first ship swaggered up carrying one of the biggest rifles Geddy had ever seen. Thick yellow tusks wormed out from under his sneering lips, curling into a tight spiral that stretched outward like a bony mustache. Thin patches of greenish brown fur dotted his thickly muscled arms. A leather patch covered his left eye, and the right one sized up Voprot as he pulled up a few meters short of the platform.

The other scoundrels fanned out behind him, deeply wary. The smell of multiple species, long at space and short on money, wafted up Geddy's nostrils.

— Uf. These hombres smell worse than my uniform.

— *Makes me glad I don't have a nose.*

— Any Nads?

— *Not so far.*

Geddy stepped forward to meet the Gethenian, who towered over him. "Welcome to the *Stalwart*." His voice echoed across the hangar. "I'm Captain Starheart, and this here's my crew."

"Aezog," growled the big guy. "Queen Tymeri said you needed men."

Geddy raised his finger, giving Oz some side-eye. "And women. And ... whatever. The Alliance doesn't discriminate based on–"

"Alliance?" sneered the Gethenian. "There is no Alliance."

"These sweet-ass uniforms say otherwise. Well, and the battle cruiser we're standing in. Surely you noticed the insignia."

Doubtful murmurs rippled through the sea of unwashed heathens.

"Gethenia never joined the Alliance. Neither did half our worlds."

"Oh, you mean the *old* Alliance," Geddy said. "This is the *new* Alliance. It's a real branding challenge."

He looked down his wide, flat nose at Geddy. "And who's in charge of this ... *new* Alliance? You?"

"Me? Nah, I'm barely in charge of this ship. That would be Commander Verveik."

"Verveik?!" He threw his head back and laughed. Dozens of others joined in while the younger exchanged confused looks. "Verveik's been dead for decades."

"Don't believe everything you hear," boomed a voice from Geddy's left.

As soon as Verveik heard about their guests, he hopped in one of the Berzerkers and jumped from his command battle cruiser, *Gallant*, to the *Stalwart*. He emerged from the shadows beside the holding platform, looming above even Aezog, who took a couple steps back as though he beheld a ghost.

Verveik let the stunned silence hang in the air for a long moment as he surveyed the motley assembly. "My name is Otaro Verveik, Commander of the Alliance."

The rabble's collective recognition appeared to broaden at the historical cue. However, the Screvari, Ghruk, and Kailorians among them visibly stiffened at mention of the War that cost their forebears so dearly. The Triad planets had every reason to hate the Alliance.

"Whatever you think of me or the Alliance, none of that matters now. We have a bigger problem," Verveik continued.

He climbed the steps onto the platform, each giant footfall rumbled up through Geddy's boots. His thick fingers curled around the top of the railing and leaned over, seemingly locking eyes with all of them at once. The exhortation to fight for the Alliance needed to come from him.

"I'll give it to you straight. The entire galaxy faces extinction. You, me, and every other intelligent being. Despite our histories, we are now united by a common enemy."

"The Zelnads," said Aezog.

Verveik issued a grave nod. More murmurs percolated around the flight deck, louder now.

"Can't hear you in back!" someone shouted.

Verveik expelled an irritated breath through his nose and spoke louder. "The Zelnads want to wipe us all out. The Zelnads created civilization, and now they want to end it. It's happened in other galaxies, and it'll happen in this one unless we fight back."

Verveik lowered his head and looked over the tops of his eyes at the skeptical crowd. He clutched the edge of the railing so tightly Geddy thought he might rip it free like a staple.

"We've all lost people to the Zelnads. But whatever you think they are, you're wrong. They want us gone, and they are legion. They have technology we can't begin to fathom, and we don't know where they are. I won't lie to you — the odds are steep."

The same hush that marked Verveik's initial appearance descended over them again, and he let it hang in the air.

Aezog turned back toward his crew, everyone searching each other's faces for clear agreement or dissent. There were still too many skeptical looks for Geddy's taste, but no one left, either.

As muttered conversations continued, Aezog gave a grunt and brushed past Geddy and the crew en route to the platform. Verveik stepped back from the railing and squared up to him. Aezog only came up to the middle of his chest, but if he was intimidated, he didn't show it at all. Nothing rattled Verveik.

"We don't fight for causes, Commander," he sneered. "We fight for money."

"I don't just need fighters, Gethenian," Verveik growled. "I need your anger. Your spite. I need you to be mean, and underhanded, and nasty as hell. You give me that and your loyalty, and I'll pay you well."

"If it's anger you want, Commander, well ..." Aezog's weird face twisted into a self-satisfied grin around his swirly tusks, and he offered his massive hand. "I'd say you just bought yourself some."

CHAPTER 3
HORDE HOUSE

A week passed, during which time the pirate horde managed not to kill one another or the crew. Not a high bar, but Geddy was trying to temper his expectations. Thus far, they'd cooperated pretty well. Their fifty-eight ships amounted to a hundred sixty-two recruits, and between them and the clones, it was a lot to manage.

Even so, they needed to train more pilots and find support staff who knew their way around a military vessel. Since receiving the batch that Tymeri sent, Geddy and Jel had put out a call on the band of thieves, a narrow set of subspace frequencies used mostly by criminals and various planetary undergrounds. By then, everyone knew that Verveik was rebuilding the Alliance, so that wasn't a secret, but the *Stalwart's* location was still neutral enough that no one would suspect where the rest of the fleet was hidden.

While Doc and Denk taught a large Zelnad 101 session in a corner of the hangar, Geddy accompanied Verveik back up to his Berzerker. A wide set of metal steps led up to the mezzanine level and the secure elevators to the bridge and the much smaller executive hangar where the *Armstrong* was also parked.

In a few days' time, they'd be headed to the summit, a meeting of top brass from Gundrun, the former Triad planets, and maybe Xellara — a collection of worlds known as the Coalition. The so-called Zelnad Nation had played them like a fiddle, saving Gundrun from destruction by a killer asteroid while simultaneously showing the other military powers their withering might. Verveik hoped to convince them of this, and to invite them to join the Alliance.

The prospect of being in a room with the Coalition should've made him nervous, but the outcome wasn't in any serious doubt. Even if they wanted to join the Alliance, they had good reason to fear reprisals from the Nads. Given their firepower, it wasn't unfounded. But they were quickly running out of time. According to Arbizander, Verveik's old chum from Gundrun, the Nads had largely gone dark. Geddy feared they were ramping up for their attack on Sagacea.

"Thanks for coming," Geddy said as they stepped into the executive elevator. It was large enough to fit Verveik's giant body, which was clearly by design. Had it been put into service, the ship would've had to accommodate myriad races. "I knew you'd get them on board."

"They're only hired guns. If we can buy their cooperation, so can the Zelnads."

He had a point, but the Nads didn't need to buy an army. They'd already taken over millions.

"Everything still on track for the summit?"

"Yes. Which reminds me — the Committee is going to meet on a research station over Afolos the day prior."

The elevator opened, dumping them out in front of the hangar door. The two Berzerker gunships sat beside each other. They proceeded through the airlock.

Geddy blinked, surprised by the change in plans. He

thought he had another day. "That's tomorrow. Why's the Committee meeting? And why Afolos?"

The commander paused next to his ship and turned to face Geddy. "Because that's where Parmhar Tardigan set up his scanner prototype. It doesn't work in atmosphere. I asked him brief the Committee on his progress so we all know the score."

Hope surged through Geddy's body. The scanner was still their best shot at locating the Zelnad base. Over the past few decades, the Nads had snatched up most of the galaxy's tukrium in search of its rare variation, shinium, which was the only substance that could pass through the barrier around Sagacea. They needed it to build their weapon, whatever that meant.

The Zelnad called the Metallurgist, who he'd met on Aku, was likely in charge of the refinement. The fact that Geddy and Eli's ship was covered in the stuff was the reason the Nads' wanted it, which was how this all started. If Parmhar's scanner could find a massive concentration of tukrium somewhere, it might point them to the Zelnad base.

"Afolos it is, then," Geddy said.

"Who's coming with you?"

He'd given that some thought. Denk could manage the clones, and Voprot could help keep the pirates in line. That left him, Oz, and Doc. "First Officer Nargonis and Dr. Tardigan."

Verveik pursed his lips and nodded, seemingly satisfied by the response. "Very well. I'll meet you there first thing in the morning."

"Sounds good, Chief. See you tomorrow."

Verveik turned and climbed the ramp into his ship. Meanwhile, Geddy receded through the airlock and opened the hangar doors, watching until he'd zoomed off toward his battle cruiser, *Gallant*, on the other side of the ion storm.

Xellara, ostensibly the Zelnads' closest allies, was the biggest wild card of the summit. In terms of sheer numbers, they had the galaxy's largest army by far. A million ships, maybe more. Fifteen million cybernetically enhanced soldiers. Infinite production capacity. Would they come to the negotiating table? If so, it could change the whole game.

He'd find out soon enough.

CHAPTER 4
WHAT'S IN A NAME?

Geddy curled his fingers under the shallow depression in the wall beside the sink and pulled. The whole panel hinged open from the bottom. A sticker revealed a series of visual instructions for how to properly clean and fold his uniform.

"Huh. Who knew?"

— *People who clean their uniforms.*

He lifted his arm and took a whiff. Recoiling, he let out a low whistle.

— *Did you think she was kidding? I can nearly smell you from in here.*

"How do I not know about this? I must've slept through orientation."

Following the instructions, he placed the uniform inside, secured it with straps, and closed the panel. As promised, a chime indicated the cleaning process had begun.

His underwear, at least, was fresh. That kind of stuff went in the chute and was delivered clean in a couple hours by a laundry bot. Why there weren't bots that did the same for the uniforms, he didn't know.

Morpho slipped through the vent overhead and rolled stickily down the wall beside the cleaning unit. As with the *Fiz*, he'd taken it upon himself to learn his way around the guts of the *Stalwart*, though it didn't need nearly the same level of attention. Otherwise, there wasn't much for him to do.

"Hey, Morph. Haven't seen you since what — Tuesday?"

The black synthetic blob gave what might've been a shrug. Sometimes, Geddy's left shoulder felt a bit naked without him there. Almost like a security blanket.

A knock at the door gave him a start. Figuring it was Oz, he hit the open button without so much as a glance at the little screen.

It was Ninety-Two.

"Oh," Geddy said. "Hi."

"Hello, Morpho," said the young clone, spotting him on the floor. Morpho saluted and hopped up onto the edge of Geddy's sink.

If Ninety-Two was embarrassed to see Geddy in only his underwear and a T-shirt, he didn't betray it. "I am sorry to bother you, sir. Have I interrupted something?"

"Nothing pressing, heh, heh. How can I help you?"

Ninety-Two glanced down the hall, then back at Geddy. "I was hoping we could speak in private."

Geddy stepped back and gestured toward the two chairs in the corner which he'd never used. The officers' rooms on the *Stalwart* were legit, with a bed that could accommodate him and Oz comfortably, and they could testify to its build quality. A wall of closets and cabinets provided more storage than he could ever use, and it had a private shower four times larger than the Ghruk-sized one on the *Fiz*.

"Sure, have a seat." Ninety-Two obliged, sitting bolt upright as usual at the little table. Geddy closed the door and sat in the other chair. "Hey, let me ask you a quick question.

How often do you clean your uniform? A couple times a week?"

"Every day, sir. I take pride in a clean uniform, and the sims make you sweat. Especially the new scenarios Lieutenant Junt programmed."

— How long has it been since I took pride in something?
— *The Penetrator?*
Geddy brooded on that for a second.
— You're talking about the ship, right?
— *Oh, good grief. Yes!*

"What's on your mind, Private?"

Ninety-Two shifted in his seat and folded his hands politely on the table. "Well, sir, I was wondering if you'd heard back from the IJC about giving us legal status."

In fact, Verveik had convinced them to legally recognize the clones, but neither party committed to a timeline, and Geddy hadn't prioritized it. Honestly, it seemed like a hassle if the world might be ending. But it was a fair question, and the boys had certainly earned real names.

"Not yet," he said, which was stretching the truth. "Did you have a name in mind?"

"Honestly, I don't know many names." Ninety-Two's countenance darkened briefly, but then a smile spread across his face. "But I would greatly enjoy choosing one."

"Just don't pick Geddy or Edgar. What about the others?"

His doppelgänger gave a sheepish shrug. "I couldn't say. I don't feel we have that much in common."

Geddy coughed to cover his reflexive laugh. "Tell you what — start looking into a name for yourself. 'Soon as I'm back, I'll poke the IJC and we'll make it official. Sound good?"

Ninety-Two rose excitedly, a broad grin splitting his maddeningly young, smooth face. "That means a lot, sir. Thank you."

Geddy patted the younger man's back. "You're a good pilot and a model soldier, young man. The Alliance is lucky to have you."

His cheeks reddened as he drew himself up, standing at attention. Geddy hated this part of being in the military. All the pomp and circumstance made no sense to him, and neither did the seriousness of the rituals. Oz had taught the clones all that stuff, which suggested her time with the Xellaran resistance was more regimented than he knew.

"You and the lieutenant are excellent instructors, sir."

"Is there anything else?"

His cheeks reddened as he cleared his throat. "Umm …"

"Please speak freely." If he'd ever been as innocent as Ninety-Two, it was when he was a kid. Probably not even then.

"There is a rumor among the men that you … know the woman we were all conditioned to desire. Her genetic parent, anyway."

Now it was Geddy's turn to be embarrassed. The clones were force-fed a combination of pheromones, erotic imagery, and who knew what else to hardwire a powerful sexual response to Tatiana. Apparently, a few had seen them talking through the glass of the enclosure at the Myadan Xoo. At the time, they were just this side of feral and Tati was a medium-rare porterhouse.

"Was there a question in there somewhere?"

The kid's blush deepened. "What was her name? Our programming never identified her."

The purity of the question caught Geddy off-guard. He half expected to be asked what it was like to have carnal knowledge of her, which would've been both awkward and difficult to explain.

"Tatiana," he replied, smiling. "Her name is Tatiana."

"Tatiana … A lovely name." A dreamy look settled on Ninety-Two's face.

A cheery tone sounded next to the sink indicating Geddy's clothes were clean. As much as he hated breaking Ninety-Two's reverie, he needed to get ready.

"Hey, so I was thinking, while I'm at the summit, maybe you could help the lieutenant train up our guests on the bubble drive."

Ninety-Two's face lit up. "I would be honored, sir. Thank you. I won't let you down."

"Carry on, then." The uniform cleaner issued another urgent beep. "I'm gonna go ahead and put on some clothes."

His charge saluted, then turned on his heels and disappeared down the hall. Geddy closed the door and fell against it.

— *You're turning out to be quite the softie.*

"That's your fault, you know."

— *You're welcome.*

Geddy gave ample clearance between the *Armstrong* and the *Stalwart* before engaging the bubble drive, which was now integrated into the ship's navigation system. Zirhof of Zorr's army of nerds and mechanics had outfitted the entire fleet with them and delivered scores of portable units to distribute to volunteers as they showed up. Among his tech's recommendations was that the drive should only be engaged once you were about half a click clear of other ships.

Oz sat beside him in the largely extraneous copilot's chair with Doc in the back. Once they were safely away from the *Stalwart*, Geddy entered the coordinates for Afolos' outer markers and executed the jump. Spacetime briefly warped around them like it wrapped around the inside of an invisible funnel, and the planet materialized on the screen in front of them. Unlike going through a jumpgate, which was hard on the body and made him black out on the way to Old Earth, this was only jarring to the mind. To pack a bag, board a starship, and arrive at your destination one point three parsecs away before your seat warmed up was bonkers.

Afolos was a relatively small planet with thick rivers that crisscrossed the surface like veins beneath leathery skin, collected into a colossal southern ocean. The planet's water bubbled up through deposits of mineral salts, frosting the riverbanks in white and pink and baby blue. Solar-powered desalination plants, plainly visible from space, pumped fresh water into reservoirs, around which its few dozen cities were constructed.

Braaphis was the largest of these, home to the university where Dr. Ehrmut Krezek worked. After helping Geddy and the crew solve Durandia's crypsid problem and later deal with the Myadan situation, he'd returned to continue his work. He'd likely helped arrange their meeting aboard the university's research station, *Anako*.

A thick central disc formed the bulk of the station, tapering at the bottom to a field tether that connected it to the surface like a glowing yellow thread. Tubular rings ran down its length, which maintained the field's integrity. Apparently, this was to shuttle supplies and maybe even suited-up personnel back and forth without the need for ships.

"In terms of continuous use, this is the oldest station in the galaxy," Doc informed them. "Dr. Krezek convinced the university to let Parmhar use it for his scanner."

"Have you spoken with him?" Geddy asked.

"Perhaps two weeks ago. He is encouraged by his progress so far."

The thin ring around the front screen flashed green as they approached the station, indicating a hail. Geddy opened the channel and to his great surprise, was greeted by Dr. Krezek's smiling face.

"Greetings, Captain Starheart. Dr. Tardigan. Ms. Nargonis. It is wonderful to see you again. Commander Verveik, it's an honor."

"Likewise, Dr. Krezek," Verveik said. "The Alliance appreciates your help."

"I trust your journey was uneventful?"

Geddy chuckled. "Seems like we just left. Are you on board?"

"No, no. I'm in my office on Afolos, but I wanted to welcome you personally to the station. The rest of your colleagues are waiting."

"Well, it was good to see you again, Doctor," Geddy said, consulting the display. "Thanks for arranging this."

"Of course, Captain. Dr. Tardigan, Ms. Nargonis, I wish you a fruitful meeting."

He blinked out. Since the station was unfamiliar, Geddy set their approach to auto and leaned back. He felt Oz's eyes on him and turned his head. "What?"

"You're in a suspiciously good mood."

He gave her a warm smile. "Ninety-Two came to see me last night."

"Oh? So, who went down on whom?" she teased.

"Actually, he asked to have a real name."

Oz flared her eyebrows. "Really? What did you say?"

"I told him to pick one he liked, and that we'd get it sorted after the summit. I figure the others will do the same."

The corners of her lips bent downward as she gave a slow nod. "Good for them. We're still gonna need the name tags, though."

He had to laugh. "No shit."

The *Armstrong* lined up with the docking port that jutted from the station and eased itself in. Verveik's ship was already docked on the other side.

A soft shudder passed through the ship as the magnetic

seals engaged around the airlock on the port side. Shortly after, the screen indicated a successful connection. Geddy rose and smoothed his uniform.

"Show time," Geddy said.

CHAPTER 5

DUCKS IN A ROW

Anako station's advanced age was evident from the moment Geddy stepped into the hold. Old ships like the *Fizmo* had a certain smell, like dirty metal and industrial lubricants with a flutter of B.O. *Anako* added a note of reheated food to the mix.

They were greeted by a young Afolosian graduate student. Her wiry, jet-black hair was piled into a careless bun atop her pale green head, and her apparel was closer to pajamas than real clothes. She slurped noodles out of a small bowl as she walked as though it was perfectly normal, which explained the smell of food.

"Sorry to eat in front of you. It's always an afterthought."

"Ah, the life of a graduate student," Doc said knowingly.

After walking through the maze of corridors and offices, they reached a door labeled CONFERENCE 2A.

"This is you," she said with a pleasant smile.

"Thanks." Geddy's eyes briefly met Oz's and Doc's, and he tapped the old control box that opened the door.

The room was larger than he expected, with two long, curved tables that nearly touched at the ends. Zereth-Tinn, the enigmatic Soturian, sat on the end closest to the door with Verveik across from him. He rose and shook Geddy's hand. "Greetings, Captain."

"Hello, Z."

Even though he'd proved his loyalty to the Alliance, Zereth-Tinn always made him a bit uncomfortable. Shooting his half-brother, Sammo Yann, dead in front of him didn't exactly help matters.

Parmhar Tardigan sat to Zereth-Tinn's right, followed by Geddy's good friend, Zirhof. Across from them was Smegmo Eilgars, the Ceonian trillionaire funding the Alliance, the flamboyant Everett Hau from Caloth, and Geddy's old boss from the Double A, Tretiak Bouche. The usual suspects from the Triad and Xellara were also there, none of whom had anything to do with their respective governments. That alone raised their stock with Geddy.

At the far head of the table sat Tatiana, who was dressed down in a businesslike blouse. A surprising choice. Geddy hadn't spoken with her since Myadan. He expected she was still sore that he'd blown up her carefully laid plans with the Xoo's well-heeled board. However, the sudden disappearance of its chair — the Zelnad named Marcourt — left something of a power vacuum which Tatiana had stepped in to fill. She looked up implacably at him.

Geddy greeted the other Committee members, shaking hands with Parmhar and Zirhof as they worked their way toward Tati on the opposite end. She had a two-seat buffer to either side and seemed happy for it. Doc sat beside Zirhof, which meant either Geddy or Oz had to sit next to Tatiana. They moved for the chair next to Doc at the same time, but Oz beat him to it. Tatiana sneered at him as he lowered into the seat. He sent her a wink in return.

— You know what they say about playing with fire.

— *If you can't take the heat, get out of the pool?*

— Something like that.

If Eli had eyes, Geddy would be hearing them roll. It brought a smile to his face.

As ostensible head of the Committee, Tretiak cleared his throat. "Tomorrow, the summit between representatives of the New Alliance and the Coalition of Independent Worlds is taking place on Gundrun. The purpose of today's meeting is to get us all on the same page. He gestured toward the opposite corner of the table. "To start us off, Dr. Parmhar Tardigan is going to update us on the status of his deep-space scanner. Doctor?"

Parmhar, clearly nervous to be in such powerful company, rose and activated a holobar on the table. "Yes, thank you, Mr. Bouche. And thanks once again to Miss Semenov, for her lead investment and of course to Mr. Zirhof and Mr. Eilgars for their continued support."

Tati only folded her elegant fingers expectantly in front of her.

"Well, then," he said, skipping past the awkward beat. "The good news is that the scanner is working as we'd hoped. Initial testing took place in our own galaxy, and as of three days ago, it was able to accurately discern the composition of Old Earth's crust from nearly seventy parsecs away."

The display showed a telescope-like device sending pulses through space at a very distant planet. The readings closely matched those in a second column representing Old Earth's own data.

"But distance isn't the problem," Parmhar continued, his voice growing heavy. "This test was only successful because we know exactly where Old Earth is. Scanning the heavens hoping to find a large quantity of tukrium presents a different challenge."

The animation illustrated how only a tiny pinpoint of space could be scanned at a time. Even with the most powerful processing available, which it had, a complete scan would have to take ten forevers.

"What kind of time are we talking?" Tretiak's tone was clipped.

"There's no telling. We could find what we're looking for tomorrow, or it could take months. Years, even."

— It's like throwing a dart into open space in the hope there's a bullseye somewhere.

— *That's actually a decent simile.*

— Thank you, Eli.

— *You take those, I'll take metaphors.*

— What do you mean, 'take?'

"But it's still a prototype, right?" noted Zereth-Tinn. "Can't it be made to work faster somehow?"

Parmhar's face reddened. "You must understand — I designed this system almost a decade ago to build a database of prospective sites for deep-space mining. It wasn't made to work quickly."

Verveik heaved a sigh, rubbing his face in his hands. "It'll be difficult to prove the Zelnads are amassing an army if we can't find them."

Everett Hau cleared his throat and waited until all eyes were on him. "How much truth do we have to tell? If it's only a matter of time, do we really need to say how *much* time?"

Zereth-Tinn cocked an eyebrow and turned to Verveik. "The spin doctor's got a point."

"It could work, unless they call our bluff." Verveik's eyes drifted to the starfield outside the room's unfortunately narrow window for a long moment.. "We may have no choice. I'd like to sleep on it. Thank you, Doctor."

Parhmar returned an apologetic half-smile, turned off the holobar, and sat back down. Verveik turned toward Tati.

"Miss Semenov, any updates on the Xoo situation?"

She stood and tucked a misbehaving strand of platinum-blond hair behind her ear. A look of confusion settled on Geddy's face. Tatiana Semenov was wearing pants.

— Do my eyes deceive me or did she cover her legs?

— *Maybe she got dressed in the dark.*

"The board knows Marcourt was behind the cloning operation and that he's a Zelnad." Her dropped down to Geddy. "Despite our best efforts, it seems they know nothing of our involvement. Basically, we got lucky."

— Lots of people got lucky that night.

— *Congratulations on not saying that aloud.*

"What are they doing about it?" Tretiak pressed.

"As you know, Myadan is a protectorate of Xellara. This happened right under their noses, and it doesn't look good. The board is pressuring the Xellaran government to publicly condemn the Zelnads for their cloning operation."

"My contacts reported the same thing," agreed the Xellaran businesswoman, Geminaya. "The government must respond, but not before waiting to see if it blows over."

"Will they be at the summit?" Verveik asked.

"If I knew, Commander, I would tell you. Do you have a sense of what Gundrun and the Triad worlds will do?"

Verveik leaned forward and planted his elbows on the table. "I have good reasons to believe Gundrun will join us. As for the others, I'm not hopeful. They still consider the Zelnads the lesser of two evils."

"We can't wait for them," Geddy jumped in. The wheels of diplomacy were maddeningly slow. "We need a real fighting force now."

"We all share your sense of urgency, Captain," Verveik said. "This will be our final overture to them. If they walk away from the table, we'll have to approach the warlords."

Everyone exchanged nervous looks. After the Alliance collapsed, several member planets' governments either toppled altogether or settled into corrupt alliances of their own with violent factions. When Sammo Yann was running weapons, that's where most of them were going. Pirates and mercs could be bought. Warlords only cared about power.

The updates continued. Smegmo was almost single handedly keeping the Alliance afloat financially. Everett Hau had skillfully fanned the Myadan flames into a full-blown scandal that had all fingers pointing at the Nads. And Zirhof's factory was cranking out bubble drive units around the clock.

Finally, it was Geddy's turn to talk about the clones.

"They're fast learners. A select few will captain some of the big ships. We've also received our first volunteers — a fleet of fifty-eight pirate and merc vessels willing to fight for us."

Zirhof gave a pained look. "Pirates and mercenaries? Are we really that desperate for soldiers?"

"They showed up and pledged their loyalty," Geddy replied. "That's good enough for me."

"What's *that* costing me?" Smegmo asked. His tone and look were more serious than Geddy had ever seen. Was he having financial problems? The Ceonian barked a laugh at Geddy's blank look. "Just kidding. I don't care."

"Is there anything else?" asked Verveik. They all looked at each other, but no one spoke. "Very well." He rose, and the others all followed. "We've got a long day at the summit tomorrow. Meeting adjourned."

Verveik had little patience for meetings, which Geddy appreciated. Murmurs of good luck and handshakes traveled around the room while the rest of the Committee filed out.

Tati placed a hand on Geddy's arm as he turned to leave. "Hey Ged, you got a minute?"

He glanced at Oz and saw trust in her eyes. "I'll see you back on the ship." She smirked at Tati, then followed the others out.

"Open or closed?" Geddy pointed at the door.

"It's not important."

He shoved his hands in his pockets, fearing more of her wrath. She'd been playing a long game on Myadan in order to expose the Zelnad operation there, and he'd screwed it up royally. They hadn't spoken since then. They faced each other across the corner of the table where they'd been sitting.

"What's up?"

Her eyes drifted down to the table. "I'm shutting down the salvage platform over Earth 2. I thought you'd want to know."

The question caught him off-guard. He'd expected a tongue lashing, and not the kind that made his toes curl. "Really? When?"

"A week from today."

Tati's father, Ivan, had exclusive rights to collect and sell scrap from Laguna if the situation ever arose. Thanks to the explosion Geddy and Eli inadvertently caused, it had. But based on how long it had taken the bots to chew up the city thus far, he figured the project still had weeks or months to go.

"You can't be done already," Geddy said.

"No, but I'm shutting it down anyway. There's not much left of any value, and the seismic activity is messing with the space elevator."

He remembered all too well riding the cage full of jagged scrap into space while wearing a leaky replica space suit. What he didn't remember, even following the explosion of methane and sulfur dioxide that turned it into The Deuce, was seismic activity. The planet was much older than Old Earth and had already gone through that phase of its evolution.

"Seismic activity? Really?"

"I'm only telling you in case you wanted to be there. I know how sentimental you are."

She had his number there. It was hard not to be sentimental when your mom adored history. "Thanks, but I kinda already said my goodbyes to The Deuce. Besides, I've got the summit, the clones, the crew … I don't know if I can get away."

She smiled pleasantly and nodded as she slipped past him en route to the door. He resisted the urge to sniff the air after her, fearful of the effect it could have.

"I kinda figured. Like I said, it's not important. Say hi to the clones for me."

"They ask about you all the time."

A smirk appeared over her shoulder. "I bet. I'll see you around."

He stopped her as she reached the door. "Hey, are we good?"

"Why wouldn't we be?" She shrugged indifferently. "Good luck at the summit. We'll see you around."

Her heels clicked and clacked as she took off down the hall toward the other side of the station. Their interaction left him feeling cold. Ordinarily, she had the opposite effect.

— *It would mean a lot to her if you came.*

— It meant more to her if *she* did. And me, if I'm being honest.

— *How do I always walk into your juvenile traps?*

Geddy looked back down the hall toward the docking bay, but Tati was already gone.

CHAPTER 6
PUSH FOR THE SUMMIT

The morning of the summit, Geddy and Oz woke early, picking up Doc on their way to the hangar. Not surprisingly, Verveik had already departed from the *Gallant*. The three of them boarded the *Armstrong* and plotted a course for Gundrun. When they were well clear of the *Stalwart*, Geddy pulled up the bubble drive controls. EXECUTE POINT TO POINT? appeared onscreen, and he tapped YES.

He merely blinked, and when he opened his eyes, the empty front screen was filled by Gundrun's shattered moon, Valniuq. That it still retained enough of its mass to remain in orbit was surprising, though physics wasn't exactly his strong suit. After a lifetime of seeing ordinary round planets and moons, its fractured form appeared fake. At least a quarter of it had been shaved off by the asteroid's impact, leaving a colossal concave depression.

The moon itself had no atmosphere or outposts, thank the stars, but it was plainly visible day or night from the ground. Forevermore, its irregular form would serve as a stark reminder of the Zelnad-made cataclysm that almost destroyed the planet.

As the *Armstrong* glided past, Geddy noticed that chunks of the moon had settled into low orbit. The lives of space rocks were strange.

"Damn," Oz said, shaking her head. "Can you imagine the force?"

"You should've seen it through a face shield," Geddy said. Terrible though it was to behold, he'd never forget it. He was lucky to have survived it.

As they skirted past the ruined moon, Gundrun itself came more fully into view. The only larger planets in the galaxy were lifeless gas giants. Over eons, the massive planet's incredible gravity had only drawn more material into its pockmarked surface. As they drew nearer, the khetaka, the massive network of asteroid-pulverizing satellites, came into view, a shell of gray dots.

"I still can't get over how big it is," Oz said. Geddy felt her eyes on him, presumably expecting a juvenile rejoinder, but he was too on edge to dip into his usual well. "Really? Nothing?"

"Too easy. Maybe I've moved beyond dick jokes."

"Since when?"

The ring around the screen flashed green, and he opened the hailing channel. A young, serious-looking Gundrun officer appeared.

"Greetings, *Armstrong*. My name is Lieutenant Kamern from Khetaka Central Command. Please state your business."

Geddy smirked and turned back to look at Verveik. "C'mon, Commander. I kinda want to see the look on his face."

The famous Gundrun straightened in his chair. "I suppose."

Geddy switched the camera to point at Verveik. "Good day, Lieutenant."

As expected, the young officer's face went slack as he immediately recognized the speaker. "Commander Verveik."

He shook his head in disbelief as though he'd seen a specter. "My stars, I thought it was a rumor."

"Commandant Arbizander is expecting us."

The lieutenant's eyes darted back and forth between the camera and his screen. "Of course, but your transponder code … it says that's an Alliance ship."

"That's correct. Now will you kindly open up the khetaka for us?"

He blinked his way out of his starstruck stare. "Yes, sir, of course. Sector 78. Sending you the landing vector."

"Thank you, Lieutenant."

"Welcome home, sir."

About halfway between the Ularac military spaceport and the building they were headed for, Oz paused to adjust her antigravity anklets. They were less chunky than the ones Geddy remembered, but that didn't make them any easier to walk in. It was an odd sensation because Gundrun's powerful gravity still was acting on your body. The anklets artificially reduced the effects, a bit like walking through water.

"Is there a problem?" asked their Gundrun escort, a female whose name Geddy instantly forgot.

"This thing's pinching me," Oz muttered largely to herself, digging her fingers between the cuff and her leg. "That's a little better."

Red dust coated every horizontal surface on the short, industrial-looking buildings of the military compound. The khetaka, the system of asteroid-pulverizing lasers arrayed around the planet, turned thousands of approaching rocks into much smaller ones every day. Those that made it into the lower atmosphere became dust before they reached the ground. You couldn't see it falling, but if you spent enough time outside, your mouth tasted like iron.

As a rule, the Gundrun only moved from one fortified building to the next. But down to the last, the soldiers who were outside stopped in their tracks upon seeing Verveik lumber past. A quick nod was all they got, if that.

— *Not what you'd call a people person, is he?*

— Sixty-six years in the desert will make a guy a little surly.

Two enormous guards stood to either side of the administrative building's equally imposing entrance. It, and most other buildings, were trapezoidal in shape, like a pyramid cut off at the knees. Everything here looked sturdy and overbuilt, not unlike the Gundrun themselves.

Even the guards, who were apparently used to staring straight ahead, did a double take upon seeing Verveik. Again, he breezed past them and into the building with scarcely a look. At least he wasn't in love with his own legend like Tretiak.

"This way," grumbled their chaperone, leading them down a long hallway to the right. It ended at a heavy door that hummed open as they approached.

The room beyond was some kind of command center with a high ceiling and tables arranged in a triangle. Three Gundrun, including Verveik's friend, Arbizander, were seated along one side. At another were representatives from the Triad — Ghruk, Aku, and Kailoria — but not Xellara. Geddy's heart sank.

Verveik lumbered across to the empty table and sat, followed by Geddy, Oz, and Doc. The Gundrun-sized chairs were comically large, though foot rests had been placed underneath them to accommodate their guests' shorter legs. Geddy felt like a kid sitting at the grownups' table.

"Welcome home, Commander," said Arbizander. "And

welcome to our guests from the Coalition. Let's get right to it. We've invited you here to present new information regarding the threat of the so-called Zelnad Nation. Commander Verveik?"

The big man folded his hands on the table. "Thank you, Commandant. First, allow me to address the—"

The door to the chamber slid open with a noisy hiss, interrupting Verveik. A petite Xellaran woman whose very eyes resembled mirrored sunglasses marched stiffly through with military precision, carving a straight line across the tile floor before stopping at the empty chair beside the Kailorian.

"Holy shit," Oz muttered under her breath.

"My thoughts exactly," returned Geddy out of the corner of his mouth.

The woman's translucent metallic eyes met with everyone's for a fraction of a second before she spoke. Geddy got the feeling she was recording them, storing their faces in some database for review later.

"Forgive my tardiness," she said mechanically. "I am Rabhu, senior director of interplanetary affairs. My superiors are interested in these proceedings to the extent they concern our economic interests."

Arbizander got up and gave a tidy bow. "Gundrun welcomes you to the summit, Rabhu. Please have a seat."

She pulled the chair out and eased herself into it like she was being graded. A faint tilt of her head at the others from the Triad was her only greeting, then she stared expectantly at Arbizander. "Shall we continue?"

— *Tati was right. Xellara has to stay in the loop.*
— *Let's hope Verveik has a hidden reserve of charm.*

Verveik got up, towering over the table. "Fine, I'll get right to the point. The Alliance agrees with the IJC that the Zelnads were responsible for the cloning operation on Myadan. We're convinced they caused the near-annihilation of Gundrun."

The Xellaran didn't react at all. The Triad emissaries exchanged incredulous looks.

"We're all aware of the IJC's findings," said the Kailorian. "Only I seem to recall the Zelnads *saving* Gundrun."

"It was all a show," Verveik asserted. "They threw that rock themselves in order to demonstrate their firepower and used the Coalition as an excuse to take our most powerful armies off the table."

"That's quite an accusation," noted the Ghruk. "Surely you have proof."

"We have a recorded confession from the man that delivered the asteroid into Valniuq, along with ample evidence of their efforts to hasten our extinction."

"Such as?" asked the Screvari.

"They've been experimenting with deadly creatures like the ranse. And crypsids, a Durandian species." He paused. "And humans, as you know."

"Hmph. Who could possibly want more humans?" asked the Ghruk, glaring at Geddy.

— *That's a fair question.*

— No argument here.

"The clones were engineered to reproduce — like, a lot — and eventually take over planets," Geddy interjected. "We think it was just a distraction. The Zelnads are ancient aliens from a distant world who aim to reset the universe to its original state."

Once again, Rabhu didn't react at all. Either that, or her face was so full of tech that it couldn't form expressions anymore.

"I'm curious," Verveik said, looking around the group. "What is the current status of your relationship with them? What did they promise you?"

The Screvari visibly tensed before answering. "Tukrium is the Triad's shared heritage. The Zelnads now control almost the entire supply, therefore it benefits us to ally with them."

"I see. And how has it benefited you?"

The Kailorian jumped in, "Aside from supplying us with tukrium, they've given work to countless thousands of our people."

The Ghruk and Screvari nodded in agreement.

— *More like taken them over.*

Geddy and Verveik exchanged a look of grave concern. This was news to both of them.

"Work?" Geddy asked. "What kind of work?"

"The kind we've always done. Mining, refining, and shipbuilding. A new generation, working together like the days of old to rebuild our fleets," said the Ghruk. "We owe the Zelnads our gratitude. Back-room dealings such as this jeopardize that."

"Where is this work taking place?" asked Doc anxiously.

"Throughout the galaxy," the Ghruk replied, as though this should be obvious. "Wherever large deposits of tukrium are found."

"Like Temeruria?" Oz asked.

"I'd imagine so."

"Temeruria would never employ workers from the Triad. Not with native slave labor so readily available," she asserted.

Doc jumped in before they could protest. "Miss Nargonis is right. The northern peoples, the Ophir, have been exploited by the Temerurians for centuries. Your people are not there, I assure you."

"It doesn't matter," answered the Screvari. "They've been given work. Purpose. All we could offer them was despair and hopelessness."

Those seemed to be recurring themes among those who joined the Zelnads. Jeledine's younger sister, Oraisa, was suicidal before she disappeared and was presumed to be a Zelnad now. He'd heard similar stories from others. Could any races in the galaxy feel more hopeless than those in the Triad? Their fall from pride and prosperity had been steep.

A century earlier, the Triad controlled ninety percent of the tukrium trade. Ghruk mined it from an asteroid belt called the Exiod Ring. Kailoria and Aku turned it into ships and weapons. But as the tukrium dwindled, their cooperation devolved into a power struggle that erupted into the Ring War. The Alliance intervened with tragic results, only later to fall apart and leave the Triad in tatters.

Meanwhile, the Zelnads became very good at finding and exploiting tukrium elsewhere in the galaxy, like Temeruria. They introduced novaspheres, enabling true intergalactic travel and enriching themselves beyond reckoning without anyone knowing who and what they really were.

But while Zelnads understood things like spacetime and exotic matter, they still relied greatly on the knowledge of their hosts.

"In other words, the Nads took away thousands of your people, and you're grateful for it?" Geddy asked.

"They were offered a brighter future," said the Kailorian. "Can your Alliance offer the same?"

"It's bullshit," said Geddy. "The Zelnads are using your people to build out their own fleet."

The Screvari's eyes narrowed suspiciously. "Another accusation. So where is this fleet? Have you seen it?"

"Not yet," Verveik answered. "But we're zeroing in on its location as we speak."

"How?"

"By following the tukrium."

"You've been unusually quiet, Arbizander," the Screvari said to the Gundrun. "What say you to these audacious claims?"

Arbizander's eyes slid from him to Verveik and back. "What the Commander said about the asteroid is true. The chances of that rock slipping free of the Elenian Belt and striking our moon are infinitesimal. Our early warning systems would not have missed it otherwise."

"Precisely the point," the Kailorian asserted. "One cannot simply send an asteroid on such a precise collision course. Your confession holds no weight."

"It was jumped there," Verveik asserted. "Using the same Zelnad-made bubble drive as the new Hovensby line."

"Jumped." The Screvari gave a bemused chuckle. "A rock that size? Impossible."

"Not impossible," interjected Rabhu. All heads turned toward her.

"What do you know of it?"

"The Hovensby jump systems are manufactured on Xellara to Zelnad specifications. Given enough power, the bubble could envelop an asteroid."

The Ghruk leaned forward to peer into her metal eyes. "Can't you see this is a desperate ploy to rebuild the murdering Alliance?"

She paused before replying. "We know precious little about the Zelnads. Where they came from, what their true intentions are. Neither do you. Our dealings with them are purely business."

The Ghruk huffed as though insulted, but they couldn't refute this. Plainly, the Nads had taken advantage of their desperation. Convincing the Coalition of that was another story.

Verveik continued, "The New Alliance, however, knows a great deal about the Zelnads. Captain Starheart is right. You are being deceived. What do you have to show for your cooperation with them?"

The men of the Triad bristled and exchanged fraught looks, but said nothing.

"Join the Alliance," Verveik said. "Help us stop them. If we don't, our entire galaxy will fall."

Arbizander stood and gave his jacket a tug. "Gundrun doesn't need to deliberate further. Effective immediately, we are withdrawing from the Coalition of Independent Worlds and joining your New Alliance."

A broad smile split Geddy's face. Having Gundrun on their side was huge. Verveik had played his cards exactly right. The Triad men appeared shocked by this and more than a little troubled.

"Then it is Gundrun that is being deceived," sneered the Ghruk, his expression hardening. "Resurrecting a dead association of warmongering zealots is beneath you. I urge you to reconsider."

"And I you," said Arbizander.

Rabhu abruptly stood and gave curt bows to Verveik and the others. "Xellara thanks you, Commander, for the information. Good day to you all."

As her shoes clicked across the floor, the angry Ghruk stood as well, followed by the others. "Ghruk is unmoved by your claims. Your invitation is rejected."

The Screvari and the Kailorian seemed less certain but nonetheless rose themselves.

"Aku knows what the Alliance really stands for," the Screvari said. "We will remain with the Coalition."

"Your evidence of this supposed Zelnad threat is flimsy at best," said the Kailorian. "Then perhaps we will have more to discuss."

The three men made their way toward the door, and all anyone could do was watch them go.

CHAPTER 7
TRIAD YOU'LL LIKE IT

After leaving the military building, they were escorted back to the spaceport and immediately cleared for takeoff. The trip from there to the inner markers of the khetaka took perhaps fifteen minutes, during which Verveik hadn't spoken. The front screen flashed to indicate the hail incoming from Khetaka Central Command as they neared the protective sphere.

Geddy turned to face the stoic Commander. "You want to request our departure vector? Make some other guy's day?"

"No, thank you, Captain. I've got a lot on my mind."

His eyebrows arched at Oz, and he put the hail through. It was an older man this time, perhaps not much younger than Verveik himself. "Greetings, *Armstrong*. I trust you enjoyed your time on Gundrun."

"You might say things got kinda heavy," Geddy managed with a weak smile.

"Ah, a gravity joke. Never heard one of those before. Sending your exit vector now. Remember to watch your velocity."

"Thanks." He cut the feed.

The outcome was disappointing though not unexpected. *And* Xellara actually came to the table, which was encouraging.

— Should I say something?

— *Ask him what next steps are. That should reveal his state of mind.*

Geddy locked in the vector, set the ship to a half burn, and spun around in his chair. "So, chief ... what happens now?"

"When the time comes, Gundrun will fight at our side. Until then, we keep training new recruits as best we can."

The ship passed between a diamond-shaped gap between the powerful lasers of the khetaka, and Geddy slowly accelerated. He'd jump back once he cleared the outer marker.

"Speaking of time, where the hell's Jeledine?" Oz asked. "We should've heard from her by now."

He didn't make a habit of worrying about Jel. She could handle herself just fine. Still, she was a full week overdue and hadn't been in contact. Three weeks earlier, she'd left to find the mysterious Lestiko, a Basoan who supposedly understood Zelnad tech because he used to be one. That phrase, "used to," was critically important. If it was true, they needed to understand how he escaped their control and recruit him to their cause.

"I'll give her three more days," Geddy said. "If we don't hear from her by then, you and I'll go find her."

Oz appeared to think this was a reasonable suggestion. EXECUTE POINT TO POINT? appeared onscreen, and he tapped YES.

In a snap, space deformed and reformed around them, and relief flooded his body when he saw the *Stalwart* was exactly where he left it. Only now it was surrounded by at least two hundred ships. Most were older Screvari Scythe GL-7s, but he spotted more than a few Kailorian Starstrikes and Ghruk Rippers. Eighty years ago, it would've looked like a precursor to a great battle. Now, it filled him with nostalgia.

"What the hell is this?" Verveik growled. "A classic ship show?"

"New Alliance," Geddy said, "meet the New Triad."

The Screvari ship that followed the *Armstrong* into the hangar was familiar to Geddy, which was how he knew they weren't a threat. It belonged to his old friend, Balzac, who he hadn't seen since their fateful trip to Aku. That was where he'd learned that the Zelnad called the Metallurgist had stripped his beloved *Penetrator* of all its shinium save for the small piece he kept in his closet like some pathetic souvenir. He hadn't looked at it since moving it from the *Fizmo* into his quarters.

"How do you know this Screvari?" Verveik asked.

"We did some business together when I worked at the Double A," Geddy said. "He's got no love for the government, I can promise you that."

"You're leaving out the part where he knowingly led you into a trap," Oz reminded him.

"He didn't have a choice. They would've exposed his counterfeit weapons operation."

"Sounds like a real solid individual," Verveik said.

"He also bought our entire cargo hold full of Old Earth junk and saved us from destitution. As far as I'm concerned, we're square."

Balzac's people were former shipbuilders and artisans who reverse-engineered certain Zelnad weapons and sold them as authentic on the black market. They were anti-government and anti-Zelnad. It stood to reason that others on Kailoria and Ghruk felt similarly, especially being three generations removed from the Ring War.

As heartening as it was to see more recruits, it might quickly become a monster. He'd expected a slow trickle of volunteers at best. What were they going to do with all these people? Building a whole new interplanetary organization from scratch, as it turned out, was complicated.

Since the doors to the main hangar were already open, Geddy decided to land the *Armstrong* there instead of its usual spot in the executive hangar. It settled onto its landing pad beside the doors, which had already begun to close. Balzac's ship took the spot next to it. They were running out of room. If this bunch was here for the long haul, they'd need to put them on another ship. Perhaps even one under Balzac's command.

"Let's hear what he has to say," Geddy said to Verveik.

The big man mumbled an incoherent reply as the hangar finished re-pressurizing. Geddy opened the ramp and walked down, then waited for the others to do likewise. By the time they were all out, Balzac was striding toward them.

"Geddy Starheart. Why am I not surprised?"

They shook hands. Screvari weren't exactly huggers. "Hey, ball sack. Have you been tanning?" He gestured toward Doc and Oz as they came up beside him. "You remember Oz and Dr. Tardigan."

"How could I forget?" He nodded a greeting to both of them.

Verveik's heavy footsteps approached, and Balzac's eyes drifted up to him with nearly the same disbelief as the pirates, younger Gundrun, and anyone else who'd grown up believing he was dead.

"I didn't believe it. Even now, I barely can," he muttered, giving his head a slow shake. "Hello, Commander."

"Mr. Balzac, welcome to the *Stalwart*."

"It's an honor to meet you."

Verveik's face registered surprise. "A rare thing to hear from a Screvari."

"As far as I'm concerned, my father's resentments died with him," Balzac said, which seemed to please Verveik.

Geddy heaved a sigh. "I wish your leaders felt similarly. We haven't had any luck bringing them into the Alliance."

Balzac seethed, shaking his head. "Cowards, every last one. They're afraid of what the Zelnads would do."

"Gundrun wasn't," Oz said.

His eyes widened, and he came dangerously close to smiling. "Gundrun's leaving the Coalition? Interesting ..."

"Indeed. What can we do for you, Mr. Balzac?" Verveik asked, a bit impatiently.

"I heard you needed people. Here we are."

Geddy nodded toward the pirates scattered around the forward part of the hangar. "They got the same memo."

"Guess things are tough all over," Balzac said.

"Apart from pilots and crews, we need people for just about every job on a starship that an AI can't do."

He held out his pale gray hands as though that suited him. "The Circle ran us out of the tunnels. We were on borrowed time anyway. But between us, we've got former soldiers, engineers, mechanics — pretty much whatever you need."

"Sorry to hear it, but we're sure grateful for the help. I understand you know their technology," Verveik said.

"The Z's?" Balzac asked. "Sure, to a point. But they've got a power source we don't understand."

Geddy and Verveik exchanged concerned looks.

"What do you mean, you don't understand it?" Doc asked.

"It's more powerful than anything we have. Like it's stored in the weapon itself. We just don't have instruments to study it. We can re-create the guts, but without that power, it's just not the same."

"Interesting ..." Doc said. "I look forward to hearing more."

"Sure thing," Balzac said. "But hey, it's been a long trip. Could you point me to a bathroom?"

CHAPTER 8
ARE YOU JELLIN'?

Jeledine returned three days after they returned from the Gundrun summit, and she looked tired. Everyone did after a long trip, but she hadn't been in space very long. In fact, thanks to the bubble drive, she'd barely needed to spend any time in her ship at all. Even so, her ordinarily lustrous, silky white hair appeared dull and dirty. Her clothes were sweat-stained and ragged as though she'd worn them in a jungle marathon.

The whole crew was there to receive her. She decided to forestall the shower she so desperately wanted until she recounted her journey. The officer's lounge aboard the *Stalwart* was roomy and well-equipped, with seating for twenty senior officers. It had a generous kitchen, a small theater, and even a bar, though nothing was stocked except the very basics.

— *Well, this should be a good story.*

"First off," Geddy said. "Why didn't you call in?"

"I tried, but all their intergalactic comm frequencies were upgraded to GD15."

"Let's pretend I don't know what that means."

"It's state of the art," Jel said. "And controlled by the

government. No private bandwidth. I would've had to check in from a public station."

"Which was monitored," Oz said knowingly.

Geddy waved off the question. "Doesn't matter. What did you find out about Lestiko?"

Jeladine took a long pull of her water, wiping the excess carelessly on her sleeve. "I think he's on Basoa. And I'm pretty sure he's a local."

Geddy and Oz exchanged a look of mutual relief, though neither ever seriously doubted this. "You think? You're pretty sure?" he asked. "But you were there for–"

She wagged a warning finger in his face. "Don't start with me, Geddy. I've had a shitty few weeks. You ever been to Basoa?"

"A couple times. Never for more than a day. Why?"

"They're not what you'd call helpful."

Geddy could have told her that. Basoans made Verveik look like a charm-school valedictorian. They were grotesque, often corpulent humanoids whose toad-like brown-green skin bore an oily sheen evolved to repel the planet's voracious insects. Whatever the substance was, it was foul-smelling to the point of distraction. They were openly disdainful of outsiders, quick to anger, and completely untrustworthy.

However, their engineering prowess was second to none. Electrical, materials, mechanical — if it was Basoan-made, it was dependable and elegant. Wealthy governments were frequent consumers of Basoan tech. If a city needed a major bridge built or a new network designed, that's where they went.

Indeed, his own experiences there hadn't been great. If memory served, he'd gotten in a fight with the personal bodyguard of the collector he was delivering to over the terms of the deal. Geddy put a smoking hole in his shoulder with the PDQ.

"Yeah, so what happened?"

Jel had people everywhere. People who could get her things like access or schedules. People with connections or who owed her favors. She knew which wheels to grease when, and he'd never once seen her fail. Maybe that's why the defeated look on her face was so disconcerting.

"I spent a few days asking around, making sure people knew I had money to trade for information. Nobody heard of anyone named Lestiko. By then, it was pretty clear he wasn't in the city, so I decided to widen the search. Trouble is, vehicles without Basoan registry can't leave the city limits, so I had to hire a very expensive pilot to take me. I didn't know anyone out there, so I was basically going door to door asking if anyone had heard of this guy. It's pretty, y'know, the Basoan countryside. Not what you'd think.

"Anyway, a week and a half later, I finally got a break. The pilot stopped at his cousin's farm to look at some issue with his irrigation system. Only these bumpkins aren't engineers, they're farmers. It was an easy fix, and once I got it working, he warmed up to me.

"Anyway, we get to talking, and I tell the farmer who I'm looking for. He *had* heard of Lestiko. Said he's some kind of shaman who lives out in this desert they call the Empty. I'm like, 'Great, let's go.' But the pilot refused. I offered him more money. Still no dice. I got all the way to a *million credits*. He didn't budge."

"What was he afraid of?" Oz asked.

"I dunno. He just said it's too dangerous, it's too dangerous."

"What if we ignore the approach protocols and head straight for it?" Geddy asked. "The *Armstrong's* sensors could probably deep-scan the whole area and get out before they even knew we were there."

Jel gave her head an emphatic shake. "And cause an

intergalactic incident involving the Alliance? Now? Verveik would kill you himself."

"Did he say how far it was to get to Lestiko?" Oz asked.

Jel shook her head. "Honestly, I don't think he even meant to tell me as much as he did."

Like small exterior parts on the *Fiz*, their options for dealing with the Nads were falling away. Tymeri had no reason to lie about this Lestiko character's supposed "breakthrough." And if it was true — if he'd somehow managed to get the better of the Zelnad squatting in his skull — then it could be a game-changer. If there was some kind of treatment or technology that could enable a host to retake control, then there was a path to defeating them.

One way or another, they had to find Lestiko.

"How good are Basoan scanners?" Denk asked Jel.

"The kind that detect unauthorized atmospheric entry?" She shrugged and pursed her lips, tilting her head from side to side as she searched her formidable memory. "Near as I could tell, the nodes are pretty standard ADS semi-directional. Nothing too hardcore. Ten-thousand meter ceiling, maybe a five-hundred meter floor. Why?"

"Well, just playin' off what Cap said, I think the *Armstrong's* stealth mode could slip by ADS, no problem."

"Sure, but the drive signature would light it up," Jel countered.

"Not if it was turned off." Geddy grinned like the Cheshire Cat.

Oz leveled her big yellow eyes at him and squinted. "Say what?"

"Back on Old Earth, they used these space shuttles to launch satellites into orbit."

Her eyes popped open again, glinting with recognition. "Like the *Challenger*."

The pleasure of her recollection spread warmth through

Geddy's chest. They'd talked about the space program when they were at the Jet Propulsion Laboratory months earlier.

"That's exactly right. Well, anyway, the shuttle's return to Earth was basically a controlled fall. No thrusters, no nothing. Just standard aircraft controls and gravity."

"The drive powers all the ship's systems." Concern darkened Denk's beady eyes.

"But defense and life-support systems can run on aux power," Geddy excitedly reminded him. "Including stealth. We'd need to, you know, power them up after we've dropped below the floor but before we barrel into the ground at a few thousand kilometers per hour. Just like I did at the bottom of–"

"Suicide Plunge at Ponley Point?" Jel finished sarcastically. "It'd be great to hear about that again."

— Do I really talk about Ponley that much?

— *Let's say it's a greatest hit.*

"Captain," Doc said with a clearing shake of his head. "Are you suggesting dropping into Basoa's atmosphere — sovereign territory — in a cloaked Alliance ship that will only have five hundred meters in which to arrest its fall?"

It might not be the best plan, but it was the only one they had.

"Well, when you put it like that it sounds reckless."

CHAPTER 9
ALL ABOUT THAT BASOA

As viewed through the front screen of the *Armstrong*, Basoa had a pronounced bulge at its equator and was speckled with dazzling colors. Most of the terrain was pleasingly varied and the climate temperate. Were it not for its unpleasant inhabitants, it might have been as much a vacation spot as Eicreon or Temeruria. Geddy didn't notice that sort of thing when he was working for Tretiak, but he did now. Maybe it was because some part of him knew the end could be near.

Given the influx of volunteers and the battle exercises Verveik wanted to conduct with Gundrun, only Doc, Morph, and Jel accompanied Geddy to Basoa. If this so-called Empty was as dangerous as the pilot indicated, there was no sense in putting the whole crew at risk.

"Basoa is actually quite unique among exoplanets," Doc said as the green, tan, blue, and white marble dangled in front of them. "It rotated much more quickly in the time of its formation than it does now, hence its ovoid shape. In fact, its days are quite long. There are many other unusual properties, of course, which I'd be happy to expand upon."

"What do you know about this 'Empty' Jel was talking about?" Geddy asked.

The question delighted him. "Ah, yes. The Empty is a colloquial term for an arid region approximately one point two million square kilometers in size. The surrounding mountains create a high-pressure bubble around it, preventing the formation of rain clouds. The region only receives a few centimeters per year of moisture."

"Other than that, what's dangerous about it?" Geddy asked.

"That, Captain, is an interesting question. I do not know, but Jeledine's account certainly invites speculation."

"The farmer said something about rumbling and lights," Jel piped up from her seat in the rear. "I think it's got something to do with Lestiko."

"I've really gotta meet this cat. Speaking of which, Jel, where's the nearest ADS installation? I wanna drop in behind a mountain if we can."

Jel swiped through screens on her tablet until she found a scan of ground-based signals, which she threw to the front screen. The planet's surface lit up with dozens of gently pulsing concentric rings in a rainbow of colors.

"So, this is the whole network. Now lemme filter for ADS only …"

A few taps on her holoscreen and the number of signals shrank by more than half. Atmospheric defense systems were common on planets with valuable IP like theirs. Keeping tabs on who or what was coming into their airspace was smart business. However, not many dictated entry and landing points. Basoa was among them.

"Cherie," Geddy called out to the ship's AI. "Highlight the area called the Empty and overlay topo."

The planet on the screen rotated so the Empty was in the middle, then overlaid it in light green. Geddy hoped to spot a gap in the ADS coverage, but there were none — not where he needed them to be, anyhow. Still, the topographic data indicated that a three-thousand meter mountain stood between them and the installation to the northeast. That would buy them at least another five hundred meters, maybe more, in which to stop without being detected.

— Is this a dumb idea?

— *Risky, but not dumb. Of course, the bar for dumb ideas is quite high now. Or low, depending how you look at it.*

"Cherie, any settlements in the Empty?" he asked.

"The area is uninhabited," cooed the female voice. "The ruins of an ancient prison colony can be found in the northwest."

Cherie enlarged the Empty and panned right to another highlighted area at the base of a mountain. However, nothing seemed to indicate ruins.

"I don't see anything."

"Historical records indicate the colony was carved into a cliffside," Cherie explained. "Satellite imagery cannot discern it."

"How far from our LZ to the colony?" Jel asked.

"Approximately four hundred and twenty kilometers."

In anticipation of this, they'd brought an Alliance skim-rover. The battery-powered vehicle fit perfectly in the *Armstrong's* cargo hold and was designed for all-purpose ground transportation, either in gravity or zero G. It had six seats and could operate as a hovercraft or with tracks depending on the need. The distance was comfortably inside its operating range.

Geddy leaned back in his seat. "All right, so we drop in behind the mountain, fire up the engines once we're below the scanner floor, and get to these ruins."

"If Lestiko is in the Empty, the ruins are the most likely place," Doc said in agreement. "The colony's location has tactical advantages and must once have been near a source of water. It would not surprise me if it was a prison without bars, offering only the opportunity to survive. Crossing the desert or the mountains would have been impossible."

Geddy turned to look at Jel, who still looked skeptical. "That's good enough for me, but you get a vote, too."

She rolled her eyes. "Obviously, we're doing this."

He smiled. "That's what I hoped you'd say."

Geddy's only real experience flying the *Armstrong* in atmosphere was landing on Stemir back when he and Jel were looking for Oz. That had been mildly complicated by some pretty significant winds, but otherwise it was fairly straightforward thanks to the ship's sophisticated avionics and pilot-assist features. Unfortunately, none of that stuff would be available without the engines. It wouldn't be dead-stick, exactly, but it would be close.

Doc double-checked Cherie's recommended approach angle and her conservative range for firing the engines. She figured it would take at least a thousand meters to reach a safe landing velocity after accounting for wind resistance. That only gave him a very small window in which to flip the ship around and fire the thrusters. The moment he did, it would be spectacularly unstable.

Back when he'd done the same thing at Ponley Point, it was hard to keep the *Dom* upright as he slowed. But that was in the stillness of the volcano. Now, it would be with a much larger ship and with the potential for crosswinds.

As the time for insertion approached, Geddy found himself second-guessing the plan. They could still try to find another pilot willing to bring them and the skimrover near the Empty. But that would take days, and it risked tipping off the Basoan government that a bunch of yahoos were traveling into a region that everyone else fastidiously avoided. He could practically see Verveik blow his top.

It would raise too many questions and take too long. Not his style, and they didn't have the time.

Cherie's approach vector had him entering the atmosphere about four thousand kilometers west of the LZ. To be safe, he'd kill the engines at ten thousand meters, leaving a very long glide toward the mountain ridge to the northeast. As soon as they were comfortably below the floor, he would flip it around and give her hell, using the tiny positioning thrusters to keep the ship upright.

He was *Geddy Muthafuckin' Starheart*, still the best pilot he knew. He'd pulled stunts in the cockpit of a starship that even he couldn't believe. He'd raw-dogged more entries than a frat president, and he'd beaten a repeat champion at Ponley flying an antique ship. But most of that had been done alone or under familiar conditions. Nothing about this was familiar, and he was responsible for the crew. The sweat that under his bushy eyebrows spread to his forehead, his armpits, his crotch.

— Am I really this nervous?
— *Apparently. How is that sitting with you?*
— It sucks.
— *Well, try not to die. Remember, we are–*
— Bound together. I know.

The *Armstrong* entered the green tube of the approach vector about a hundred kilometers outside the markers, beyond which traffic wasn't logged.

He took a deep breath and let it out in a long, thin stream. "All right, gang, now would be a good time to cinch up those restraints."

"How rough is this gonna get?" Jel asked.

He consulted the atmospheric data along the vector. Stratospheric crosswinds were pushing forty kilometers per hour. Not terrible, but they'd be a factor. He was far more worried about the inversion maneuver.

"We're gonna shake like a paint can," he said. "Engaging stealth."

— All right, pal. Hope to see you on the other side.
— *Your fate is my fate.*
— And maybe everyone else's.

CHAPTER 10
JUST DROPPING IN

At ten thousand meters above Basoa, Geddy killed the *Armstrong's* engines. A jarring silence followed.

"Warning," Cherie intoned. "Without thrust, flight control will be difficult. Are you certain you want to keep emergency protocols disabled?"

"Thanks for the tip on flying, Cherie. I only need you for the final landing sequence."

They were accelerating faster — *much* faster — than he'd envisioned. He only had the backup-powered instruments to go by, and a thick layer of clouds obscured the ground. The ship's descent through the upper atmosphere was so buttery smooth that it felt more like floating than it did screaming toward Basoa at nearly two thousand kilometers per hour.

"You are doing beautifully, Captain," Doc said.

Once again, the *Armstrong's* flyability impressed him. The rigidity of the airframe combined with its weight and aerodynamics had thus far made him wonder if his hand-wringing had been for nothing.

"Altitude five thousand meters," Cherie said. "Immediate deceleration recommended."

"Stay out of it, Cherie. Just warn me when we get to–" They broke through the clouds, and the sight of the mountain stole his voice. It was snow-capped and thick with trees. Absolutely beautiful.

"Three thousand meters," said Cherie. "Strong crosswinds detected."

No sooner had Geddy's grip tightened on the controls than the wind slammed into them. Apparently, the hot, high-pressure bubble over the Empty held a jet stream aloft over the surrounding mountains. The ship, which had been rock-steady, lurched suddenly to the right. The merest tap on the stick sent it yawing the other way. He righted it before it turned into an uncontrollable spin.

On his right shoulder, Morpho had compressed himself into a tiny, shaking ball, and he was pretty much indestructible. Not a great sign.

The best way to invert was to pitch her nose-up and spill some velocity first. His eyes slid over to the altitude. Two thousand meters. Almost showtime.

The crosswinds over the Empty disappeared as quickly as they came, and the air smoothed out.

"Here we go."

"Fifteen hundred meters," Cherie warned.

Geddy's middle finger gave the stick a tap, and the ship pitched upward. The moment he did, it shuddered so violently that the front display became a complete blur. G forces shook his cerebrospinal fluid like a beer can.

— *Hurry, Geddy. I can feel you losing consciousness.*

"One thousand meters," said Cherie. "Ground impact in five, four …"

One more twitch, and the ship fully inverted. It took every ounce of strength to reach the thruster lever, a reddish smear on his vision. He felt his fingers close around the handle and he shoved it forward.

The forces on his back squeezed the air from his lungs as the engines fired, pushing against gravity with everything she had.

"Two hundred fifty meters," Cherie said, her voice increasingly distant. "Final landing sequence activated."

His vision had already gone black as he fought to retain consciousness. Had he waited too long to invert? Would a bloom of fiery hell on his back be the last thing he ever felt?

The force of an impact traveled up through his bones, and he was certain the heat of an explosion would follow. But it was only the rear skids slamming into the ground. The nose began to drop, now cradled by the landing jets, and it settled onto the ground.

"Landing sequence complete," Cherie said.

Geddy's limbs refused to move, and the pinpoint of light at the center of his vision remained fixed like a lone star. Every joint ached like he'd endured ten novasphere jumps. The whine of the engines as they shut down came to him as though through water, dreamy and indistinct.

Something sticky smacked his right cheek, sending his head lolling to the side. Then it slapped the left like a ribbon of half-cooked pappardelle.

Morpho.

— *Geddy, can you hear me?*

Hearing Eli could only mean one of two things. Either he was still alive or they'd both merged with the infinite.

— Yes.

— *We made it. Good show.*

At last, the pinpoint in space widened and separated into two expanding apertures that filled with white light.

"Captain, Jeledine, are you okay?" asked a man's voice, calm and even. Doc.

Geddy opened his jaw but only managed an "Unnnnh."

Jel said, "Everything hurts."

"That is because your vascular system is expanding. Your bodily fluids are being re-dispersed."

As Geddy's vision widened further, he could only see crusty white sand, or maybe salt, extending to the horizon. The shadow of the mountain stretched out ahead of them.

"Why do you seem fine?" Jel asked Doc.

"Ornean physiology is uniquely able to handle high G-forces."

"Cherie," Geddy muttered as pins and needles spread through his extremities. "How's my ship?"

"All systems nominal. Impact to rear skids exceeded recommended operating range by two hundred and sixteen percent."

Following a sharp inhalation, a surge of oxygen flooded his brain. He sank back in his seat and let out a long breath.

"Anything on the scopes, Cherie?"

"Negative."

It took a solid thirty minutes for Geddy and Jel to feel steady on their feet, during which time he watched the scopes for signs that Basoa had scrambled ships to their position. But none came, and he could finally let himself believe that they'd gotten away with it.

The next thing was to prepare the skimrover. Most of their supplies had already been loaded before on the *Stalwart*. It was 45C in the shade with seven percent humidity, which was borderline for needing suits, but for now he only wanted to feel the wind in his hair. Other than Gundrun, which barely counted, he hadn't been outside since Myadan.

A blast of hot, intensely dry air hit them as Geddy opened the cargo hold door.

"Look." Jel pointed behind the ship.

Geddy turned around to see a wide crater behind them where the full-blast engines had carved an enormous glass bowl out of the desert, the ground pushed up along the edges where the sand had melted. At least Cherie had the good sense not to land in it. But it was close enough that the edge of the ramp fell inside it. He thought about moving the ship forward so it would be easier to back out the skimrover, but now that they'd made it to the surface undetected, he was loath to power up the engines again until it was time to skedaddle. Besides, if the vehicle couldn't make its way out of a shallow crater, they'd have bigger problems.

Mostly, Geddy looked forward to opening it up with nothing between him and his destination but an ocean of crusty sand. In space, you could approach light speed and hardly know it. But on ground, even a couple hundred kilometers per hour was exhilarating beyond compare. He never felt more alive than when his hair was pinned back by the wind.

Geddy climbed into the driver's seat and powered it up, Morpho on his shoulder, as usual. Jel took the seat next to him, and climbed in back while Hughey floated beside her. It was a longish ride, made more so by the need to approach carefully. Basoans had their peccadilloes, but they didn't bullshit you. If the farmer said it was dangerous out here, then it was. This Lestiko cat had to be taken seriously.

He turned to Jel and Doc, making eye contact with both of them in turn. "Last call. Once we roll out, we've only got what's on the rig. We got everything we need? Water, supplies, weapons?"

"Made a list and Doc checked it twice," Jel replied, nodding.

"We are as well-supplied as we can be, Captain," Doc said.

Geddy gave them a tight nod, then casually opened the little storage compartment between the seats and withdrew a silky black scarf. An absolutely essential accessory that came with the dress Oz wore at the IASS gala. She'd sent it along as a stern reminder to come back to her in one piece. Beneath it was a pair of sunglasses he'd pilfered from the Myadan Xoo's gift shop right before the first wave of IJC investigators swooped in.

The funny thing was, he actually felt guilty about it. What did that say about who he was now?

He doffed the sunglasses, then looped the scarf around his neck with a flourish.

"The end of the world might be around the corner, people. Let's get some bugs in our teeth."

A quick nudge of the stick and the skimrover pivoted right, its shapeshifting wheels making for a silky smooth descent down the hold's short ramp. He backed it down into the glassy crater. A shockingly symmetrical mini mountain range had formed around the edge, shiny and black and jagged as a stone knife.

"Over or through?" Geddy asked no one in particular.

Jel blinked incredulously. "You have to ask?"

Geddy flared his eyebrows, his eyes sliding up to the two meter-tall ring of fresh igneous rock surrounding them. "Through it is."

Two independently rotating pulse cannons adorned the skimrover's force field-capable roll cage while an internal gimbal system kept the seats perfectly level. Considering his bones still felt like it had been ground into meal, he was grateful for the feature.

The cannons seemed like overkill, so he instead drew the long barrel of the PDQ from its holster and stuck his arm out the side, looking right down its big, beautiful length.

He squeezed the handle for one full second. Two. Three. And he let go. Before the pistol's awesome power, the jagged wall of black glass might as well have been a fat swirl of whipped cream atop a Mulwak Mountain Mint shake, because he fucking destroyed it.

"Cool," he mumbled.

A hole like a missing tooth appeared through a glittering shower of glass. He engaged the force field and floored it, barreling toward the steep side of the crater and the gap he'd just made. The shards that fell on top of them bounced harmlessly off with barely a sound.

"The Alliance made some good shit, I'll give 'em that!" Geddy laughed with glee, the ground before them finally free of debris. "Cherie, you still with us?"

"Yes, Captain, my transfer from the ship went smoothly," said the AI. "Unlike yours from space to here."

Jel's mouth flew open, her eyes peeling wide. "Oh, *damn*! Now that's a full burn!"

Even Doc laughed, an odd yet unrestrained bark of delight that was somehow as apt as it was surprising.

— Is this what it's come to, E? Getting dissed by the ship's AI?

— *Considering the women in your life, you should be able to handle a bit of sass by now, don't you think?*

— A very fair point.

"How about a power recommendation on that front field, my beautiful helper?"

"I'm assuming at maximum hover velocity?"

"You know it, darlin'. Just enough to pull my cheeks back into a big ol' grin."

"Ready when you are," said Cherie.

"Then by all means, engage hover. Let's see what this puppy can do."

CHAPTER 11
BIG EMPTY

Urging the skimrover ever faster across the baked earth of the Empty was fun for approximately seventeen minutes, after which the region's moniker truly started to hit home. Doc explained that its life began as a shallow and very salty ocean. But time and heat had taken their toll, and now it was only endless flat stretching to the horizon. The only thing that could hide their approach toward Lestiko's presumed location was darkness, which would be arriving shortly.

That there was nowhere to hide was part of the point, of course. Like Doc said, it made sense to sandwich the prison between impossible mountains and deadly desert.

"Are we there yet?" asked Jel, her long white locks trailing playfully behind her.

"I wonder what lots go for out here," Geddy mused.

Twenty percent permeability turned out to be the sweet spot for the shields, though the rarefied air dried your mouth, your nostrils, and even your throat. The twin Basoan suns dipped low on the horizon behind them, lengthening their shadow to grotesque proportions.

Once the suns were swallowed by the now-distant mountains in the east, darkness came quickly and the temperature plummeted. Geddy had Cherie secure the shields, and the night display popped up. Thirty-eight kilometers to go.

A structure soon appeared on the scopes, and not at the edge of the mountains. At first blush, it looked almost like an Old Earth lunar lander. When Geddy trailed off, Jel leaned closer and squinted.

"What the hell's that?"

"I don't know. Maybe we ought to go around."

He slowed the vehicle, wishing to hell he had some other cover. Unlike the *Armstrong*, there was no stealth mode.

"Try infrared, Captain," Doc suggested. "Perhaps there is movement we cannot see."

"You heard the man, Cherie."

The display changed to infrared, and immediately Doc's hunch was proven correct. Two forms were discernible inside. One was seated and not moving while the other flitted around it.

"Is it a ship?" Geddy asked no one in particular.

Doc said, "I do not believe so."

The closer they got, the more detail the scopes picked up. The shape reminded Geddy of a virus, with a globular, multifaceted structure on top and supports like splayed legs underneath. A vehicle was parked beside it, but the lack of a heat signature suggested it had been there a while.

Geddy let the skimrover glide to a stop and fixated on the holoscreen. It appeared that the person standing was having a conversation with the seated one. That lasted a few minutes, then the standing person left and descended a set of outer steps. He or she boarded the vehicle, which resembled a smaller version of the skimrover, and sped away in the direction of the cliff.

— What do you make of this?

— Your guess is as good as mine.

"Cherie, switch us to electromagnetic."

She did, and the elevated globe shape glowed as though it was on fire.

"Whoa," Jel said. "Whatever that thing is, it's got plenty of power."

"Sure does," Geddy said.

"The structure's isolated position and power capabilities suggest it presents a danger. It would be wise to keep your distance," Cherie said.

Could this be what the farmer was talking about? Was Lestiko testing some kind of new weapon?

"Well, guys, I think I'm gonna take the long w–"

"Look, Captain," Doc said, pointing at the screen. "Power appears to be increasing."

Indeed, the bright purple glow around the structure brightened further, verging on white.

"Cherie, full power on the force field," Geddy said.

The urge to get even further away from the mysterious construction was strong, but before Geddy could turn the vehicle, night turned quite suddenly to purple-tinged day. He shielded his eyes with his hand. The shockwave from the explosion raced toward them like a tsunami, ripping apart the sun-baked sand. It didn't even seem real until it smacked them like the hand of a vengeful god.

The skimrover's controls wrenched upward as the energy wave flipped them end over end like a toy. As they tumbled backward, the leveling system struggled, but mostly succeeded in keeping them upright in their seats, which was surreal in itself. The first flip was on the vehicle's long axis, but once it canted sideways, they turned over at least twice more the other way. When the rover finally stopped rolling, they were facing south, nearly perpendicular to the blast.

It all happened so fast that Geddy could only sit there

motionless, taking deep breaths to calm his racing heart. They were almost forty clicks away when the thing blew, yet the blast reached them in seconds. Was this desert some kind of bomb testing site for the Basoan government? The same government that didn't have the opportunity to ward them off? Had they just been blasted with a deadly dose of radiation?

His heart took a long time to slow.

When the fine dust was finally carried away by the evening breeze, they'd rolled and skidded at least fifty meters back from where they were. Where the strange structure had been, there was now only a crater ten times larger and much deeper than the one the *Armstrong* made. The structure was gone.

Finally venturing a glance to his right, Geddy watched Jel give her head a cleansing shake, her slender fingers drifting up to her temples.

"You okay?"

"I've taken a few poundings in my day, but never like this," she mumbled. "What the hell was that?"

"A big-ass explosion, that's what. Doc, you all right?"

Doc's amplitude rarely varied, but he appeared shaken. "Yes, I ... think so."

"Morph, you still with us?" After a moment, he popped up from under the seat, then hopped from Geddy's leg to his left shoulder. "Got your cage rattled like the rest of us, huh? Cherie, how are radiation levels?" Geddy asked hesitantly.

"Negligible," she replied.

"Then what was that?"

"Energy signature unknown."

The questions assailed him. What was that structure? Who

was in it when it exploded? Was that part of the plan? What the hell was going on out here?

"Look," Jel said, pointing a shaking finger at the far side of the crater.

The scanners were in the process of recalibrating, so there was nothing to see on the holoscreen, but rather, through it. A set of powerful lights in the distance, beyond the edge of the crater, headed straight for them.

With the systems temporarily offline, Geddy didn't even need to justify doing this the old-fashioned way. He disabled the force field around the frame, unfastened his restraint, and climbed out of the skimrover.

"What're you doing?" Jel asked.

"I'm tired of sitting," he replied, drawing the PDQ and holding it along his thigh, the long barrel brushing his pant leg. It was quite cold now.

"Hughey, go with him."

The shifter bot drifted from the back of the rover and formed into its standard cylinder at his side. Having it and Morph along with the PDQ gave him a sense of bravado he might not otherwise have had. He took several cautious steps away from the rover.

The approaching lights grew larger and brighter, not moving especially quickly, until the vehicle skirted the perimeter of the crater. It stopped briefly, then continued a bit more, rolling to a stop fifty meters away. A few seconds later, a figure emerged and stood silhouetted by the powerful beams.

"Cherie, activate floodlights," Geddy said, and when they came on, he started walking forward, his own long shadow trailing out behind him. The silhouette was revealed as a squat figure in a thick, high-collared jacket. "You guys stay here."

— *Are you sure about this?*

— That's Lestiko. I don't know how I know, but I know. Question is, is he a Nad or not?

— *It is still too far. But do not take that as a suggestion to ... and you're moving closer anyway.*

The stranger also took tentative steps forward, quickly closing the gap between then as he came into view. As suspected, he was Basoan, but by that standard he was unhealthily thin with extra toad-like skin hanging off his lower arms like a shawl. His head nearly resembled the planet's flattened oval, but was pockmarked like a dead moon.

— *I can sense him now, Geddy. He has the harmonic.*

— Are you saying he's a Nad or that he just has the harmonic?

— *I cannot tell. It is different from the others somehow.*

"That's far enough," came his wary voice. They sized each other up for a few moments, perhaps twenty meters apart. "Who are you?"

"Captain Geddy Starheart of the New Alliance." It felt empowering to say but rang strangely in his ears. "I'm looking for Lestiko."

"You found him, but this isn't the protocol," he said flatly. "Who told you to come here?"

"You sold a terrestrial gravity beam to an acquaintance of mine. Queen Tymeri. I asked her where it came from."

He paused. "You're not alone."

"It's just me, two of my crew, a bot, and a synthetic."

He paused. "You saw the explosion?"

"Up close and personal."

The Basoan gave a tuneless whistle, and the air around him lit up like a thousand fireflies. Clouds of tiny, shimmering drones had already surrounded them like bees wearing headlamps. Until then, Geddy had no idea they were there.

"You shouldn't be here. I'm going to need all your weapons."

"Or what? You pollinate us to death?"

"Any one of these cluster drones has twenty ways of killing you. Drop your weapons or die where you stand."

As much as it galled him, he tossed the PDQ in the sand a few feet away and said over his shoulder, "Toss out your weapons, guys."

The man took a few steps forward and picked the pistol up out of the sand, the drones flowing around him like a river around a boulder. He investigated it in the light and pursed his lips, impressed.

"This is good work." Turning it over in his hands, he read the inscription. "Property of Geddy Muthafuckin' Starheart."

Geddy held out his open palms. "What can I say? I was going through some stuff. At least you know I'm on the level."

"Two crew, a bot, and a synthetic, you say?" He reached up and tapped his head, smirking. "Aren't you missing someone?"

— Oh, no, he didn't.

— *He did.*

"It seems you and I have much to discuss, Captain Starheart."

CHAPTER 12
CLIFF DWELLER

Lestiko's vehicle was an old-school hovercraft cobbled together from at least three or four even older ones. It had two narrow seats and a modest storage area in back. Not exactly the kind of vehicle Geddy expected from the guy who supposedly made the gravity beam that Queen Tymeri used to snatch Oz away. After introductions were made, they followed him at a distance past the far edge of the crater on a beeline for the remote corner of the Empty where the ancient colony had once been.

They were fifty clicks beyond the crater when the hovercraft slowed, and a pair of automated lights activated along the top of a sandstone promontory. Dwellings had been carved into it by long-dead hands, the square windows indicating four compact levels.

He pulled up alongside Lestiko as he climbed out of the hovercraft and powered down.

"Welcome to Cliffside," Lestiko said, gesturing grandly. "Please hurry — I don't like having the lights on for long."

"When do we get our weapons back?" Geddy asked.

"Once I feel I can trust you."

He'd wrapped the PDQ, along with Jel and Doc's blasters, into a bundle tucked under his arm. As much as Geddy hated to be without the pistol, Lestiko held the cards here. Plus, he wanted to tread lightly.

"I am sorry you weren't able to obtain an audience with me, Miss ..." Lestiko began, looking at a very surprised Jel before he turned and strode toward the entrance, which was covered by a simple metal door suspended from a track.

"Jeledine's good enough," she said. "How did you ...?"

"Privacy is sacrosanct to me. I take great pains to maintain it."

"You mean making Zelnad tech?" Geddy asked.

"I do dabble in technologies that exceed our current understanding. But only to fund my more important work. Please." He pulled the creaky door aside, and dim lights activated within. "That's not why you came, though, is it?"

"What makes you say that?" inquired Jel.

"Call it a hunch," he said, giving Geddy a wink as he passed.

Neither Jel nor Doc had heard Lestiko say he knew about Eli. He'd decided to keep that to himself for now.

The room they'd entered was small and boxy, all stone, with a narrow set of steps leading up to the left and a door covered by a blanket to the right.

"Let's talk in my quarters. It's warmer in there," Lestiko said, gesturing toward the blanketed door.

Geddy pulled the blanket aside and stepped into a slightly larger room with more rounded edges. A narrow bench had been carved out of the wall on three sides, and the floor was littered with pillows and rugs. At Lestiko's behest, they settled onto the benches, and he took a seat near the corner. The raw sandstone was more comfortable than it appeared, but not by much.

"So if you know we didn't come to buy from you, then why do you think we're here?"

"Because you wanted to learn about the Process."

"And what process is that?"

"These ruins have been here for nearly two thousand years," he replied, ignoring the question. "The history books say it was a prison colony, but that's a bit of an exaggeration. Its true purpose was closer to what you might call a mental hospital."

"So what is it now?" Jel inquired. "A day care?"

"Oh, many things. A home. A rehabilitation center. A place of healing. Isolation is critical to the Process."

Doc said, "I am eager to learn more."

"Of course you are, Dr. Tardigan. But before we go further, I'd appreciate some information from you." He turned to Geddy. "Queen Tymeri must've told you more about me. What else did she say?"

Geddy replied, "That you used to be a Zelnad but that you 'broke through.' We need to know what the hell that means."

In lieu of an answer, he said, "'Breaking through' describes the final stage of the Process. But first, I'd like to learn more about your entities. Something is very different about them."

They exchanged quizzical looks. "Entities?" Geddy asked.

"I sense two of them. One in you, Captain, and the other, I believe, in your peculiar little companion there." He pointed to Morph on his shoulder.

— *Oh, this guy is* good.

— A little *too* good, maybe.

The only other features in Lestiko's room were a pit toilet in another corner, a bedroll, and a small table. A square woven mat sat at the center. Not remotely what Geddy was used to seeing from a weapons guy.

"So," Lestiko began, his eyes twinkling with interest, "your entities. How long have you had them?"

He wasn't sure how much truth to tell. All Eli knew for sure was that the guy had the harmonic. That could mean anything. But he didn't see any angle to the question, either.

"Almost eight years," Geddy said. "As for Morph ... I guess I couldn't say. He's not a big talker."

The ridge of warts over his eyes arched. "Eight years. That's among the longer inhabitations I've heard of. Has it told you its name?"

"Eli."

He chuckled to himself. "They shorten their names so we can pronounce them. Suffice it to say, they don't have much faith in our intellect. Mine is named ..." he uncorked a long stream of mouth noises that sounded like a mix between mating birds and scatting. It rose, and fell, and rose again but not in any melodic way. "But I call it Rai."

— *I don't suppose that rings a bell.*

— *This may come as a shock, but not all Sagaceans know each other.*

Lestiko laughed, seemingly for no reason.

"What's funny?" Jel asked.

"I must admit, I didn't know they were capable of humor. I knew something was different about yours."

While Jel and Doc were thoroughly confused, Geddy was suddenly on high alert. Somehow, Lestiko had heard their internal conversation.

"You ... *heard* Eli just now?"

He held up his fat hands. "I didn't mean to eavesdrop."

"How did you do that?"

"Harmonic tuning takes practice and discipline. But the

energy behind yours is somehow ... gentler. Like a lower wattage. Not like anything I've encountered."

Doc leaned forward. "What do you think the entities are?"

Lestiko leaned back. "I regard them as spirits, though that isn't exactly right. Old as time, maybe older. Incorporeal beings of profound insight to whom we are only vessels. Unfortunately, they are parasites. Thieves of the soul."

— *What the hell is he talking about?*

— *Relax, E. I'll handle this.*

"What the hell are you talking about?" Geddy asked.

"Were you a Zelnad or not?" Jel quickly added, suddenly making it feel like an interrogation.Her sister, Oraisa, had disappeared a few years earlier, and Jel was certain she'd become a Zelnad. It weighed on her conscience.

He expelled an exasperated stream of air and shook his head. "Zelnads! I'll never know where that came from."

"It roughly translates to 'reset' in their language," Geddy said.

Lestiko's jaw hit the floor. "Eli *told* you this?"

"He's an open book. Most of what we know about the Nads came from him."

He cocked what passed for an eyebrow, a skeptical look settling on his face. "You don't say?"

Something in his tone filled Geddy's chest with ice. He didn't like it one bit. "Is something amusing?"

"Let me guess." His voice pitched upward mockingly. "He told you all about a mysterious world named Sagacea, and how they seeded the universe with knowledge."

Geddy's heart sank along with the tone of his voice. "Yeah ... that's right."

"Did Eli also tell you that they see all outcomes? That they know what we'll do before we even do it?" Lestiko asked pointedly.

Geddy could only stared at the man, unable to voice the answer.

Lestiko looked at the floor and heaved a long sigh. "Oh, Captain, I'm so sorry."

"Why?" Geddy leaned anxiously forward, his ire growing. How dare this weirdo patronize him?

"Everything about that story is true except for one critical part." He leaned forward and took Geddy's hand, not unlike the way Colonel Pritchard did before he told him his parents were dead. "The only 'seeds' they plant are the ones in our minds." He tapped his head for emphasis. "The ones that make us think they want to help us. See, the truth, Captain, is that they all want the same thing — a clear slate. A dead universe that may or may not ever rise again from the primordial soup. If Eli is telling you differently, it's a lie."

— *That's not true!*

— Easy, E. I know.

Only he didn't know. Not for certain. Lestiko had planted a seed of his own in Geddy's mind. A seed of doubt. And it had already rooted and grown like a weed. What if he was a pawn in a much bigger and longer game? What if Eli hadn't wound up in his brain by chance? What if Morpho's job was to keep his dumb ass alive for some purpose he wasn't even aware of? Wasn't Eli always nudging him this way or that? Was any choice truly his own?

No. If he could trust in anything, it was Eli's goodness and Morpho's dedication. This was some kind of test, and for his own sanity, he had to pass it.

Geddy emphatically shook his head. "That's not true. Eli's one of the good guys. He's been on our side from the beginning."

— *You tell 'em, Ged! I'm not like the other spores!*

"Eli, please. You see, Captain, manipulation only works if the victim can't see their role in the scheme. They count on that. You know what you know for a reason, and it's not to help save the world. If I had to hazard a guess, I'd say it's to make you believe you actually have a chance of doing it. That must be part of the whole plan. See, to them, we're just the butterflies. They're the storm."

Geddy jerked his hand away. "Not Sagaceans. Sagaceans want us to live. To get better and move forward. " Until a moment ago, he'd believed this to his core. Saying it now, his voice wavered.

Lestiko leaned back and threw up his arms, his blistered skin shaking. "I see. So countless millions of 'bad' Sagaceans are out there trying to end the world, but the only two 'good' ones I've come across in almost eleven years belong to an officer in a very fragile New Alliance?" He narrowed his eyes at Geddy. "Even you seem smarter than that."

— *Geddy, I know how this sounds, but he's the one being manipulated. I need to have a word with this Rai.*

— Something tells me you will.

— *We are a unit. The universe brought us together because only we can do this.*

Lestiko let out a sneering laugh. "My stars, is that how it talks to you all the time? You must not have much of an ear for dialogue. I mean, 'The universe brought us together?' Wow."

The ice in Geddy's veins turned molten, his cheeks reddening. He didn't seriously believe anything Lestiko was saying, but he did know an awful lot. His mouth was a desert.

Judging from the looks on Doc and Jel's faces, they couldn't entirely reject what they were hearing, either. Hughey still hovered inertly near Jel's feet.

— *Oh, come on. Not them, too!*

"You think we've already lost." The words passed Geddy's clenched jaw with an audible hiss.

Lestiko's face softened, and he leaned forward. "I don't think it, Captain. I know it." He raised a cautioning finger. "In every galaxy they have wiped out, there has been a clear progression. First, a great and terrible war splinters the galaxy into factions. In its wake comes mistrust and blame. Tribalism, injustice, and hopelessness inevitably follow. Soon, civilization can't recognize existential threats from without or within. By then, the die is cast. All that can follow is an apocalypse."

Geddy stopped breathing and his mouth went instantly dry. Nearly all of this had already transpired. The Ring War. The collapse of the Alliance. Hopelessness. Even now, precious few worlds could recognize the Zelnad threat, let alone unite behind it.

"They don't have to destroy us," he muttered. "We'll do it ourselves."

Lestiko nodded grimly.

"But they were breeding deadly creatures," Jel protested. "We stopped them. That had to buy us some time."

"It's all a game to them, Captain. Like cats playing with a bird they're just going to eat anyway. Since the moment they came to our galaxy, they've been pulling little strings. My guess is, every strange occurrence over the last few centuries has been engineered to bring us precisely to this point."

"Wait, back up now. Are you trying to tell me the Zelnads started the Ring War?" Doc asked.

Lestiko's shrug nearly brought his shoulders to his ears. "Who's to say? Could it be a mere coincidence that this business with deadly creatures and cloning took place in the galaxy's most popular tourist attraction? One that happens to fall under the purview of the Xellarans, the world with the most people and the largest army? I suppose.

"But at this point, is it really that hard to imagine your New Alliance and the Coalition of Independent Worlds coming to blows? A war of that magnitude would doom the galaxy to fizzle and die. I can't even imagine how many times it's played out. This galaxy's destruction is imminent. A fait accompli. All we can do is make the most of it."

The awful truth of Lestiko's words dug into Geddy's chest like talons and ripped it from his chest. The Alliance was beyond fragile, a loose affiliation of a determined few exiles, miscreants, and refugees bankrolled by one person. To that point, only a single world had joined them. A powerful one, to be sure, but not nearly powerful enough to hold against the Coalition if it came to that. The galaxy already stood on the brink of self-destruction, and the only ones who knew it were Zelnads.

No wonder they could talk their hosts into doing just about anything. They knew the world was going to end. The Nads just threw them a lifeline called Eternity in Sagacea.

"Well ..." Jel began, "... if you think we're all screwed, why bother with all this? Whatever *this* even is?"

"Because I don't intend to share however many years I have left with one of them. You have your fight, and I have mine."

— Could all this be true?

— *I don't know, but it sounds plausible. It is more difficult to help civilization evolve than to foment its collapse.*

— We may have less time than we thought.

"You're both right," Lestiko said, having heard Eli's comment.

"This Process ..." Doc said, "What is it, exactly?"

That got Lestiko really excited. He leaned forward and pulled up one of the rugs. After smoothing an area of sand with his big hand, he drew a three-level pyramid with his fingertip.

"The Process has three main steps. The first is Realization." He drew an R in the bottom level. "I help the host see how much power they've already lost. They have to want it back or they'll never cross the Bridge."

He drew a B in the second level.

"That's step two. Entity-to-entity negotiation. Hosts learn to reassert dominion over their mind and body, but it must be done alone. Every entity is different, and so is this part of the journey. But if they apply all they learn during Realization, the entity will be sufficiently weakened to proceed to the third step."

He drew a slow D at the top.

"Dominance. Full host control of body and consciousness must be wrested from the entity's grip like candy from a child. By then, it has no choice but to yield. That is the ultimate goal of the Process."

"What about the ones who don't make progress?" Jel asked.

Lestiko's eyes darkened, and he rose, brushing the sand off his hands. "That is the problem I am trying to solve. With some, the entity is too strong. It results in a stalemate that leaves both entities diminished, especially the host. The only way to fix that is to break the connection entirely."

"You can do that?" Doc asked.

"Yes ... but I don't yet know how to control the release of energy."

Suddenly, the apparent weapons test out in the Empty was making a lot more sense. But that wasn't the only cataclysm they were trying to avoid.

CHAPTER 13
MORE OR LESTIKO

No sooner had Lestiko referenced the explosion than a woman's pained scream met their ears from somewhere overhead, distant and muffled by Cliffside's thick stone walls.

"What is that??" Jel asked, alarmed.

"Please don't be alarmed," Lestiko made a calming motion with his hands as though this was perfectly normal. "Vocalizations make the fight easier to bear."

It was a portentous punctuation to what Lestiko blamed for the explosion — a failed attempt to separate a Zelnad from its host by technological means. What if it could be weaponized?

"So you mean that explosion ..." Geddy began.

"Another failed experiment, " Lestiko said, clearly troubled. "The bond between the entities and their hosts is incredibly powerful. It's a form of energy I'm still trying to understand. Breaking it is relatively easy, but the release is always catastrophic. I can't do it without killing both of them, and I can't contain it. I can only capture some of it in a battery."

"So who was the guy inside that structure?" Geddy asked.

Lestiko looked away, seemingly regretful they knew about that. "A fellow Basoan, I'm sorry to say. As some do, he became ... stuck in the Process, unable to assert full control. He chose to risk death rather than remain in that limbo."

Geddy exchanged a concerned look with the others, who seemed equally unsure what to make of their new acquaintance.

"How many trials have you conducted thus far?" Doc asked.

"That was number fourteen," Lestiko admitted, visibly embarrassed. "Perhaps an Ornean mind could help me crack the code."

Jel jumped in before Doc could respond to the flattery. "Whoa, hold up. Did you say you've killed *fourteen people?* Remind me never to ask you for help."

His smile flattened and his whole body bristled with indignation. "Mind your tone, Miss Berwynd. What I've done is no worse than assisted suicide. People with these ... *things* inside them are sick. I don't have the cure, but until I do, I have the closest thing there is. The cure comes by moving the science forward a little bit at a time. That's what I'm doing, and that's what the volunteers signed up for."

Doc, being Doc, tried to steer the conversation in a more useful direction. "Mr. Lestiko, if I may ... if fourteen people died in your experiments, how many people have made it through this Process of yours?"

Lestiko paused for a long while before answering. "Including me ... one."

The three of them exchanged shocked looks.

"But the fourteen–" Geddy began.

"Only one host from the original cohort is left."

"One," Jel said flatly.

"As I indicated, they know exactly how to manipulate us. I designed the Process based on my own desire to protect my mind from Rai. But my mind is exceptionally strong. I failed to account for that, so my subjects, so far, have all succumbed to a sort of madness."

— *This guy's a real barrel of laughs.*

— Dude, he can hear you …

"He's almost charming, your entity," Lestiko said. "Overcoming its influence might prove difficult. Assuming, of course, you still wanted to attempt the Process."

"Are you kidding me?!" Geddy asked. "Sorry, but succumbing to a 'sort of madness' and getting blown into dust aren't exactly what I'd put on a brochure. Besides, Eli and I are a team until the end."

— *You tell 'em, Ged!*

Lestiko gave a pained smile. "Of course." He leaned in to inspect Morpho, who tightened into a ball on Geddy's shoulder. "Perhaps your friend here would be interested. What is he?"

"He's a Zelnad-made synthetic who's also host to a Sagacean like me."

"Zelnad-made?" He gave his chin a thoughtful scratch. "Mmm … perhaps."

The *Fizmo's* late Captain Bykite claimed to know Morpho's origins. When they first met, he told Geddy that Morph was a Zelnad weapon designed to wreak havoc inside enemy ships. For unknown reasons, he instead began repairing the *Fiz*, eventually earning the crew's trust. Since then, Morpho had saved his life multiple times and rarely left his side. He was clearly a Sagacean like Eli, which left a gaping hole in Bykite's account.

"I owe Eli and Morph my life," Geddy said. "If they're exploiting me, they're doing a shitty job of it."

Lestiko gave a soft "Hmph," and extended his finger as though to poke Morph, but a flat tendril reached out and slapped it away with a wet splat. Lestiko pulled back and barked a delighted laugh. "Ha! It's a feisty one!"

"You have no idea."

"Do you communicate with it? You must."

Jel gave him a cautioning look. She was as protective of Morpho as she was of Hughey. Geddy was appropriately wary of the man, and he couldn't have been more wrong about Eli, but he clearly knew things about the Nads that they didn't. Or, at least, he understood them in a different way.

"He kind of plugs into my brain sometimes," Geddy admitted. "In fact, he and Eli used to have entire debates in my head while I slept."

Lestiko's eyes sparkled with wonder. "Fascinating. Can he do it with others, as well?"

In fact, he had. After secretly constructing an escape pod on the *Fiz*, Morpho linked the whole crew together, Eli included, and told them what they meant to him.

"Morph can do just about anything. Isn't that right, pal?"

Morph gave a little salute, his body relaxing slightly.

"Well, then he could help us all have a chat. A little host-entity mixer, if you will."

— *I am not sure this is a good idea.*

— I get that, and I know he's a little off, but I don't see much risk.

Eli and Lestiko hadn't exactly hit it off. He'd basically accused Eli of being a closeted Zelnad, an argument Geddy instantly rejected. But that aside, there was the question of trust. They'd only met this guy, and when they had, he was vaporizing some rando in the desert under the pretense of an experiment.

"I understand your hesitation, Eli," Lestiko said, inviting

Geddy to sit across from him on one of two large pillows he'd arranged in the center of the room. "But I'm willing to be wrong about you and Morpho. Either way, we both have much to gain from this communion."

Both Doc and Jel appeared nervous about all this, Jel especially, but they also understood that he had to do it. It was reassuring to have them there in case things went sideways.

Lestiko crossed his legs as he lowered himself gently to the pillow, a feat of strength and flexibility that seemed impossible. Geddy did his level best to fold his similarly beneath him, though he still had to grab his ankles to pull them closer. He'd gotten relatively flexible doing sesehlu with Doc and the crew back in the *Fiz*, but it hadn't stuck.

"I don't suppose you have a beanbag?" he asked, wincing as one of his knees crunched in protest.

"*Lahp na suyu*," he said, smirking at Doc.

Doc gasped. "You know sesehlu?? I suspected it by the way you sat."

"What's that mean?" Jel asked.

"Entropy is the enemy," Doc replied. "One of the classic meditations for masters of the practice."

"Which is to say, Captain, that because the universe favors chaos, we don't have to help it."

"So that's a no on the beanbag?" Geddy asked.

Lestiko allowed a laugh and locked eyes with him. The thinly veiled hostility he was used to seeing in Basoan faces was utterly absent. It made him an easy man to trust, if not to like.

"Shall we begin, then?"

"Yeah, all right. But fair warning, it's a weird sensation."

"Morpho, I am ready when you are."

Of course, Morph didn't take orders from Lestiko. He shifted his position as though waiting for the high sign.

"Go ahead, Morph. See you on the inside."

Morph snaked a tendril into his left ear like a black, room-temperature tongue. As his hearing disappeared, he resisted the urge to yawn, which only made it that much more jarring. As Morpho wormed his way past the delicate organs of his inner ear, Geddy watched another tendril shoot across to Lestiko, who merely closed his eyes and surrendered to the experience.

Geddy did the same and found himself in a room as dark as Morpho's body. There was no light source, yet somehow he could see Lestiko clearly, still sitting like a wart-covered pretzel on the nonexistent floor across from him.

Lestiko let out a deep sigh and briefly examined his surroundings. "Very minimalist. I approve."

"He's not much for decorating."

"The captain is correct," came Morpho's 'voice' from nowhere and everywhere. Like Eli's, it was androgynous and gentle, yet assertive.

"Is that you, Morpho?" Lestiko asked.

"Yes."

"E, you here with us?"

"Yes, Geddy." Eli's voice had an almost childlike quality by comparison and a warmer tone.

"Rai?" Lestiko's bulging eyes roamed about the space. "Don't be rude, now."

"I am here." Lestiko's Zelnad entity replied flatly, as though being here was beneath it.

"How extraordinary!" Lestiko exclaimed.

Geddy had to agree. To date, he'd never shared psychic space with a Zelnad. It felt like talking to the puppet and not the puppeteer.

But the fathomless, velvety blackness was already too disorienting. He couldn't be here for more than a few minutes.

"Morph, maybe we could slip into something a little more comfortable?"

From all sides, a scene rushed in to fill the space around them. It was a quiet study in a modest Old Earth home, dripping with warm light and wood and overflowing bookshelves. A fire crackled in the hearth, and the two pillows on which they sat had been replaced by overstuffed chairs. An oval woven rug underfoot covered the hardwood of a reassuringly solid floor. It seemed absolutely real, and Geddy could feel his blood pressure lower.

The space was, in fact, quite comforting, but it wasn't any room he recognized. It was from Old Earth. How could Morpho possibly conjure such an arcane setting?

"I'd say we have a quorum!" said Lestiko. "Shall we begin?"

CHAPTER 14

A MEETING OF THE MINDS

The tension in the realistic room Morpho conjured for the bizarre meeting between the five of them was so oppressive that it had a presence all its own. At least it wasn't pure black like when they started.

"Rai, we are guests in this consciousness, which is a synthetic being called Morpho. Captain Starheart claims that neither his entity, Eli, nor Morpho share your desire for the Reset."

"Then they are not my kindred," Rai said flatly. Its voice was just as androgynous as Eli or Morph, but older somehow. Darker.

"We are born of the same energy," Eli said in his more childlike voice. It had substance here, almost like he was in the room, though only Lestiko was visible. "We differ only in our beliefs. That does not make us enemies."

"'Enemy' is a construct. There is only our purpose and those who would stand in our way."

If Lestiko was troubled by the sneering contempt in Rai's voice, he didn't show it.

"Well, you seem fun," noted Eli.

"We know what *you* want, Rai," said Lestiko. "We are here to understand what Eli and Morpho want."

"We want what true Sagaceans want," Morpho said. "To guide and inspire. Our original purpose."

"Our guidance is the only reason they have made it this far," Rai sneered. "Without it, they would only reproduce and kill."

Before Eli, Geddy wouldn't have disagreed with that. Now, it kind of pissed him off. The galaxy was full of assholes, sure, but on balance, there were fewer of them than Rai seemed to believe. Or represent.

"Just because you're old as fuck doesn't mean you know the future," Geddy offered. "There can be no hope without uncertainty."

"That's actually really good, Geddy," Eli said.

"See? He gets me."

Rai's laughter dripped with the same cynicism. "A human speaks of the future as uncertain when it is mathematically assured."

"Why bring math into this?"

Lestiko interjected, "Rai, you said you would beha–"

"Maybe we don't have the greatest track record," Geddy said. "That doesn't mean we're hopeless."

"You destroy everything you touch. You use knowledge only to acquire and subjugate. How can any species secure its future when it barely considers the present?"

"We only destroyed two planets, thank you very much. Considering how many there are in the universe, that's *mathematically* the same as zero. Eli, Morph, back me up here."

"Do we have to?" asked Eli.

"The point is, you can't know the future with any certainty. There are countless galaxies out there. Countless habitable worlds. Someone's gonna figure it out eventually."

"There *were* countless habitable worlds," Rai said. "I believe your galaxy is among the last."

That stopped the conversation cold.

"Um, what?" Geddy asked.

"Did you not know? Your galaxy is among the last bastions of civilization in the entire universe. Congrats on making it this long."

Geddy couldn't allow himself to believe this. Scholars across the galaxy agreed that the universe must be full of others, distant and unknowable. But now, with the advent of the bubble drive, there was already talk of expeditions to find them as the worlds within their galaxy had found each other.

"You ... didn't know this?" Lestiko asked.

"It's a lie," Geddy asserted. "They need us all to be as hopeless as they are."

"Hope is for fools. We have watched the same pitiful tale play itself out since the dawn of time," Rai said. "Once Sagacea is gone, this galaxy will return to dust. Then the universe will finally be pure again. Matter and energy will dance their beautiful dance, governed only by the laws of physics."

Eli said, "Geddy and I are a team. I offer sage advice, and he tells me to shut up. That, too, is a beautiful dance."

"Then I suggest you enjoy it while you can."

Acid flooded Geddy's stomach. He was so sick of listening to Zelnad BS, he could scream. But as a result, he knew their pitch well. Maybe he could trick Rai into betraying something useful by pushing its buttons.

"Then what are you waiting for?? Oh, unless you still don't have enough shinium to get the job done."

Rai paused. "You ... know of shinium?"

"Oh, I know all your evil plans. Mainly because you brainiacs can't go ten minutes without running your mouth about them. I even think that's a little too cocky, and I'm Geddy Muthafuckin' Starheart."

"What is shinium?" Lestiko asked, deeply interested.

"It's tukrium impregnated with Sagacean spores," Geddy replied. "It's the only thing that can penetrate the barrier around Sagacea, so they're building a weapon out of it. Apparently, they're about as good as finding it as they are finding nice things to say."

"We have been refining shinium for eons, human. We know precisely how and where to find it."

"Then destroy Sagacea and let us live out the rest of our pointless lives in peace!"

"That's the spirit!" Lestiko said.

"You swore an oath," Eli said, and the room fell silent. "Or have you been stewing in spite so long that you've forgotten?"

"The oath became null and void when the gifts we bestowed upon the world were used to conquer and destroy," Rai spat.

"Okay, first of all, you people really need to lighten the fuck up. And second, what o–" An anguished woman's wail, the same they had heard earlier, cut Geddy off. His head spun to Lestiko. "Look, man, I don't care what you say. That ain't normal."

He heaved a sigh. "Very well. I suppose there isn't much else to say, anyhow. Thank you, Rai, as always, for bringing sunshine into our lives."

"Eat shit and die, skinsuit."

"Thanks for the meeting space, Morph," Geddy said, his lips curled into a distasteful sneer. "It was a real hoot."

With a wet, painful pop, Morpho withdrew from Geddy's ear, and the darkness was instantly replaced by the dim light of Lestiko's room. As he reoriented himself in the real world, he noticed pained and baffled expressions on Doc's and Jel's faces.

"That was like watching two old dogs have the same nightmare," Jel said drolly.

Lestiko scratched at his ear, seemingly disappointed in how their little meeting had gone. "I stand corrected, Captain. Eli and Morpho are not the same as Rai. As for the ... disturbance from overhead, I suppose I owe you an explanation." He got up from the floor and gestured toward the door. "Please follow me."

CHAPTER 15
RUINED

Lestiko led them out of his quarters and toward a narrow set of steps leading to the next floor. The tallest Basoan only would've come up to Geddy's chin, which was probably why there were places where his head scraped the carved ceiling. The only real solution was to penitently lower it as they walked.

"Historians still regard this as a prison," Lestiko said over his shoulder. "I hoped it would be where people became free."

The bottom of Lestiko's tunic swooshed back and forth as he climbed the first short flight, then pivoted left to climb a second. It ended at an open steel door. He gestured that they were welcome to look inside. "This is the Realization level. We'd have group sessions, they'd meditate, eat, and sleep. That's thirty days. Everyone made it past that."

A corridor even narrower than the stairs stretched a short ways in either direction. None of the doorways, which seemed quite close to each other, had doors or curtains. The hallway was utterly silent. Geddy threw a look back at Jel, who was clearly on edge.

"This way, now."

Lestiko continued up the next flight, paused at the small landing to ensure they were right behind him, then kept going. The entrance to the level was protected by another metal door, only it looked an awful lot like Gundrun steel and it was closed tight.

"The Bridge level." Lestiko's tone was heavy. "Don't let the door's sturdiness alarm you. It's a bulkhead door from an old Basoan fishing vessel. It is only for noise control."

Another anguished scream emanated from behind the door, followed by sobbing. Again, Lestiko appeared more apologetic than troubled.

"That is the sound of my last living subject trying to 'cross the Bridge' so to speak. I'm hopeful she'll be able to move upstairs soon."

"Sounds to me like she's being tortured," Jel said pointedly.

"The entities have fiendish and even cruel ways of resisting the Process. The poor woman you hear has been stuck on the Bridge for a long time, but she's making tremendous—"

"How long?" Geddy asked.

Lesitko held Geddy's gaze for a long moment, then turned to continue up the stairs. "If you please ... the view of the stars from the roof is simply aw—"

Geddy reached the landing with one giant step and grabbed a fistful of his tunic, shoving him hard against the wall next to the door. His bug eyes widened in shock.

— *So much for subtlety.*

"What's really going on here, Lestiko?" Geddy hissed. "How long has that woman been your prisoner?"

"Captain, as I've explained, she's not a—"

Geddy gave his chest another shove. "*How long?*"

"Almost two years," he croaked.

"Screw this," Jel spat. "Hughey, unlock the door."

Hughey flowed out of her jacket pocket where he'd hidden and funneled into the crude lock. A click came, and Jel threw it open to the sound of anguished sobs coming from the right side of the corridor. Doc followed her through.

"No, please!" Lestiko implored.

Geddy held a shaking finger in front of his face. "Stay out of our way."

He released the man's tunic and watched him closely as he proceeded into the corridor. Here, the rooms all had similar steel doors, but they all stood open save for one at the very end. Blankets had been stuffed into the gaps around it.

He caught up to Jel and Doc as the woman clearly screamed, "Help! Is somebody there?! Please let me out!"

Jel's hand flew to Geddy's jacket, gripping it so hard he thought it might rip.

"What? What's wrong?"

"It can't be ..." she muttered. Then she raced to the door, yanking the blankets out from around the door. "Hold on! We're gonna get you out!"

"The Bridge requires complete isolation!" Lestiko protested from behind them. "You're ruining everything!"

"Please, please help!"

Tears streamed down Jel's smooth cheeks as she began to sob. "Ori? Ori, is that you? Please tell me it's you."

A pause came. "Jel?"

Geddy held still for a moment, attempting to process what was happening. Jel tugged frantically at the locked door.

"Ori, I'm here! Hughey, get it open."

"Stop right there."

Lestiko walked slowly toward them brandishing a smooth metal object about the size of a cigar with a glowing blue tip. Geddy reflexively went for his sidearm, but of course, the PDQ was still down in Lestiko's quarters. His face flushed with rage.

"You left me no choice. Now move away from the door and let me explain."

"Fuck you and your bullshit explanations. She's my sister!" Jel said through gritted teeth.

He seemed genuinely shocked by this. "Your sister …"

"On second thought, Hughey …" Jel muttered. "Disarm him."

Before Geddy could protest, Hughey shot like a bullet toward Lestiko. A blue blob of energy spat forth from his weapon and enveloped the cloud of nanobots instantly, freezing it in place like a still frame in a movie. The faintly colored field around it shimmered silently in the hallway.

To that point, little had stood in Hughey's way. Whatever technology Lestiko wielded must be powerful indeed.

"Now …" he said, moving his other hand in a calming motion. "Let's all take a deep breath here and talk."

Geddy could tell that Jel wanted to tear away and murder him with her bare hands, but even she was intimidated by whatever had immobilized the great Hughey. He might've dispatched Morpho if he didn't fear the same outcome.

Lestiko continued, "There's no way around this part. She has to cross the Bridge alone."

"Jel, are you still there? What's happening?" asked Ori through the still-closed door.

— *Oh, Geddy, this is so wrong. She is suffering needlessly.*

"She was already suffering," Lestiko asserted. "I want that to end as badly as you do."

"As long as it doesn't disturb your sleep," Geddy grumbled, glancing down at the pile of blankets.

"Believe me, Captain, I wish there was another way. The Process isn't perfect, but it works. I'm living proof."

"Let Hughey go," Jel said. "We're just gonna take Ori and leave."

"Very well." He paused for a moment. The corners of his lips upturned in a way Geddy didn't like. "Alpha configuration, authorization zero nine two. Enable."

Whatever field had been holding Hughey dissipated, whereupon his nanos gathered into a sphere the size of a golf ball and dropped to the stone floor as they watched in stunned horror. Because the stone was uneven, the Hughey-ball rolled tight against the wall, motionless.

"There," he said, heaving a relieved sigh as he lowered the device. "I did say no weapons."

"What did you just do??" Jel demanded.

"I deactivated him. I build failsafe protocols into all my bots."

"*Your* bot?" Jel asked.

"Jel, talk to me! Please let me out!" Ori pounded on the door.

Geddy's heart ached for her, too, but there wasn't much they could do.

"How did you come by it?" Lestiko asked Jel. "The bot."

"Payment from a lying Basoan," she growled. "Hughey, can you hear me?"

The metal ball sat motionless.

"I'll reactivate him once we've reached an understanding. Now listen, I know this must be incredibly difficult, but by interrupting the Process, you've set your sister back immeasurably."

"Say 'Process' one more time," Jel spat, her hands curling into fists.

Doc took a couple slow steps toward Lestiko. "Jeledine, please. This is not getting us anywhere. Lestiko, we are men of science and reason. Let us speak as such."

"That's all I'm asking," he replied.

"Enough talk," Jel said. "We're doing this the old-fashioned way. Ori, hang on, I'm coming!"

She reached inside her short-waisted leather jacket and withdrew a long, small pouch. Her pick set. Not many doors had regular locks anymore, but Jel kept the fine old tools anyway, if for no other reason than to scrape food out of her teeth.

Lestiko opened his mouth to protest, but he didn't have the heart to stop her.

A metallic click came from behind Geddy, and he whirled to see Jel fling the door open. Oraisa fell into her arms, sobbing uncontrollably. She barely resembled a Stemiran woman. Her face and hands were covered in bruises. Her hair was the same pure white as Jel's but longer and ratty, and she was alarmingly thin.

Geddy turned back to Lestiko. "I think I would've volunteered, too. What else have you been lying about?"

"Nothing," he said, defeated. "I swear."

"We'll see."

CHAPTER 16
A LOT TO PROCESS

After they freed Ori from her cell and Lestiko restored Hughey to his typical form, his entire persona shifted from that of a confident, self-styled messiah to that of a broken man whose audacious and well-intended dreams had collided violently with reality.

Geddy had known a few guys like that. Many were businessmen for whom the Next Big Thing was always right around the corner. Others were tinkerers forever on the verge of a breakthrough. All had a preternatural tolerance for repeated failure.

He wasn't some shyster or con artist. Only a liar protecting his outsized ego like a dragon guarding its hoard. However questionable his methods, they'd worked for him. The main difference between him and Geddy was that Eli was happy to be a passenger from day one. Rai, not so much. Was that what all the Zelnads were like? Hateful and bitter? And what was this oath?

Eli had taken the wheel exactly once in a moment of desperation. In an instant, Geddy wound up in the back seat of an ever-lengthening limo. It was scary as hell. He only made it out because Eli let him. If Rai was even half that powerful, then the fact that there even *was* a Lestiko seemed almost miraculous.

Ori was so weak that Geddy had to carry her back down to Lestiko's quarters. She lay on his bedroll, clenching Jel's hand like a life preserver while she helped lift her head to a cup of water.

"Many came, at first," Lestiko said ruefully from the stone bench near the door, his elbows on his knees. "Just getting them to understand what was happening to them and why was a major accomplishment. Most had thought they were going crazy. But after that, the Process broke down. That was difficult to accept."

"It's not his fault," Ori said as Jel dabbed away a trickle of water from her mouth. "I had every opportunity to leave."

Jel looked up at Geddy, her face twisted in confusion. "What're you talking about? You were locked up and begging to be let out."

"That wasn't me. It was my entity. At least, at first. But then I recognized your voice, and it gave me strength."

"Because you're strong." Lestiko sounded like a proud father.

"Strong? She's half starved!" Jel said.

Ori shook her head vigorously. "I'm not. Lestiko's taken good care of me. Really."

"The fight leaves the hosts drained, mentally and physically," Lestiko said. "You've seen what kind of energy the entities have to work with. It's more powerful than you can imagine."

Jel's ice-blue eyes narrowed at him. "All right. so How do we know that's her talking?"

"You don't." He nodded to Ori. "But she does."

"It's me, Jel. I swear it. Thanks to you, I feel better now than I have in months. I can't explain it."

Jel didn't talk often about Oraisa. All Geddy knew was that

she'd battled a deep depression and vanished. It was a familiar enough story that he didn't think the details were important. But Dr. Krezek, the Afolosian scientist who they'd rescued from Tymeri along with Oz, shared a similar experience with his research assistant turned Zelnad, Milbart. Both had fallen into profound despair before disappearing.

A very half-assed theory he kept at the back of his mind came to the fore, taking a more defined shape but unready to emerge.

"Ori, what actually happened to you on Stemir?"

Her eyes drifted away from him up to the ceiling, then she sat up with no help from Jel. In the space of ten minutes, fresh energy had surged into her as though her Zelnad had relaxed its grip. Or had she wrested away control?

"Maybe you should lie down," Jel suggested.

"No, I'm fine. You deserve to know." She took a breath and gently tucked an unruly lock of hair behind her ear. "I'd always struggled with depression, but a few years back, it got bad. Jel was off doing her thing, my circle of friends was shrinking ... I was in a dark place. Some days, I didn't even get out of bed. I lost my job ... I even thought about ending it.

"One day, I dragged myself to the park. I figured maybe a little sun would do me good, y'know? As I'm sitting there watching birds play in a fountain, I heard this voice in my head. I don't mean the little voice everyone has. I mean an *actual voice*. It told me it was an ancient alien from a place called Sagacea, and that it needed my help to get back home."

The hair on Geddy's arms stiffened. The exact same thing had happened to him, albeit under very different circumstances.

"After the initial shock, I started to feel like ... like I mattered to someone. Like I had a purpose. This hand plunged through the darkness and grabbed me as if to say, 'I've got you.' I felt like I owed her my life, and I was ready to do anything she asked of me."

"She?" Doc asked.

"Ahnea." Her tone was a curious mix of fondness and contempt. "It's easier for me to think of, well, *her* that way."

"So what happened?" Geddy asked.

"She told me to board a transport to Aku. That I'd find others like us, and together we would journey to Sagacea."

"And what did she say would happen there?" Lestiko asked, clearly knowing the answer.

"That we would all become one. That the doors to the universe would open and we would only know peace."

"Such a beautiful lie," Lestiko said ruefully. "But a lie just the same. The only difference is, I was too cynical to believe it."

"I wanted to believe it," Ori said. "But then I started to feel myself slipping away. It was subtle at first, like losing a few minutes here and there. Ahnea tried to convince me it was my imagination. *We are bound together*, she said. Only I didn't consent to that."

"Oh, Ori, I had no idea ..." Jel lamented.

"I couldn't tell anyone or they'd think I'd lost it. Ahnea kept insisting I go to Aku. Screaming it, practically. One day, I found myself at the spaceport with no memory of how I got there. I got so scared, I bought a one-way ticket to Basoa because it was in the opposite direction as Aku.

"Anyway, without novaspheres, it's a three-week hop, right? One night, I was trying to sleep, and I kept hearing this heated conversation. Like two people screaming at each other right next to me. I opened my eyes to ask them to be quiet, but it's one guy sitting there with this look on his face ... the same look I'd seen in the mirror. Haunted. Desperate. I realized I'd heard the conversation in his head. Between him and his entity."

"That's the harmonic tuning," Lestiko reminded them. "I encouraged my subjects to practice it."

That checked out. Eli could only sense Zelnads, but Oz could very nearly hear Eli. Rarely did a comment pass that she didn't notice, though she couldn't quite tell what he was saying. Maybe Ori had a similar ability.

"Was he on his way here?" Jel asked.

Ori nodded. "He'd heard through the grapevine there was a place for people like us. That a man had learned how to take back control and could help us do the same. I came with him. We ... became close."

"Where is he now?" Doc asked.

Ori's eyes looked past Geddy out the open window that fronted the Empty. "He, ah, decided he wanted out. One way or another. So he volunteered for one of the separation tests."

Knowing that she had cared for the man who got blown up in Lestiko's contraption made it all the more sad. His heart went out to her.

"I'm sorry," Geddy offered.

"I was almost there myself." She turned to Jel and smiled before leaning against her. "Until you came along and gave me hope for the first time in ... I don't know how long."

Geddy leaned forward on the bench, his eyes darting back and forth between Doc and Lestiko. "I think I know how to fix your Process."

Lestiko sat up, his eyes widening with interest. "You do?"

"Hard to believe, I know. But Zelnad hosts all seem to have something in common. They've lost hope. That makes them easy to take over. They're basically selling Sagacea as a version of heaven to people whose lives are hell."

"But most aren't as strong as Oraisa or me," Lestiko said. "How do we convince them it's a lie?"

"We give 'em something better to believe in. The host *and* the entity."

CHAPTER 17
PARTING GIFTS

Ori's condition improved dramatically over the next few days. Lestiko had stores of frozen food squirreled away in a vault hollowed out of the rock beside the compound. And, as Doc predicted, Cliffside sat at the edge of a deep aquifer. Ori ate and drank like she'd wandered in from the desert and transformed into a completely different person.

Whatever malaise had made her so susceptible to the bullshit Ahnea fed her had given way to buoyant optimism. Almost annoyingly so. Geddy sincerely loved Jel — once as a friend with benefits and now more like a sister — but Ori was a bit much.

No one could blame her. She'd been through something he couldn't even imagine, alone, and seemed better for it, if not exactly *because* of it.

But holy shit, could that girl talk. She talked so much, her sentences overlapped. *Remember when we ran into that albino guy at the thing we went to with mom and he was like how old are you girls and we totally played him until mom showed up and was like who's your friend oh my god I can't believe we did that.*

That Jel, who wasn't a big talker, could endure such a firehose of musings and memories for three straight days was a testament to her love for Ori.

After the third day, they decided to leave early the next morning and get back to the *Armstrong* before the sun got too high and Geddy went insane. They gathered in Lestiko's quarters for a meal of Basoan tayra he'd set aside for a special occasion and an assortment of root vegetables from the north that would've made Denk jealous.

For most of the past year, Ori's room was at the opposite end of the hallway from the friend she'd met aboard the transport, whose name was Ghavrus. The main idea of the Bridge was that there was no one to talk to besides your entity, but Ori learned she could tune into Ghavrus if she pressed her head tightly to the door, as though it acted as some kind of psychic antenna.

If Ghavrus eavesdropped on her conversations with Ahnea, he never said. They'd barely gotten to know each other before being separated. But lying there in the dark with her head wedged into the corner where the door met the floor, she could hear Ghavrus talk to his entity, whose name she never learned. That was what she meant when she said they were "close."

After a time, she learned that Ghavrus had actually followed his entity's order to board a transport to Aku, where Ori had stopped short and gone to Basoa instead.

"You have to understand, Ghavrus' entity was very manipulative and cruel. Any time I tuned in, it was trying to make him give it full control. It would say stuff like, 'Only I can get you out of here' or berate him for using his free will to walk right into a prison. Just a constant drumbeat of castigation.

"So late one night, I'm listening in, and the entity is going on and on about how Ghavrus betrayed it. Like, 'What kind of gutless coward turns away from his destiny?' Shit like that. Ghavrus tried to defend himself, but it was relentless."

"'Destiny' referring to Sagacea?" Doc asked.

Ori shrugged indifferently. "I assume so."

Geddy's eyes darted to Doc. "Did it ever mention a base, a fleet, a weapon — anything like that?"

Her lips swished thoughtfully back and forth as she searched her memory. "Don't think so. But it talked a lot. Like, *a lot*. All while I was supposed to be talking to Ahnea. I kind of learned to tune it out after a while, y'know?"

"Oh, I definitely know."

A tear ran down Jel's cheek. "I can't believe you've been fighting this for so long."

Ori put a comforting hand on her shoulder. "But I'm stronger for it. I'm back in charge again. I can feel it. Lestiko helped me, and you put me over the top. Now it's time to go back home."

Jel visibly tensed. Her relationship with her family was fraught to put it mildly. Geddy didn't know the details. "Home? I can't go home right now."

"But Mom and Dad miss you. They worry about you."

She gave a derisive laugh. "That would be a first."

Geddy could only handle so much talk about feelings. He got up and pretended to stretch. "Well, sounds like you two have a lot to talk about. I'm gonna get the rover ready."

The barren, windswept expanse of the Empty was cast in the bluest, flattest light Geddy had ever seen, making it look more like a foley than an actual landscape. The breeze felt surprisingly cold on his cheeks, making him glad it would mostly be at their backs.

Terrestrial mornings were always a mixed bag. Compared to being in space, the slow rise of a sun could almost seem miraculous. But he'd been cold for three days and was about to get colder still. That shit was for the birds.

As he secured the last of their gear to the back of the skimrover, Lestiko sidled up to him.

"If you're done, I'd like to show you something before you leave."

Geddy closed the buckle on the storage box and followed Lestiko around the right corner of the sandstone promontory. A modern door with an access panel awaited.

"Wine cellar?" Geddy asked.

Lestiko passed his hand over a scanner, and the door slid open. He looked over his shoulder with a sly grin. "Not quite."

Geddy followed him inside where lights had already activated. The room had been excavated through modern means, its corners sharp and right. Rows of workbenches along the walls, and two long ones in the middle, were littered with all manner of gear and weapons in various stages of completion. It all looked cutting-edge.

Lestiko gestured about the room before setting his hands on his hips. "Welcome to my workshop."

Geddy felt like a kid in a candy store. He loved to rub elbows with tinkerers of all sorts. He knew many of them through his work for the Double A, but very few who had a pulse on Zelnad-caliber tech. His Screvari friend, Balzac, probably came closest. But he didn't recognize any of this stuff.

"Whoa. So this is where Tymeri's gravity beam came from."

"Among many other innovations, yes."

"It's impressive."

Lestiko's four-fingered hand swept across the workshop. "Take your pick."

"Whoa, really?"

"I am genuinely sorry for deceiving you. Consider it a gesture of good will."

"I don't even know what most of this stuff even is," Geddy

said, running his fingers over something that was either a small missile or a curiously sturdy marital aid.

"Weapons, mostly. As I recall, the Alliance loved those."

"There's only one thing in this workshop I want."

"What's that? A new shifter bot, perhaps?" He held up a smooth metal ball like the one he'd turned Hughey into earlier. "Yours is a few generations behind."

Geddy leveled his gaze at him. "You." Lestiko barked a laugh under the false assumption he was joking. "You understand the Nads. You know their technology. We need to press every advantage we've got. Plus, it seems to me you've run out of reasons to stay."

Lestiko regarded him curiously for a moment. "Why do you still think you can prevent the Reset?"

"Because I'm too arrogant to think otherwise. And even if I wanted to give up, Eli wouldn't let me."

— *Damn skippy.*

"If only all the entities believed in their hosts as Eli believes in you."

"What if they did?" asked Geddy.

"What do you mean?"

"The Nads believe we're destined to make the same mistakes over and over. That we can't save ourselves. This is our last chance to prove them wrong."

A bemused grin spread across his frog-like face. If he was merely cynical, he wouldn't be doing what he was trying to do here. The notion clearly intrigued him.

"That's rather optimistic, don't you think? Bordering on naïve."

"Does that mean you disagree?"

"Tell me, Captain — let's say you somehow manage to find this base of theirs in some distant and dead galaxy. What then?"

"We ... stop ... them?" Geddy wished it didn't have to sound like a question.

Lestiko shrugged. "How? They have superior technology, they know how you will think and act, they are resolute, and they are legion."

"All the more reason to help us."

Lestiko's look was a combination of admiration and pity, like a parent might give a child with a surfeit of determination but a dearth of ability. "I can't help but admire your vision, Captain, but I must complete my work."

"What work? All the hosts are dead."

"Not all." His lips turned gravely downward.

Geddy's heart sank. "You'd sacrifice yourself to get Rai out of your head?"

"I don't expect you to understand, Captain. My relationship with Rai is a constant, bitter fight. One way or another, we must part company, and soon."

Lestiko was right. He couldn't know what it was like to be at war with the voice in his head. But as far as he was concerned, that was the point. Zelnad hosts either surrendered or fought, but there was a third option.

"Eli and I built a ship together. It took years, but we did it. Together. We accepted each other."

Lestiko put a patronizing hand on his shoulder. "I admire your vision, Captain. I do. But you have your path, and I have mine. If I can figure out how to separate hosts from their entities, I'll share it with the world. That includes the Alliance."

Part of him wanted to keep trying. To convince Lestiko that theirs wasn't a lost cause. But he couldn't fault the guy either.

"Then I wish you well," he muttered.

"Now," Lestiko brightened and clapped his hands. "What can I get you?"

"You know their technology," Geddy said. "Is there a

weapon they've never seen? Something they can't defend against?"

Lestiko brightened and raised a knowing finger. "Now *that's* something I can help you with."

He shuffled away, squeezing his girth between two adjacent tables of half-finished projects until he arrived at a smaller table along the wall. A flat gray capsule about the size of Geddy's forearm was nestled on a folded cloth.

"This," Lestiko began, "is a gravity weapon. Essentially, it creates a temporary black hole from which even the largest of ships cannot escape. A direct hit will suck a ship, and possibly any ships near it, right through. Suffice it to say, it should be fired from a healthy distance."

"Like with a torpedo?" Geddy asked, and Lestiko nodded.

"Precisely. It's not the kind of weapon they would ever expect you to have, let alone use. Shields or no shields, it'll work."

Geddy's plan was to somehow free the hosts and break the Zelnads' power, not to pull them into a black hole. But if it ever came down to the Nads or his crew, he'd have no other choice.

"Thank you," Geddy said as humbly as possible. "You're sure I can't convince you to come with us?"

"Very sure, Captain. But again, I wish you and the Alliance well."

They shook hands, and that was that.

CHAPTER 18
SOLDERING ON

A fierce battle raged right in front of him, yet Geddy did nothing. With the *Armstrong's* stealth mode engaged, he merely leaned back in his seat and watched.

The clones were in a live-fire exercise against the pirates and Balzac's Screvari. Using disruptors at half power, it took dozens of direct hits to wear down a decent shield, but they still felt the hit. Since they didn't know what Zelnad ships were capable of in battle, the best they could do was pit them against seasoned pilots who knew how to fight dirty.

Though the Basoan scanners had certainly detected their drive signature as they left, they'd reached outer space and jumped back to the *Stalwart* before they could react. Ori could scarcely believe her eyes.

After recounting the details of their bittersweet journey with the rest of the crew, Geddy went to bed but wasn't able to sleep. The Lestiko business had him in knots. Despite finding Jel's long-lost sister, the risky visit to Basoa hadn't exactly paid off.

Since the scrimmage was scheduled to begin early that morning, he'd just gotten back up and parked the *Armstrong* a safe distance away, engaging stealth so he could watch from afar. Even a battle involving hundreds of ships looked insignificant from where he was.

— *Did you ever fight in a battle like this?*

"No."

— *So ... should you be practicing, too?*

Prior to his adventures with the crew, he'd only been in a handful of space combat situations. Even then, he was mostly being chased by angry warlords or pirates on his way to his jump vectors. His go-to maneuver was to lead them into a situation that required fancy flying like a canyon or asteroid field. That's where he shined.

Of course, he'd pretty much always been alone in such scenarios. The *Auctionaut*, Tretiak's custom-built and well-armed starship, could only handle two people, and save for a handful of occasions when Jel was along, it was just him.

The *Fiz* was the first ship he'd actually lived and worked on with a crew.

"Sometimes I wonder what would've been different if we'd met earlier."

One of the best parts about being completely alone was talking out loud to Eli. It made him seem more like a flesh-and-blood being.

— *I have wondered that, too.*

"I think I would've gone insane."

— *Why?*

"Because I wouldn't have wanted another voice in my head."

— *What changed?*

"My own inner voice wasn't very nice."

Self-loathing colored much of his time alone after the evacuation of Earth 2. Not to mention a couple extra coats of guilt for his role in making the planet inhabitable. If he hadn't inadvertently huffed Eli into his sinuses where he eventually took residence in his frontal cortex, Geddy would have probably died on the planet, and he would've been cool with it.

"Do you think Lestiko will change his mind?"

— *I don't know. He seemed very resolute. And yet ...*

"And yet what?"

— *I sensed conflict both in him and Rai.*

"I'd be pretty cynical, too, if I was him."

— *You already are cynical.*

"You know what I mean. I get where he's coming from."

A live-fire scrimmage was a lot better than running sims all the time. Accurate though the training systems were, there was nothing like the real deal. Still, he knew it was going to be woefully inadequate. The Zelnads had observed galaxy after galaxy, star system after star system, for eons. They knew exactly what posed a threat and what didn't. The chances of surviving a full-scale confrontation with the Nads were infinitesimal, and he knew it. Everyone saw what happened over Gundrun. The idea that they could fight something like that was folly.

And yet, they couldn't do nothing. If a few things broke their way, they'd find the Nad base, Sagacea, or both. If they could do that, then maybe there was a way to win. A way to restore hope to the hosts and break the Nads' spell over them like Jel had done for Ori.

He opened a frequency back to the *Stalwart*. A few seconds passed, and Denk's jolly round face appeared. "Hey Cap. How're they lookin' out there?"

Geddy gave a genuine smile. Despite his misgivings about the Alliance's strength and readiness, he was proud of the fellas. They'd worked hard to please him and Oz, and they were starting to carve out their own identities, which was equal parts cool and weird.

"Chips off the ol' block," he said. "Could you patch me through to Jel's quarters?"

"Sure thing, Cap."

The screen switched to an animation that read, "BRIDGE TO BERWYND, J." Jel appeared shortly thereafter with her mostly packed duffle on the bed behind her.

"Hey," she said. "Enjoying the war games?"

"Taking careful notes. You packing for Stemir?"

She heaved a sigh. "Against my better judgment."

"For how long?" he asked.

"A week. Two at the most."

"Well, you're still a free agent. You deserve the break. How's Ori?"

"She's ... I don't know ... at peace, I guess. Like when we were kids, but stronger somehow. Almost like she and Ahnea are a team now. Does that make sense?"

— *Kind of like you and me.*

He gave a knowing smile. "You know it does."

She visibly relaxed at his endorsement of the idea. "Hughey Twoey's staying here."

As though on cue, the silvery bot cloud rose into the frame.

"How come?"

"For you-ey," she said, smiling. "And because I don't figure I'll need him."

He knew better than to protest. Besides, Hughey wouldn't do anyone any good cooling his heels on the *Bogart* while Jel and Ori were patching things up with their family. They had plenty of use for him here.

"What does he eat and what's his bedtime?" Geddy asked with a smirk.

"Nothing and never. Not even you can screw it up." She snapped her fingers. "Oh, I almost forgot. I think Doc's almost done retrofitting that warhead of yours."

"Oh, good. I'll be back in a few minutes to see you off anyway."

"Sounds good."

The forward magazine was a room several decks below the bridge where torpedoes, missiles, and countermeasures were stored and loaded. Like engineering, it was fully automated. The *Stalwart* carried three types of missiles and two types of torpedoes, none of which had ever been fired in a combat situation or otherwise. It was hard to not have doubts about their effectiveness after sitting for eighty years, but Verveik assured him the triple-walled, argon-filled ordnance would work when the chips were down.

Geddy was as curious about Lestiko's gravity weapon as he was intimidated by it. Plus, he'd never seen a military-grade torpedo up close. So he joined Doc to watch him replace one of the existing warheads with the new one.

Their torpedoes were antimatter and plasma, either of which could tear a hole in a ship big enough to fly through. But that assumed the shields were down or weak, a problem torpedoes compensated for by traveling at incredible speeds. Both tapered to a needle point, which maximized shield damage.

The outer housing was made of solid thedrine fuel, a close cousin of the industrial explosive labrozite. On impact, the nose would shatter and momentum would carry the inner warhead through the shield or hull, whereupon it would detonate.

Geddy looked over Doc's shoulder as he expertly applied a final solder. "You don't have military experience. How the hell do you know how to do this?"

"The Alliance ships have extensive documentation," he replied matter-of-factly. "I simply read the technical manual for this LS-430a antimatter torpedo. Of course, I had to make some assumptions about the gravity weapon's detonation mechanism and adjust accordingly, but otherwise the procedure was quite simple."

One layer at a time, he replaced the parts of the torpedo he'd removed in order to install the new warhead, carefully screwing each one back into place as Geddy looked on.

"I gather Jeledine has departed?" Doc asked.

"Right before I came down here."

"I'm happy for her and Oraisa."

"Me, too. Speaking of siblings, any news from Parmhar?"

Doc nodded. "We spoke briefly this morning. He is working as fast as he can, but he's feeling pressure from the Committee."

Geddy had as much a role in creating that pressure as anyone. When he and Doc snuck into Ornea to meet with him, he was an associate professor close to being shown the door. He would have had to enter the private sector, which on the shame scale was only a couple notches below Doc's exile. At the time, it felt like they were saving him from that fate. But maybe they'd only thrust him into an impossible situation.

As Parmhar had explained, his deep-space scanner wasn't designed to work quickly. Now, he was expected to find a *specific* point in three-dimensional space, possibly hundreds of parsecs away, that may or may not be the Zelnad base.

It was both a big ask and a shot in the dark. As far as Geddy was concerned, they couldn't bank on it. Finding Sagacea was the bigger prize because chances were, not even the Nads likely knew its location. Like Eli, they'd merely been ejected into space millions of years ago, ostensibly never to return.

"How's he holding up?"

"He is managing," Doc said. "Of course, our father is not helping matters."

Doc and Parmhar's father, Pyrus, was a well-regarded but odious professor of philosophy back on Ornea who had disowned Doc and was on his way to doing the same for Parmhar. Parmhar was sworn to secrecy about his work with the Alliance, which must have made it seem like he gave up his academic career for nothing. What lies did he have to tell Pyrus?

"That's got to be hard on him," Geddy said.

"My father could make anything difficult for anyone." He drove in the last big screw and ran his fingers over the smooth seam.

"Safe to say that something that creates a temporary black hole is a weapon of last resort?"

"That would be safe to say, yes," Doc said with a faint smile.

They stepped back, and Doc activated the system that loaded the enormous torpedoes into their tubes. Hydraulic arms lifted the phallic weapon to tube height and slowly eased it inside.

They turned away and strolled back toward the door. "Are you still going to visit Tatiana on Earth 2?" Doc asked.

"Yeah, Voprot's prepping the *Armstrong* as we speak. I'll pop over there for a couple hours and come right back."

"Perhaps it will give you a sense of finality," Doc offered. "A literal and figurative 'cutting of the cord,' so to speak, with your former life."

Geddy gave a rueful chuckle. "Wouldn't that be nice?"

Doc lowered his eyes and came right up to him, his expression somber. "Captain, I've ... meant to thank you."

"For what?"

"For restoring my dignity."

"What are you talking about?"

"The time I have spent with you and the crew has been the most thrilling and rewarding of my life. Not financially, of course, but in other ways."

"Of course," Geddy admitted.

"You have given me purpose and taken me from exile to belonging. That is a longer journey than you know."

Geddy's heart swelled. This was as emotional as he'd ever seen Doc, which still wasn't saying much. But he could relate.

"That's great, Doc, but why are you telling me this now?"

He nodded at the torpedo tube. "Because inside that tube is a weapon of last resort. We may be running out of time to speak our minds. The closer we get to finding the Zelnads, the more danger we invite."

Geddy wiped away a tear and opened his arms. "Captains aren't supposed to ... Goddamnit ... bring it in."

Doc hesitantly took a step forward, and they awkwardly embraced. A few seconds in, the door opened and Voprot came in.

"Geddy, your ship is r–" He stopped in his tracks and cocked his head, his ears twitching as he looked curiously at them.

He and Doc released each other. "Thanks, V. I'll be right there."

"It is okay to hug," Voprot said. "Not on Kigantu, but okay with me."

Geddy laughed and shook his head. "It's not like that, pal. Doc was sharing his... um, feelings."

Voprot's eyes darted back and forth between them. "Then ... how it not like that?"

"He was thanking me for giving him something huge."

— *Geddy, don't torture him.*

The lizard took a couple slow steps backward. "I am get uncomfortable now."

"I'm talking about dignity." He gave Doc a sly wink. "What did you think I meant?"

CHAPTER 19
FOR OLD TIME'S SAKE

Eight years earlier, starting from the day he returned to The Deuce, sold the ship he stole from Tretiak, and went to work in the geothermal tunnels, Geddy didn't leave the surface even once. The closest he got otherwise was Tati's penthouse, basically the highest point in Laguna. Since then, the only time he'd seen the planet from space was on his harrowing elevator ride up to the giant Semenov salvage processor in geostationary orbit, and then again when he was ejected into the vacuum with a bunch of jagged metal.

He'd been to Old Earth more recently than Earth 2, which was kind of ironic.

Unlike Old Earth, however, it wasn't a pretty planet, even from afar. Practically all of its water was deep underground or frozen except for the lake around which the city of Laguna was built, and that was manmade. Other than the lake itself, a tiny blue dot sandwiched between Herschel Crater and the nameless hills to the west, the planet's only colors were tan, the sickly green of a ubiquitous shrub called brickbrush, and the blue-white of the Ice Castles, the polar region in the North that covered nearly a quarter of its surface.

Seeing it now from the bridge of the *Armstrong*, it could've been any half-dead exoplanet like Durandia. Were they really lucky to have found it they'd been told as military brats? Or was that as much a lie as the story about how the transports came to this galaxy?

Tatiana's salvage platform was essentially a colossal plant for the sorting, processing, and packaging of valuable materials, mostly metal. It was almost entirely automated, from the heavy demolition equipment and bots on the surface to the space elevator that hauled it into orbit and the machinery that broke it down. Semenov Planetary Systems owned and operated four such platforms.

The green ring around the front screen flashed, and he opened the channel. A barrel-chested man with a five o'clock shadow and a buzzcut came on screen. Geddy knew a former PDF soldier when he saw one.

"Greetings, Captain. I'm Chief Sworles. Miss Semenov is expecting you. I trust your journey wasn't too long."

"Went by in a flash, Chief. Where do you want me to stick this big hog?"

Sworles gave a bemused smirk. "Dock 1B. We'll see you in a few."

Once he blinked out, the docking sequence replaced his face on screen, and Geddy set the system to auto. He visited the small bathroom beside his quarters, wetted his hands, and ran them through his unruly brown hair.

— Is grooming really necessary?

"It's not for her, it's for the occasion."

— Mmm hmm.

By the time he came back out, the ship was nearly lined up. He waited by the airlock until he felt a gentle vibration travel up through his feet, and a chime indicated the connection was made.

"Docking sequence completed," cooed Cherie. "Airlock

pressure equalized."

The door slid aside on his end, and a moment later the one on the platform hissed open as well. Sworles was waiting to greet him. He was about Geddy's height but burlier, the kind of guy he felt comfortable around. He could pretty much guess the story. Put in his time with the PDF, got bored, and took a lucrative gig in the private sector that he could do in his sleep.

"Welcome to *SPS-2*, Captain." Sworles' grip was sturdy and reassuring.

"Thanks, Chief."

"C'mon, I'll take you to the ops center." He gestured down a long, nondescript corridor and they began to walk. "Ever been in one of these rigs?" asked Sworles, smirking. "Other than your brief tour of the intake bay?"

Geddy grimaced as the memory of the day flooded back. "You know about that?"

"I reprimanded the men who ejected you into space. If it's any consolation, they felt badly about it."

"Y'know, it all worked out for me."

The corridor ended at an elevator which Sworles ushered him inside. "Ops level. Authorization M-three-Q-two."

The door closed, and they hummed upward.

"How long you been on board?" Geddy asked.

"Since the very beginning. Four years, five months, and thirteen days. Not that anyone's counting."

"That's a long turn," Geddy noted.

"Better here than Earth 3."

"Yeah, that tracks."

The elevator door opened into a semicircular command center with a huge wraparound screen and a see-through floor. Two other workers, both young men, sat at the controls. Tatiana rose from a chair behind them and sauntered over carrying two tumblers of what he already knew was Old Earth — quite likely two of the last glasses in the universe. She wore blousy black pants that swished and flowed like a dress as she walked and a simple short-waisted red jacket.

She smiled pleasantly as she handed him his drink. "I saved the last of it just for this occasion."

"Yeah, right. You probably have a warehouse full of it." He took his glass, clinked it to hers, and took a welcome sip. It was as tasty as ever.

"I'll never tell," she said with a wink, then turned to her staffers. "Give us a few minutes, won't you?"

"All the checks have been run, Miss Semenov," Sworles said. "We can release the tether any time."

"Thank you, Chief. I'll alert you when we're ready."

He nodded curtly and fell in behind the two younger workers. They returned to the elevator together, and Tati watched until the door closed before turning to Geddy with a weary sigh.

"I don't know how they do it. I've only been here an hour and I'm already bored."

"Sworles seems like a solid dude," he noted.

"Then my dad was a good judge of character at least once."

He glanced down at her legs. "Again with the pants. Have you switched fashion consultants or are skirts out this year?"

Tati favored him with a demure smile. "Those men have been out here a long time. No sense in torturing them."

"That's very thoughtful."

She meandered back toward the front screen, which didn't offer half the view that the floor did. They paused over the remains of Laguna some four hundred kilometers directly below. Even knowing where it was connected to the ship, the tether used by the elevator was all but impossible to see.

"I'd forgotten how much I hated these things," Tati said.

"Salvage platforms?"

"It's like a big mechanized vulture feeding on a carcass."

"Well, someone's gotta do it. In both cases."

"Yeah, well, after this, it'll be someone else's job."

He looked up and cocked his head. "How's that?"

"This was the last salvage contract Dad signed. I'm seeing it through, then I'm out of that nasty business."

"Wow. Really?"

Big, splashy salvage ops like this were the main reason the Semenov name was so recognizable. Ivan had his fingers in plenty of other pies, but his reputation was quite literally built with scrap. The Ring War left a trail of destruction that somebody had to clean up. He always seemed to be in the right place at the right time.

"Almost every piece of scrap we hauled up is being repurposed on Earth 3."

"You're not selling it?" She shook her head. "Then how the hell are you making money off this?"

She stared back, challenging him to realize the answer for himself. "I'm not. The cable's Gundrun steel, which we need to finish the Bubbles. The rest is worth more to us than it would be on the open market."

Tati characterized it as a business decision, but she also wanted to be remembered as the one who got Earth 3 over the hump. Either she was playing a long game or she thought it was the best thing for her planet. Ivan could never have been so beneficent.

Geddy's neck was getting sore from staring down through the floor, so he took another sip and moved closer to the front screen, which looked straight out at the planet's north pole. Half the Ice Castles were in shadow, and the other half was largely obscured by thick, yellow-tinged clouds. That was weird because the region was known for the brilliant displays of sunlight playing on skyscraper-sized towers of ice pushed up from below.

"So, tell me about these tremors. The ones on the planet, I mean."

"Getting worse by the day," Tati replied. "The science nerds back home think it's new pockets of methane and hydrogen sulfide bubbling up. They say the crust is thin and unstable."

"I dunno, Tots. When I worked at the plant, they had seismic alarms. They were set pretty low, and I never heard 'em go off once."

Her face hardened. "It doesn't matter. Once we cut the cord and haul it in, I'm done with this shit."

Some of Tati's most painful memories of The Deuce involved her father. Some likely involved him, their torrid affair, and their brief engagement. But Geddy had his own memories to leave behind, never getting to say goodbye to his parents and causing the accident that forced the planet's evacuation.

He raised his glass again. "To forgetting."

"I'll drink to that."

Another clink, and he raised the silky liquid to his grateful lips.

CHAPTER 20
CORD CUTTING

Once the crew returned, Sworles explained that the tether was a relatively thin cable of pure Gundrun steel, not exactly the most ductile metal and therefore challenging to make into cable. Its value, he added, likely exceeded that of the platform itself. It was attached to an anchor the size of an office building buried deep beneath Herschel Crater. They had already begun the slow process of reducing the platform's orbital distance so there was no tension in the cable when it was released. Once that was done, they'd reel it in and drag the platform back to Earth 3, a four-month journey.

Then, humanity's last connection to The Deuce would finally be severed.

"If this is the final salvage job, what will you do with the platforms?" Geddy asked Tati.

"Lease them out. Sell them. I honestly don't care."

While Sworles and the other two workers consulted quietly over readings on the screen hovering in front of them, Geddy leaned in close to her. "Hey, I've gotta ask. Are you still pissed about Myadan?"

She looked up at him through the tops of her eyes. "This may come as a shock, Starheart, but not everything's about you."

"It's just ... you seemed kinda out of sorts at the Committee meeting."

Tati's eyes drifted back down to the see-through floor. "Laguna wasn't much, but my father built it into what it was. I can't help but feel I'm letting his legacy die. Stupid, I know, but there it is."

This admission was as much vulnerability as she'd ever shown. It was weird to hear her say it, especially to him, but she probably didn't have anyone to talk to. Living in a castle had a way of alienating people, but apparently she had yet to figure that out.

That she could still care about honoring her corrupt, greedy, and domineering father baffled him. "You have your own legacy to build."

She gave a rueful laugh. "Yeah, a legacy that started by ruining the planet and almost killing you."

The weight of this hit him like a blaster bolt. The accident in question did take place in the geothermal tunnels, which Semenov Industries owned and operated, but it had nothing to do with her. Apparently, her icy affect hid actual guilt that wasn't hers to bear. It was time to finally come clean.

— Well, shit, E. I didn't know she blamed herself for the accident.

— *You have to tell her.*

"Hey, uh, there's something you need to know. The explosion wasn't your fault."

Her eyes narrowed suspiciously. "What do you mean?"

"It was mine."

The look of doubt instantly morphed into disbelief and anger. "Geddy, my guilt isn't your problem anymore. It never was."

"I'm being serious, Tots. I caused the accident."

Her bright, bottomless eyes searched for insincerity or deceit but found none. "What the hell are you talking about?"

He recounted how Eli had helped him find a source of shinium beneath an unused utility tunnel. How he used labrozite explosive to blow a hole in it, weakening the rock that held back an ocean of toxic gas. How he was presumed dead and saw that as an opportunity to keep working on his ship with impunity, blissfully alone save for Eli and the hologram at the mall.

Back on Xellara, at the IASS show, he'd revealed the fact he had an ancient alien in his head. Tati took that pretty darn well, all things considered. This bombshell, not so much.

"So not only did you let me and everyone else believe you were dead, but you caused the fucking explosion?!"

"Miss Semenov," Sworles said, mercifully breaking the tension. "We're ready."

Tati's eyes met Geddy's long enough to bury her sense of betrayal deep into his soul. "Then let's get this over with. The Captain and I have better things to do."

"Tots ..."

But she'd already strode stiffly away from him to stand behind Sworles with her arms tightly folded. The big man's eyes briefly darted between them as he sensed the change in temperature.

"It ... could be a bit anticlimactic," he warned. "We release the clamp, and we slowly reel in the cable. Do you want to say anything first, Miss Semenov?"

"Do I seem like the sentimental type, Chief?" she asked brusquely. "Let's get on with our day."

"You heard the lady," said the chief to the taller of the two young men. "Let's release the c–"

A pointed shudder ran through the ship, so sudden that Tati stumbled backward and would've fallen on her ass had

Sworles not caught her. Alarms sounded, and the platform tilted back toward the colossal processing center where the tether was attached.

"What the hell was that?" demanded Tati to no one in particular.

"I dunno, the cable just went taut!" the young man said.

"Bring her down as far as you can without de-orbiting us and release it at your first opportunity," ordered Sworles.

"Aye, Chief, reducing our altitude."

The chief shot a look to Geddy and pointed at one of the empty chairs. "Captain, Miss Semenov, I'd feel better if you were strapped in."

Tati didn't need to be asked twice. She quickly sat on the other side of Sworles and secured the restraints while Geddy sat beside the shorter of the two young men. The platform's engines audibly strained against whatever was pulling on the tether, but it slowly eased as the platform lowered closer to the edge of the atmosphere.

"Any day now, Ensign," growled Sworles.

"The release mechanism's unresponsive." The kid shook his head. "Whatever happened down there must've damaged it."

"Shit." Sworles turned to Tati, who still seemed rattled. "The ground around the anchor must be unstable."

"Isn't there like a backup or something?" Her jaw clenched tightly.

"The backup is cutting it. It's no big deal — I'll take one of the dropships down."

"Screw that." Geddy unbuckled himself and rose. "Let's go down in the *Armstrong*. To the planet, I mean."

"You sure? We have two dropships ready to go."

He cocked an eyebrow. "What'll you cut it with?"

Sworles shrugged. "A torch."

Geddy rolled his eyes. Cutting a Gundrun steel cable that size could take hours. "Oh, hell no. I've got a better idea."

"Do you mean what I think you mean?" Sworles asked.

"I haven't shot anything in a while."

Tati unbuckled herself and got up as well. "Well, I'm coming with you."

"I don't think that's wise, Miss," Sworles warned. "We don't know what's happening down there. It could be dangerous."

"If this eyesore goes down, I'm not going with it. It galls me to say it, but I feel safer with Geddy."

Sworles glanced over at his young charges, who seemed largely untroubled by what happened. The taller one said, "It's no problem, Chief. I'll watch the slack and be ready to reel her in."

"You're sure?" Sworles asked her.

"Yes, Sworles, I'm sure."

"Alliance. As in the dead intergalactic organization?" Sworles asked, settling into the same chair Verveik had used en route to the summit.

Geddy released the locks and carefully eased the *Armstrong* out. "That's the one."

"So the rumors are true. 'Course, I also heard Otaro Verveik was still alive." His bemused grin suggested it was crazy talk.

"He is," Geddy and Tati replied in unison.

Geddy was about to plot an approach vector, but for once, he knew exactly where he was going. He swiped it away and executed a moderate burn toward the hazy atmosphere.

"Huh," Sworles said. "Guess I'm out of the loop."

If he noticed or cared that Geddy was raw-dogging the entry, he didn't say anything. The big ship vibrated briefly as it punched through the upper atmosphere, but the dampeners took most of the teeth out of it.

Morpho, who had remained inside, came swinging across the ceiling behind him and landed with a wet plop on his left shoulder.

"Hey, Pal. I was starting to wonder where you went."

"What the hell is that?" Sworles asked nervously.

"This is my first mate, Morpho. The shifter bot beside you there is Hughey Twoey."

"Um ... okay." He glanced down, looking even more uncomfortable when he spotted the silvery cloud of nanos.

"Where's your girlfriend?" Tati asked. "Catsuit shopping?"

"In fact, she's helping train the clones."

"Did you say 'clones?'" asked Sworles.

"The Zelnads made clones of Geddy so they could make babies with clones of me and speed along the end of civilization," Tati said. "I shot mine, but he's teaching his how to be more like him."

"Yeah, that's a pretty tight summary," Geddy agreed.

"I'm very confused."

Ahead, a layer of wispy clouds dissipated to reveal the south side of Laguna. The demolition machines had completely leveled it, leaving mostly chunks of beige concrete behind. It was sad enough to see up close, but from the air, it looked like some kind of super-weapon had been detonated. Cracks crisscrossed the city like a dry riverbed, an ocean of escaping gas distorting the air like an invisible liquid.

"Damn, you weren't kidding about seismic activity."

He angled to the east and the jagged ridge surrounding the crater where the tether was attached.

"Yeah," Sworles said. "My guess is the ground opened up under the anchor and swallowed it."

They skirted the rim of the crater directly over the spot where he'd made the final decision to ride the elevator into space almost a year prior. The colossal piles of metal were largely gone, as was the small army of sorting bots. The elevator platform itself was set off to the side, but the cable now protruded from a sizable hole in the ground that looked fresh. Here, too, the ground resembled an unfinished puzzle.

Geddy eased the ship closer to the hole and made a slow circle, activating the ship's powerful landing lights for a better look. The top of the anchor could be discerned inside, but it was way down there.

"Looks like your theory was right, Chief. I say we blast it." He turned to Tati. "That work for you?"

She gave a disaffected wave of her hand. "Whatever gets me back to Earth 3 before happy hour."

He pulled up the targeting reticle and zeroed in on the cable. In theory, a quick succession of disruptor blasts should do it, especially from such close range.

The channel back to the platform had remained open. "SPS 2, this is Captain Starheart. We're gonna do this the fun way."

"Roger that, Captain. We're ready when you are," said the young man.

"Cutting the cord, then." He turned to Sworles. "How many shots do you think?"

"With disruptors?" Geddy nodded. "Three."

"I say two."

Sworles offered his hand. "Fifty credits."

Geddy took it. "You're on."

"Let's go before you start comparing dicks," Tati said.

With the reticle fixed on the target, Geddy squeezed off two quick blasts. The section he'd hit frayed and glowed bright red but didn't break yet. Gundrun steel wasn't tukrium, but it was still tough stuff.

One more blast did it. Since the cable was already slack, it wasn't overly dramatic. The lower bit fell into the sinkhole and the upper hung there, swinging lazily back and forth.

"Ha!" Sworles slapped his thigh and laughed, then held out his open palm. "A bet's a bet."

Geddy dug in his pocket for a fifty-credit square, the most cash he usually carried, and plunked it unceremoniously into Sworles' waiting hand.

His shit-eating grin contrasted with Geddy's pursed lips. "Choke on it. SPS2, you're good to go."

"Glad to hear it, Captain," replied the young man. "We'll start reeling it in."

Geddy swung the nose of the ship around toward the remains of the city and began climbing. At about two thousand meters, he glanced north. The opaque, billowing clouds that had obstructed his view of the Ice Castles from space seemed like they hadn't moved.

"Hey, Cherie, what's the current atmospheric profile?"

"Seventy-one percent nitrogen, twelve percent oxygen, ten percent methane, four percent hydrogen sulfide, and three percent trace gases."

"*Ten percent* methane?" Geddy asked, his mouth hanging open.

"We're pretty sure it's from increased volcanic activity in the North," Sworles explained. "That's what's producing those clouds."

— *Are you thinking what I think you're thinking?*

He leveled out and angled the ship toward the clouds.

"Geddy, what are you doing?" Tati asked warily.

"I've always wanted to see an active volcano. Have you?"

CHAPTER 21
WHAT THE DEUCE?

The *Armstrong* streaked northward from Laguna at an altitude of only seventy-five meters. Geddy's instincts told him lower was better. Something about the opaque clouds — namely, that he'd never seen the Ice Castles blanketed by them before — had set him on edge from the moment he saw them. But his curiosity had to be satisfied.

"Geddy, come on," Tati whined. "Remember what I said about happy hour?"

"Did your dad ever take you up here?" Geddy asked, ignoring her protest.

She sighed and leaned back resignedly in her chair. "Just once when I was little."

"How about you, Chief?"

"Two or three times on the tourist transport with my ex," Sworles replied.

During The Deuce's heyday, if you could call it that, humans themselves were the main tourist attraction. But as the years rolled on, the Ice Castles became the biggest draw. The massive formations were always changing and shifting so you could keep coming back and see something new. It was also one of the only ways to see actual nature.

Geddy's dad took him up there several times in his Bayonet, a PDF fighter designed to be equally good at atmospheric and space combat that wouldn't have been especially good at either. Had Earth 2 gotten involved in the Ring War, Triad ships would've flown circles around it. But when he was a kid, he didn't know any of that. He assumed it was the deadliest fighter in the galaxy because his old man was flying it.

The barren, rocky gray hills north of the city ebbed into flat and featureless plains dotted with brickbrush. But the Ice Castles appeared so abruptly that it almost looked fake. There was a swath of rippled ice resembling a flash-frozen lake, followed shortly by the first battlement of giant crystals that pushed up out of the permafrost.

Ordinarily, the sun glinted off them like glass shards, and they were clearly visible from ten clicks away. Now, the low and unnatural clouds turned everything flat and lifeless and not spectacular at all.

Further west, the clouds were darker and streaked. The sensors indicated that wind velocity increased in that direction. A storm.

"Something's not right about this," Geddy noted. "The clouds, the seismic activity, the sinkhole ..."

"Who cares?" Tati said. "Let's leave this shit-smelling planet and have a cocktail."

"I'm sure it's just a coincidence. The planet's probably having a bowel movement." Sworles laughed at his own joke.

Geddy glanced at Tati long enough to notice her close her eyes and take a deep breath as though she was counting to ten. She thought men were crude and boorish and largely unnecessary.

The clouds thickened to the point where they clung to the ground, requiring him to activate sensor-based imaging.

Almost instantly, they disappeared like they were never there and were replaced by rendered images of the same ice formations.

"What are you expecting to find, exactly?" Tati asked, her irritation growing.

"Long story short, I think there's a chance the Zelnads are looking for a tukrium alloy here."

"Tukrium?" Sworles asked doubtfully. "There's no tukrium here."

"Oh, there is, but it's deep. Very, very deep."

"How do you know?"

His eyes slid over to Tati, whose look indicated his secret was still safe with her.

"Long story. Anyway, I'm probably wrong, so we'll make a quick sweep here and get back to the plat … form."

The scopes had picked up four unknown objects heading their way at dazzling speed. They were rendered as relatively small spheres bracketed by triangles. Not like anything he'd ever seen. Drones, maybe?

— *I don't like the looks of those.*

— And I don't like being right all the time.

— *I can see how that would get tiring.*

— Zelnads, you think?

— *I couldn't say.*

He powered up the shields, which only had about sixty percent of their strength in atmosphere. Once he did, his pulse quickened.

"What are those?" Tati asked, warily eyeing the ships' red outlines.

"I've got a bad feeling they're Zelnads."

"Zelnads?" Tati asked, disbelieving.

The ships flew in a tight diamond formation and were closing fast. Geddy was tempted to bug out, but something had appeared up ahead. At first, it looked as though a skyscraper had toppled over onto the ice. But as the scopes rendered a more detailed view, it became clear that it was a colossal machine or string of machines. Smoke or vapor billowed from one end and angled east on the wind. Whether it was the source of the cloud layer was impossible to say, but it seemed likely.

Unexpectedly, a contented grin spread across his face. "They're mining shinium. I guarantee it."

"What the hell's shinium?" Tati asked. "And why do you seem happy about it?"

"Because it means they still don't have enough of it. Cherie, weapons hot. You guys strapped in?"

Tati immediately cinched down her restraints. Sworles' were already tight.

"Weapons hot? You don't think they're gonna shoot at us, do you?" Tati asked, her voice wavering.

He was about to say he didn't know when the ships flashed bright purple at the exact same time, then again and again as their diamond formation widened.

"Shit. Hang on!"

Rather than pull up, Geddy dove below the barrage of lightning-fast energy blasts and hit the brakes so he could get a better look at them as they passed. But that assumed they could only fire forward. As they zipped past overhead, the triangular fins radiating out from the spheres rotated quickly downward and kept firing. The impact jolted the ship so violently, he nearly struck one of the ice formations as he banked hard to the left. The shots never stopped, even as the small ships abruptly changed direction and gave chase.

The *Armstrong* shuddered with each hit, and the shield integrity meter plummeted to twenty percent before his eyes.

— Ruh-roh.

"What the hell? Those aren't any regular disruptors," Sworles said.

"No, they're not."

Geddy rarely panicked, but his chest tightened as though he'd cinched a girdle. It seemed his hunch was right, and now he had a notion of what Zelnad fighters were like, but the cost of that knowledge might be steep. Shields were almost gone and he hadn't even returned fire.

"Cherie, stealth!"

"Engaged."

"Curtain bombs!"

The curtain was a matrix of high-powered bombs that put a wall of explosions between the *Armstrong* and a pursuer. They deployed from an array above the engines with a staccato metallic ripping sound, then he broke hard right. The curtain burst behind them, and instantly, the firing stopped. The ships scattered, momentarily disoriented.

"Cherie, send a mayday to the *Stalwart!*"

"Comms are offline. Reason unknown."

"So they're jamming us. Perfect."

The ships re-formed behind him, tightly following his drive signature. To their left, the storm raged. Making a break for open space wasn't an option with the shields so low, say nothing of the speed disadvantage. Considering the fighters' size, they'd have a harder time in high winds than the much bigger *Armstrong*. In theory.

He banked quickly left, darting as close as he dared between two columns of ice.

"Isn't that a storm?" Tati asked.

Her eyes were peeled wide in fear, reflecting Geddy's own worry about their situation. If this didn't work, he'd have no choice but to flip around and face them head-on, though he knew how that would go.

"Yeah, but it should give us some cover." The fighters lined up, preparing for another volley. Stealth mode couldn't fool them for long. "Hang on."

The storm resembled the wall of a hurricane. They plunged inside, and the wind slapped them like the hand of a vengeful god. The ship lurched sideways, and the front screen flickered. They weren't going to make it very far here. He needed to put her down before they drew a bead on him again.

No sooner had this thought formed in his head than Morpho, who never left his shoulder, plugged into his ear with a painful, urgent pop.

— **Go to coordinates 82.117 and 10.232.**

— That's oddly specific.

— **Just go! We can hide there!**

Morpho withdrew with a pop, and he entered the coordinates. They were forty-two kilometers away, which seemed like a light year.

"Did that thing just finger-bang your ear?" Tati asked.

"He's got a place for us to hide."

With the scopes struggling, it was hard to tell how close the Nad fighters really were. The answer came in the form of another violent shudder that almost sent them into a spin.

Twenty clicks still remained.

"Shields critical," Cherie warned. Indeed, the meter was down to two percent.

Before he could even process that, a shot slammed them so hard that it could only mean it took out the shields completely. By the way the stick felt, he knew they'd hit the rear stabilizer. He shut off the alarm after one *whoop*, his knuckles turning white as he struggled to keep her level.

His only choice but to drop even lower, still weaving between the huge pillars of ice like a pinball. The trailing ships couldn't close as fast, and thankfully, their next several shots only turned the towers of ice into snow. But the *Armstrong* had become impossible to steer with any precision.

With one kilometer to go, he made a wide circle around the point until he spotted the mouth of an ice cave sandwiched between two ice pillars. It was going to be very, very tight. He got them lined up and killed the engines so they'd be harder to track.

"Brace for impact!" He whispered a little wish to the universe.

Speed was his only friend now. He drew a bead on the widest part of the opening and angled the wings slightly to make the ship narrower, his finger hovering over the button that would fire the emergency retros and kill as much of their speed as possible. Without thrust, the ship was at the mercy of the angry wind.

To his amazement, they only brushed the two pillars as he blasted through and immediately fired the retros. The sudden deceleration threw them forward hard in their seats, followed instantly by the bone-jarring crunch of a front impact. The darkness swallowed him whole.

CHAPTER 22
DOWN TOGETHER

Geddy.

The voice was as unwelcome as his mother's when she yelled at him to stop playing the Ponley Point video game in his room. As he generally did back then, he ignored it.

— **Geddy, I need you to listen.**
— What happened? Why is it dark?
— **Your conscious mind is temporarily shut down.**

There was no crash until Morph reminded him of it, but now he remembered barreling into an ice cave at high speed. Speed they'd carried into a wall of ice.

— If I'm not conscious, then how can I understand you?
— **Because I am in your cortex.**
— Is Tati okay? Sworles? Why isn't Eli here?
— **Don't worry about them right now. I have something very important to tell you.**
— About what?
— **Dr. Nilsson and this cave.**
— The human scientist who actually invented the bubble drive? Verveik already told me about that.

— There is much he doesn't know.

— Okay ...

— The Zelnads' goal has always been to destroy Sagacea. However, I don't think they know how to reach it.

— Eli said it's at the center of the universe.

— That is a simplification your feeble mind can grasp. The universe has no center.

— Okay, but how could they not know? How could *you* not know? You're all from there.

— Sagaceans are ejected into space. There is no reason to know because we were never meant to return. That is the purpose of the barrier around it.

— Okay ...

— The universe was born from energy. Sagacea is the source of that original energy.

— Original energy?

— Are you going to keep interrupting me?

— Sorry. I'll be unconscious now.

— From the moment the *Rearview* ships jumped here from Old Earth, the Zelnads knew that whatever technology brought humans to this galaxy exceeded even their understanding. That it had the potential to reach Sagacea.

They spent decades trying to learn the tech's origins. Word got around that they were willing to pay anything to get ahold of it. Ivan Semenov took notice.

Dr. Nilsson knew the Zelnads wanted her bubble drive, and because she was host to a Sagacean, she understood why. So, she destroyed her research and hid the device in the Ice Castles.

— Why keep it at all?

— In light of what happened to Old Earth, she thought the day might come when they needed it again. She made her way deep into the North and found this cave. It was the perfect hiding spot.

By then, however, she was quite old. Her Sagacean had helped her prepare a new host for itself. A more durable form that could easily survive the cold and guard her technology. Once she died, her Sagacean transferred into it.

Decades later, a ship arrived at the cave with two people inside. A young captain and his wife. The Sagacean would not let them near the drive.

— No fucking way, Morph.

— The captain called in the cave's location to his superior officer.

— Colonel Pritchard.

— He sent a team. They overpowered the Sagacean, took the drive, and killed your parents.

In the end, Ivan Semenov never got anything from the Zelnads. It was Pritchard who delivered the bubble drive to them.

— How could you possibly–

— Because I am the durable form Dr. Nilsson created. My failure to protect the bubble drive is what brought the Zelnads this close to reaching Sagacea.

Geddy sat there in the dark with Morph for a moment, who he could feel with him but not see, and let this realization flow over his consciousness like sticky tar.

— Why are you telling me this now?

— Because you deserved to know. And because there is a very real chance you will die here.

Geddy awoke to a tsunami of pain. His head felt like it was in a vise. The acrid smell of frying electronics poked his nostrils like needles. All around him, shifting ice cracked and creaked as though alive.

— Eli, you there?

— *Yes, Geddy, I am here.*
— Did you hear all that or did I dream it?
— *I heard it. It's a lot to take in.*
— You didn't know any of that?
— *How could I?*
— You and Morph used to talk while I was sleeping.
— *Not about his origin story.*

Reluctantly, he pried open his left eye. The *Armstrong* was tilted at least thirty degrees to the right, but the controls were glowing. At least they still had power. His neck cracked audibly when he turned to the left. Tati was still secure in her seat, her head lolled to the right. For once, his eyes drifted to her chest for a noble reason. It rose and fell, rose and fell. Shallow, and more rapidly than he would've liked, but she was alive.

The front screen displayed the usual overlays, but the view was solid black. His best guess was that ice had collapsed onto the nose of the ship, but he wouldn't know until he got outside and looked.

He undid his restraint, and it became a bit easier to breathe.

"Tots, can you hear me?" He rubbed her cheek and gave it a few pats. "Tots?"

A low, painful groan escaped her lips, and she canted her head upright, a veil of platinum blond hair obscuring her face. She tried raising her right arm to brush it aside and winced, sucking air between her teeth.

"Ah, fuck! My shoulder ..."

"It's probably from the restraint. Hang tight a sec. Sworles, you okay?"

No reply.

He rose and pivoted toward Sworles behind them, who was clearly *not* okay. His head was also lolled to the right, but his eyes were half open and staring straight ahead. The sparkling metallic nanobots of Hughey Twoey rose from below the console and hovered in a cluster beside the big man.

"Sworles?" Geddy came around and gave the big man's bearded cheeks a quick pat, then pushed two fingers against his carotid. It didn't push back.

"Is he okay?" Tati asked dreamily.

"Not exactly. He's dead."

She gasped and tried to turn, but her injured shoulder jabbed her with pain, stopping her short. With her other hand, she undid her restraint and gingerly rose to see for herself.

Her breath escaped in a long sigh, and she closed her eyes. "Son of a bitch. I actually liked him."

— If we get out of this mess, remind me to take my fifty credits back.

— *You can't be serious.*

— I mean, it's not like he needs it.

— *It seems icky.*

"I'm sorry," Geddy offered. "Cherie, damage report. Critical systems only."

"Hull integrity seventy-eight percent. Life support nominal. Ion core nominal."

"*Armstrong*, you are one tough bird. Now just tell me she's flyable, and we'll be in business."

"Forward sensor array inoperable. Right rear stabilizer inoperable. VTO thrusters offline. Terrestrial flight not advised."

His head still throbbing, Geddy knelt beside the floor hatch in the rear left corner of the bridge and opened it. He unrolled one of the envirosuits and grabbed a helmet.

"What are you doing?" Tati asked dreamily, her left hand clamped on her right shoulder.

"I'm gonna see how fucked we are." As he tugged on the legs of the suit, he lifted his chin at her shoulder. "How's it feeling?"

"I think it's dislocated."

"Morph, can you help her with that?"

Morpho slung a tendril out to the console between them, then quickly coiled around Tati's dangling right arm like a sticky black vine. She recoiled in fear.

"Ew! Get this thing off me!"

"We need to pop it back in."

"Can't you do it?"

"I could, but ... turns out Morph's a doctor. Sort of."

She opened her mouth to protest again, but Morph tensed and thrust her arm upward with a hard twist. Geddy actually heard it snap back into the socket as Tati cried out in pain.

"Ah! Fuck!"

"That's how you know it's working," Geddy said with a wink. Morph remained wrapped around her arm, jutting what passed for a finger at the open emergency hatch. "Oh, right, a sling."

He dug into the duffle full of medical supplies and found the sling, then delicately placed her injured arm in the cradle, adjusting the padded strap around the left side of her neck.

"There, how's that?"

"Fine, I guess."

He slipped his legs and arms into the envirosuit, zipped it tight, and secured the beefy cuffs around the integrated boots and gloves. The helmet, which was larger and loose-fitting, went on last. Finally, he strapped the PDQ on over the suit.

"It should stay warm enough in here, but there are extra clothes in here if you need them and painkillers in the medkit." He indicated the open hatch. "I'm less concerned about the heat than the air. We only have so much O2 on board."

"We're gonna be okay, though, right?" she asked hopefully.

"Of course." Truthfully, he wasn't so sure. "Cherie, leave comms up for now."

"Yes, Captain."

"You want to talk to me, just talk. I'll hear you in here." He tapped his helmet.

"What about him?" she nodded at Sworles' body.

"I'll move him into the hold. In the meantime, try to relax so we don't burn up more O2 than we need to. Don't worry, I'll figure this out."

"Don't be long."

"I won't. Morph, see if you can fix the VTO thrusters."

Morph gave a dutiful salute and jumped from the back of Tati's seat onto the floor, disappearing through one of the heating vents like a loogie hawked into a sewer grate.

Sworles was a big guy, probably a hundred kilos. Geddy was sweating so much by the time he dragged him through the door to the hold that the suit's air exchange system could barely keep up. With some difficulty, he finally managed to zip Sworles' corpse into one of the body bags and shoved him tight against the bulkhead.

— Too bad. He seemed like a good guy.

— *I am scared.*

— Me too, pal.

He opened the little cover that protected the control panel beside the hold door and tapped the button to open it. The upper third swung upward while the lower two thirds formed a ramp and lowered, stopping just shy of the relatively flat cave floor when it ran into a mound of crushed ice.

His HUD indicated the air was even worse here, and the temperature was minus thirty-eight, which meant the suit had to stay intact or he could freeze to death.

The lights of his helmet threw a bright cone across the sparkling floor, which was covered in shattered ice crystals. Getting around in here was going to be tough. To make it a bit easier, he leveled his trusty PDQ at the ground in front of the ramp and gave it a short squeeze. The crystals exploded with a sharp tinkling sound, leaving a comparatively flat pile behind.

"What was that?" asked Tati in his ear, panic in her voice.

"Just clearing a path so I can inspect the ship."

He stepped off into the pile of ice shards and found it was easy enough to clomp around. A few more quick blasts and he'd opened up an oval about ten meters long and half as wide. He shuffled out to the edge of the cleared area and noted that the narrow-but-tall entrance was no more than thirty meters away. No wonder there wasn't time to kill their speed. The roof topped out at maybe twenty meters and coated with jagged ice crystals resembling inside of a geode. If one of them fell straight down, it would skewer him.

— *It is rather beautiful.*

— Yeah, well, it could be the last thing we see.

Turning around, he surveyed the *Armstrong's* immediate surroundings. As he'd feared, an avalanche of ice from the ceiling had broken off and buried the front third of the ship. One of the two vertical stabilizers over the engines, the starboard one, was now a stump. Whatever beams or bolts were fired by the Zelnad fighters had sliced cleanly through the tukrium skin.

A few more blasts cleared paths to either side of the ship. Visually, at least, it comported with Cherie's damage assessment. But digging it out enough to get it turned around might take some doing, especially considering Tati's busted wing and Sworles' inconvenient deadness.

"Well, the good news is, the ship's pretty intact. With Morph's help, maybe we can get her back in the air." He glanced over toward the cave entrance, beyond which the foul wind howled audibly. "The bad news is, I'm not exactly sure how to get us off-planet without getting blown to pieces."

"So what do we do?"

"Figure out a way to reach your platform or the *Stalwart*. In the meantime, Morph and I have got some work to do."

CHAPTER 23
CAN YOU DIG IT?

A folding camp shovel was the *Armstrong's* only such tool. It was designed to dig a trench around a tent or bury a fresh shit, not for clearing away a couple metric tons of ice. Geddy struggled with it for about fifteen minutes and moved roughly his weight in ice off the nose before he decided it couldn't possibly be done alone. Not without burning through all the O2 or sweating too much for the regulator.

That left them in a pickle. He could probably blast away the excess ice with the PDQ, but that would almost certainly cause more crystals to rain down, as would powering up the ion drive before it was time to leave the relative safety of the cave.

— *Where's a Zelnad gravity gun when you need it?*
— *In Doc's lab on the Stalwart, right where we left it.*
— *Thanks for the reminder.*

There was no way a signal from outside would reach them in here. His attempted SOS had been jammed, and any ordinary frequencies would be monitored by the Nads. The young technicians aboard the salvage platform probably knew something had gone wrong, but they would only know to contact someone from Semenov Planetary Systems. That didn't do them any good.

No one was coming.

"I don't hear any shoveling," Tati said in his ear.

"Talk to my union."

"Don't ever say 'union' in my presence. I'm not kidding," Tati said.

"I'm thinking, okay?"

"That's not really your area. Eli had better be helping."

— What should I tell her, o all-knowing spore?

— *I am thinking, too. It just takes me a little less effort.*

"He's pitching in."

"What've you got to eat?" she asked.

"There's a recombinator in the galley. Help yourself, but I'd avoid any dairy."

"You should eat something, too."

"I will once I have a plan."

"So, I should be working on a plan B, then?" she jeered.

— *Was she always this mean?*

— You can't imagine.

There was no sense in burning through his O2 merely thinking, so he was about to open the airlock door when he paused beside Sworles' body.

"I don't suppose you have any ideas."

The man in the shiny red bag did not reply, however, something caught his eye behind his right shoulder. The letters NAL stenciled on a small crate whose outer edge was also flush to the bulkhead. He knew it was all emergency gear but couldn't recall anything ending in those letters. An acronym, maybe?

"Sorry, I just need to peek behind you here."

He knelt along the outside of the body and reached across in order to pull it away from the wall. It took more effort than he would ever admit to Oz, but he finally pulled hard enough on Sworles' right shoulder to slide him out.

The word was TERMINAL. The acronym preceding it was TAC.

Adrenaline shot through him. Tachyon Accelerated Communication was narrow-beam tech that predated the Ring War and was generally used for emergencies — their galaxy's version of a telegraph. It sent messages via tachyon beam through a two-century-old network of relay satellites that would convert it to universal distress code and deliver it to the intended recipient. In theory, it could send a message from one side of the galaxy to the other in minutes. But only a fraction of the original network was still operable, and it required stable ground conditions and open sky. That wouldn't be possible here. But his mind had already seized on another idea.

— *Remember back on Myadan when the comms kept cutting out? Jeledine said she could use Hughey as an antenna.*

— I was thinking the exact same thing.

If Hughey's nanobots could stretch far enough, they could get outside the cave. And if they could do that, then maybe they had a shot at contacting the *Stalwart* on the long-range band of thieves, which the Nads almost certainly wouldn't be monitoring.

— He can't reach that far, can he?

— *Only one way to find out.*

Tati's use of the recombinator drained auxiliary power more quickly than Geddy expected. The batteries were full when they entered, but between that and maintaining a comfortable temperature in the cabin, they were already down to sixty-two percent. He'd asked Cherie about the levels before he came back inside so Tati wouldn't hear the answer.

"This soup is bland and uninspired," she opined. "You're lucky I'm hungry."

"That would've been good to know before I made the same thing."

He slid the steaming bowl of minestrone out of the metal box and sniffed at it. The recombinator was designed to simulate flavors and appearance, but smells not so much. Like everything else, the soup had a nondescript, vaguely artificial smell that didn't get you very excited to eat it.

Tati blushed and allowed a laugh. "I guess I shouldn't complain."

"Why stop now?" he said as he sat across from her in the small galley.

The hurt in her eyes instantly filled him with guilt. "I guess I deserve that," she said.

"No, that was a tasteless joke."

She set down her spoon and leaned back. "So how fucked are we?"

— *Well, this ought to be educational.*

He tilted his own spoon to his lips and sipped. Tati had a better palate than him, but her assessment was fair. At least it was nourishing. Supposedly. Still beat the hell out of nutrimush.

"As fucked as you were the night we got engaged."

She allowed a knowing grin, her pouty lips spreading into her rarest fashion accessory — a full smile. "That's pretty fucked."

"For my next trick, I'm gonna try using Hughey here as an antenna to extend our comm range. It's a long shot, but until I have a better idea …"

Hughey floated in the corner of the galley nearest the door. Tati regarded him silently for a moment.

"She must love you."

"Who?"

"Jeledine. Lending you her best friend and all?"

He brushed it aside. "Eh. She just knew she wouldn't need him on Stemir."

Tati shrugged self-righteously. "Call it what you want. That girl loves you."

Now it was his turn to blush. "Only as a friend."

"That still counts." She gave her head a slow, rueful shake. "Everyone seems to love you. Everyone's always loved you. Your crew does, too."

He wanted to return the compliment, but it would've sounded like the lie it was. "Bunch of suck-ups if you ask me."

"Your heart's usually in the right place. I'll give you that."

"That applies to most everyone."

"No, it doesn't," she said flatly. "You ruined both this place and Myadan, so obviously, you're a fuckup sometimes, but you're never in it for yourself. Y'know, for the longest time, I treated you like a project. I tried to turn you into a Semenov when I should've been trying to be more like you."

"Why are you telling me this?"

"Because we might die here. Part of you still hates yourself for the man you used to be. You need to be done with that. Right here, right now, because you're not him anymore."

He raised his eyes to her. "Tell you what. I'll forgive myself if you admit that you're nothing like your father and you never really were."

Tears formed in her ice-blue eyes, and in very not-Tati fashion, she didn't blink them away. After a moment, he reached for her empty bowl, and she stopped his hand with hers, giving it a tender rub.

Her head nodded imperceptibly. "Deal."

CHAPTER 24

THE MOTHER OF INVENTION

Luckily, the UDC antenna housing was in the upper rear half of the ship, a fact Geddy didn't know until he asked Cherie. A vertical row of panels behind the port wing slid aside to reveal footholds up the side, which were big enough to accommodate his thick boots. The Alliance engineers thought of everything, it seemed.

Hughey floated beside him as he climbed, his nanos shimmering in the reflection of Geddy's helmet light. He'd pulled Morpho temporarily off his work on the VTO jets, and he was perched in his customary place on Geddy's left shoulder, impervious as ever to the cold.

The teardrop-shaped antenna cover was fastened to the hull with an unreasonable number of screws that he carefully removed and tucked inside his breast pocket. He dropped a couple, but miraculously, none tumbled all the way off and into the ice.

Maybe that was a good sign.

The last screw removed, he lifted the cover free. The antenna was little more than an oblong post with copper wire coiled around and soldered to it. He took a glance back at the cave entrance, then at Hughey, trying to let himself believe this had a chance of working.

"Whaddya think, chatterbox?" he asked the bot. "Can you reach the entrance?"

As if in reply, a little cluster of nanos formed a shiny silver scab on the coil, then stretched its way toward the entrance in a mostly invisible line with several centimeters between each tiny, oblong piece of hovering metal. The nanos had near-field connections to each other, so if he could reach, then in theory, they could send and receive UDC back to the fleet.

Even in the lights of Geddy's helmet, he could only see the first couple meters of the Hughey-tenna. Dull gray light swallowed the rest.

"C'mon, baby ..."

While Hughey continued stretching toward the entrance, Geddy climbed down and entered the ship again, quickly closing the door behind him. He wanted to be ready to check the signal.

"Cherie, how's our battery?"

"Battery power forty-three percent."

He exhaled a worried breath and removed his helmet as he entered the bridge. Tati had a silver thermal blanket wrapped around her, and her breath fogged the air.

"I had Cherie lower the temperature," she said. "The heater was using too much power."

Tati sacrificing her own comfort for the collective good was as admirable as it was surprising, but they were still losing power too quickly. Soon, he'd have no choice but to fire up the engines, which came with its own set of problems — first heat and vibration, then detection if they got out.

He managed a smile. "That was thoughtful, thank you."

"Is the antenna working?"

"That's what we're about to find out." He sat and whispered a wish to the universe. "Cherie, how's our UDC signal looking?"

"UDC still unable to send or receive."

"Can you boost power?"

"Power is already boosted."

Geddy's head fell forward, and he rubbed his face in his hands. "Shut it back down, Cherie. Fuck me!" After punching the air, he looked over at Tati and quickly added, "I don't mean you."

"Don't flatter yourself. You don't get me hot anymore." She pulled the blanket tighter around her neck. "Although I kinda wish you did right now."

"I don't suppose you came up with a plan B?"

She gave a rueful grin. "Sorry. I got distracted writing my review of the soup."

He shook his head and rubbed his face to warm it a bit. "Well, we're running out of options. We can't call for help. We don't have working VTO thrusters yet, so we can't even back out, let alone leave. The sensors are fucked, so we'd be flying blind anyway, but none of that matters because we're buried under a mountain of ice."

"Can you melt it somehow?" Tati asked.

He'd already thought of that. The PDQ couldn't fire a constant beam and they didn't have anything that could. The only thing hot enough was the engines, which were inconveniently located at the rear of the ship.

"You could show it your tits."

Tati projected phony regret, "Sorry. My arm's in a sling."

"I'm gonna check on Hughey. Maybe something'll come to me."

"Good luck."

He donned his helmet and went back out through the hold, where Hughey was already waiting for him. Even though he was only a translucent cylinder, he appeared apologetic.

"Thanks for trying, pal."

Carefully, he worked his way back up the maintenance steps and withdrew the multitool that still hung from his belt. One by one, he started driving the screws back into the antenna housing starting at the corners. The fourth screw slipped free and tumbled down the fuselage, this time coming to a rest in a long, deep groove near his hips. As he tried to fish it out, an adrenalized thrill surged through him.

The groove formed part of the seal around the port side phantom, one of the drone ships designed to bolster the *Armstrong's* defensive profile. Had he deployed them against the Zelnad fighters, they'd have been shot down immediately. But they had small conventional engines and a full supply of solid fuel.

— *Yes, Geddy! The phantoms!*

A self-satisfied grin spread across his lips.

"Tots, I've said it before in a different context, but your tits are off the hook."

The largest of the three phantom UAVs hovered above the cockpit and the other two to the side, their engines aimed at the pile of ice. They couldn't run much above an idle, but they were working. Rivulets of water poured down the sides of the ship, and bluish light from the burners was starting to appear through the edges of the front screen as the ice melted.

As he feared, however, the rising heat caused more hanging ice crystals to break off by the dozens and rain down on top of the ship like flak. Most of it shattered and slid down the hot sides, but some of it added to the pile on top. All Geddy or Tatiana could do was sit and wait.

Meanwhile, the battery continued to drain. It had fallen to just under twenty percent.

Morpho appeared for the first time since the failed experiment with Hughey and plugged into his ear while Tati looked on with fascinated revulsion.

"You can look the other way if you'd like."

She leaned on her good arm and smiled. "Not a chance."

— **The VTO jets will be operational soon, but the vertical flight control module is inoperative.**

— Can you fix it?

— **I'm running a patch to enable manual control. But even if it works, the ship will be almost impossible for you to fly.**

The ship had five VTO thrusters arranged in an X shape on the bottom of the ship. Ordinarily, they worked as one, using vector thrusting to maneuver it while hovering. Without that control module to orchestrate all that motion, Morph had to code a graphical interface for the left hand, which would also have to work the throttle. Until they made it outside, it would be like playing a piano with one hand and a guitar with the other.

But that was only the first challenge. They'd then have to climb out of the storm and try to reach open space where they could use the bubble drive to jump away. Considering how nimble and powerful the Nad ships were, their chances of surviving were astronomical. Here, however, they were zero.

— I don't see another option. Do you?

— **Unfortunately, no.**

— Then keep at it. And hurry.

Morph left him with a sucking sound that always sounded ten times louder than it was then scuttled across the floor down into the vent to continue working.

Tati's bemused smile tilted into a smirk. "Durandians, Orneans ... Whatever that lizard is ... You ought to win some kind of diversity award."

Geddy laughed. "I had to cast a pretty wide net." She

returned his smile and he got up once again. "I'm gonna check on the melt. How's your arm?"

"Manageable. As you know, I like to keep a few painkillers around."

He barked a laugh. "You always were good at thinking ahead."

After securing his helmet again, he passed quickly through the hold door and glanced furtively at the bright red body bag to ensure it hadn't moved, ridiculous as that was. The constant patter of falling ice reached his ears, reminding him of the danger that awaited outside. He unfastened the lid from the TAC terminal's metal housing and peered inside.

This was their only shot at contacting anyone, but he couldn't use it here. Even setting it up barely outside the cave entrance was out of the question. The howling winds pushed eighty knots, and he knew in his bones the Nad ships were still patrolling the area even if he couldn't hear or see them.

Even so, Verveik and the crew needed to know what the Nads were doing here. If he didn't get a message out or died trying — and soon — they never would.

CHAPTER 25
MULTITASKING

Each of the five circles on the holoscreen represented one of the VTO thrusters. The further Geddy moved his fingers to the outside of the circle, the greater their angle. Controlling their thrust separately was too much to manage without lots of practice, so Morpho had fixed the throttle at twenty percent. As soon as he lit them up, he needed to be ready. With the crash, there was no telling which direction they were pointed.

"Are you sure about this?" Tati asked doubtfully.

"Nope. And even if I get us out of this cave, we'll probably be shot down instantly."

"Y'know, there is such a thing as too much honesty."

"Just trying to level with you, Tots. It ain't good."

"I thought you were some kind of hotshot pilot."

"This is a whole different ballgame. Now lemme help you with those straps." He cinched down the left strap, then paused at the right one. "Apologies in advance."

"Now that's no way to start an– Ah, fuck!" He tightened it quickly, and she grimaced with pain. "Some part of you must enjoy this."

"Believe it or not, hurting you isn't my idea of a good time. Unless it's by request." He tightened his own straps and reached out to the controls with a cleansing sigh. "Here goes nothing."

Wingtip to wingtip, the *Armstrong* took up about half the cave's width and maybe a third of its length. That left precious little room to get the feel of Morpho's manual controls, but if he couldn't keep it off the walls in here, navigating through the narrow entrance would be pretty much impossible. If it came down to it, he'd have to blast himself a wider exit and blaze out of there as fast as he could.

He powered up the VTO jets, and the ship jerked free of the cave floor, simultaneously jetting backwards. Though he was mindful of over-correcting, that was exactly what he did, shifting all five fingers quickly up on the circles. Just as suddenly, the ship reversed direction, pinning them to the seats and barreling toward the same wall they'd crashed into.

"Slow down!" Tati helpfully said.

This time, he only rocked backward with his middle three fingers. As tempting as it was to pull all the way back again, he only went a little past center, and she came to a gentle stop a couple meters short of the ice.

He let out a long breath, his heart still racing. "Okay, okay ... she's sensitive. Let's get her facing out," Geddy said mostly to himself.

With his left ring finger, he nudged the front left thruster forward, and the ship began a slow pivot to the right.

"That's more like it, Geddy," Tati said softly. "Use those fingers like I know you can."

A self-satisfied smile unfurled on his face. "See, I just needed to get a feel for the old g–"

A thunderous report came from overhead, a large chunk of falling ice that made Geddy's whole body contract, including the fingers of his left hand. The ship lurched violently left and back, slamming into the ice wall before Geddy could correct it. Then came a fresh surge of adrenaline and another over-correction that sent the ship jetting forward and to the right, smashing them into that wall with enough force that a vision of shearing vertebrae passed before his eyes.

As though sensing that this seesaw would only continue, Morpho killed the power, and they dropped the last meter back to the ground with a jarring *thunk*. Geddy's head reflexively spun to Tati, her bosom heaving from the impact.

But the now-unsettled ice cave had only just awoken. Sinister cracks hit his ears from the front right part of the cave, the last he'd collided with as he fought for control, and both he and Tati gave a start. An entire section of wall calved free onto the floor, making them both gasp. It exposed a dark gray shape, obviously manmade. A small starship.

"What the hell is that?" Tati asked.

Geddy knew what it was immediately, though the words were difficult to form. It couldn't possibly be what he thought it was, yet nothing else made sense.

"It's a PDF Bayonet," he replied distantly. "And I'm pretty sure it's the one my dad used to fly."

"A Bayonet," Tati said as though the very notion was preposterous. "Here."

Geddy abruptly rose. "I have to check it out."

"But the battery's almost dead."

He lowered his head and let out a long sigh. "We didn't just stumble on this cave. Morph guided us to it when we were running from the Nads."

She blinked in confusion. "What?"

He hurriedly recounted the story Morph told him. His

parents, Dr. Nilsson, Pritchard — everything. But her skeptical expression never crossed the line into disbelief.

Her eyes zipped back and forth between him and the Bayonet. "You're saying that's literally your dad's ship?"

"It means Morpho's story is true. Pritchard sold out the entire galaxy, and now the Nads hold the key to reaching Sagacea."

Within a minute, his helmet was back on and he headed out through the airlock. Morpho appeared through the vent and slung himself up on the seat that Sworles died in as though to ask, *What the hell are you doing now?*

The nose of the Bayonet was elevated a good two meters off the floor at a downward angle as though expanding ice had lifted it off the ground. After again removing the lid from the narrow-beam crate, he held it over his head and leveled the PDQ to the left of the old ship, blasting away ice all around it with short taps of the trigger until more than half of it was exposed. A final blast freed it, and it slid out from its cavity like an artifact, sliding to a stop no more than ten meters from the *Armstrong's* starboard wing.

The lights from his helmet couldn't penetrate the glass of the front shield, which was heavily frosted on the inside.

"Cherie, deploy the starboard phantom," he said, and again it popped free of its recessed housing. "I need it to melt this, too."

"Geddy, you just finished telling me our situation was urgent," Tati said into his ear. He could see her now through the window. "I'm sure this is hard for you, but that thing's a relic. We need to get the hell out of here."

"What we need is to call for help. This puppy's got a conventional drive. If it still works, maybe we can find a place to set up the TAC terminal."

With Cherie's help, the phantom aligned its engines with the frozen Bayonet's port side door. Within a few minutes it appeared free of ice. He folded out the handle, gave it a jerk toward him, and it swung open.

— *You don't have to do this.*
— Yes, I do.

With no power, the ladder didn't deploy, so Geddy had to grab the edge and hoist himself up. As soon as his eyes popped above the opening, he came face-to-face with the pilot's desiccated and frozen-solid corpse, still wearing an early PDF version of an envirosuit. The face shield was half missing where it had been shot with a blaster.

A captain rank insignia was plainly visible on the upper left breast of the suit, below which was a patch that read, KEPLER, L.

In the copilot's seat sat his mother, also in an envirosuit but without the name or rank. She was slumped over at an awkward angle as if she'd been unceremoniously shoved inside.

— *Oh, Geddy ...*

The urgency Tati mentioned was enough to help shove down the wave of emotions that welled up inside him. He had a reason for chiseling this old hunk of junk out of the ice, and it wasn't to see the bodies of his dead parents.

"Y'know, if the seals held on this thing and there's no major damage, it's not crazy talk that we could get her going," he said.

"Just so I'm clear ... you're talking about *flying* a War-era ship out of here, right?"

"It's a helluva lot easier to fly than the *Armstrong* right now. Plus, it's old-school. Between that and the storm, we might be difficult to track."

"If it starts," Tati cautioned.

"Yeah, if it starts. I don't think it has a block heater."

CHAPTER 26
FIXED BAYONET

Half an hour later, the flood of emotions following Geddy's grisly and traumatic discovery would be denied no longer. After gingerly removing his parents' bodies from the cabin, he placed them next to each other against the cave wall, covered them with a tarp from one of the supply crates, and had the cry he needed to have. Finding them was only closure from the standpoint of finally knowing what happened. Otherwise, it was more like picking a scab that wasn't quite ready to fall off.

— *Are you okay?*
— They're just frozen meat.
— *But–*
— Not now, E. I've gotta keep it together.

"Ged, there's seven percent battery left," Tati gently reminded him.

It should be plenty. The Bayonet's engines only needed enough juice to prime the ignition coils, which wasn't much. He'd already confirmed there was ample fuel, and Morph had given the ship's guts a quick once-over, reporting no noticeable damage. A scraping sound broke the sadness that had descended over him as his back was turned to the *Armstrong*. Morph was dragging a power cable across the ice.

"Thanks, pal."

Geddy met him and dragged it the rest of the way, then opened the left rear maintenance panel. He held it open while Morph, who was an expert at this stuff, pulled wires off a circuit board and twisted them together, then used splice sleeves to connect them to the cable. Most of what Morph did to keep the *Fiz* running took place out of sight. His advantage, other than knowing what the hell he was doing, was that he had a near-infinite number of fingers, incredible strength for his size, and didn't feel pain. By the time the connection was made, the cable damn near looked like it belonged there.

He backed away and seemed to look at him.

"Okay, get ready to flip the switch. I stay here and hold my breath."

Morph sprouted legs and skittered across to the *Armstrong*. A moment later, a loud click echoed through the chamber, and Morph poked out to give him the equivalent of a thumbs-up.

Geddy whispered a silent wish that this had to work. He climbed up into the stiff, uncomfortable pilot's seat where that had been his dad's final resting place and paused to collect himself. His old man nurtured his keen interest in the ship's inner workings. He knew the Bayonet's controls stone-cold by age nine and even got to fly it a couple times sitting on his dad's lap, a breach of protocol that would've earned him a severe reprimand.

He flipped the toggle for the ignition coils. To his great relief, it lit up red.

— Moment of truth.

— *I'm with you.*

Geddy initiated engine start. A sharp report like a backfiring motorcycle came from behind, followed by the low, if unsteady rumble of the three Hawkins BE-9909 engines. Their reassuring vibrations sent ripples of pleasure through his backside.

— *Yes!!*

— Don't get too excited yet. I've still gotta check the VTO.

The moment he hit the switch, the jets beneath Geddy's feet sputtered to life, and a gentle push forward on the smaller of the two thruster levers lifted the Bayonet off the ice. A tap left on the stick, and he drifted left. A tap right, and it went right.

He eased her back down, leaving the engines running, and climbed down the short ladder. The moment his feet touched down, Morph hopped up to his shoulder, clearly pleased with himself. Geddy held up his palm to be slapped.

"Thanks, buddy. You done good."

After their high-five, he returned to the ship to find Tati looking anxiously out the window. She'd donned an envirosuit though she couldn't quite zip it all the way on account of her arm.

The moment Geddy came in through the hold door and removed his helmet, Morpho plugged in.

— **I must fly out ahead of you.**

— Don't be dumb. We'll take what we can in the Bayonet and leave the *Armstrong* here. We've got like four hundred more just like it.

— **You cannot outmaneuver or outrun them in that ship. You need to find a place for the TAC terminal.**

He hated to admit it, but Morph had a point. Maybe he couldn't fly the *Armstrong* very well in its current condition, but Morpho could. At the very least, it would buy them time to contact the fleet.

If the Nads tracked them, none of that would be possible. The Bayonet's first-generation shields could handle bugs, birds, and small arms fire. Whatever weapon severed the *Armstrong's* stabilizer would turn the Bayonet to scrap with one shot.

— **Take Tatiana and Hughey. If I make it, I will find you. This is the only way.**

Tati appeared in the short corridor between him and the hold with her helmet in her left hand, looking expectantly at him. Morpho unplugged and hopped down, flinging himself past Tati and into the pilot's seat.

She watched him pass her with mild alarm. "What's he doing?"

The words were like sponges, sucking the moisture from his mouth. "He's going to draw the Nads away in the *Armstrong*."

Tati stood there a moment with her lips parted, seemingly trying to understand how this scenario could end happily for everyone. But it soon dawned on her that it very well may not. The best-case scenario in the Bayonet was sending a message to the fleet. All they could do then was hide and hope. Any of it was more than they could do here.

She quartered back toward Morpho, who was already working on the preflight sequence, and her eyes darkened. "I'm sorry."

He helped with her helmet and tightened the cuffs. A minute later, the system indicated good seals. Tati's right sleeve hung uselessly at her side, and the chest bulged out where her arm was folded.

"Hm," he said, stepping back. "Light gray's really not your color."

"Do you have one in fuchsia?"

He allowed a chuckle. "Hughey, you're with us."

The shifter bot appeared from the doorway over the bridge and paused there a moment, seemingly confused as to why Morpho was doing one thing while they were doing another. But after a couple seconds, he glided over beside Tati.

Geddy looked past her at Morpho. "Morph, we'll be headed for the mountains near the old geo plant. Come find us there, okay? Otherwise, just try to make it to space and jump back to the fleet. One way or another, we need to reach them."

He gave a can-do salute and continued with his labors. Not a big hugger, that one. Geddy lingered on him for a long moment, realizing he might never see his friend and protector again.

He squared his jaw and said, "Let's go."

Tati followed him into the hold and helped him carry the crate with the TAC terminal out to the Bayonet. The door closed immediately behind them, and the *Armstrong's* VTO jets roared to life. It hovered there briefly before pivoting smoothly back toward the entrance. Meanwhile, Geddy and Tati loaded the crate into the much smaller hold of the Bayonet. After closing the hatch, he helped Tati climb into the copilot's seat, then got in himself. The engines still sounded good, and he lifted clear of the ice.

"He's gonna be okay, isn't he?" Tati's eyes were fixed on the *Armstrong*.

"Morph's got a way of staying out of trouble."

A few seconds later, the *Armstrong's* blue ion drive flashed to life. Geddy raised his gloved hand in farewell. "Good luck, Morph."

The ship eased its way around a few large crystals sticking out of the ground, then shot skyward, angling between the widest part of the entrance before it accelerated into the storm and disappeared to the west.

Geddy waited for a ten count before he followed the same route through the crystals, then accelerated through and angled due east. Compared to the *Armstrong*, she felt like a toy.

"Well, here goes nothing," he said.

Tati slid her hand on top of his as it tightened around the stick and smiled. "It's gonna be okay."

He almost believed her.

CHAPTER 27
WHO YOU GONNA CALL?

The clouds thinned, the air calmed, and the old Bayonet, the only fighter model in the long-dead Earth 2 Planetary Defense Force, emerged into a mostly sunny late afternoon as it skimmed twenty meters above the ground. There wasn't a Zelnad ship to be seen as Geddy and Tati raced toward the distant mountains.

"How's your arm feeling?" he asked.

"Not as bad. Where are we headed, exactly?"

"The back side of the geo facility. The mountains are rough and steep there. I need to find as much cover as we can get."

"Morpho's gonna be okay, isn't he?" she asked.

Again, Tati's genuine concern for another's welfare gave him pause. "He's a great pilot. If anyone can make it, it's him."

The scopes remained mercifully clear as they reached the jagged mountains stretching for ninety kilometers west of Laguna. From the air, the steep-sided canyons resembled the gills of an ancient and colossal leviathan. Ten clicks in, he spotted a relatively flat clearing surrounded by boulders and circled the LZ in a descending spiral. A minute later, the skids settled onto the gravelly ground, and he powered the engines down.

"Stay here," he told Tati. "I'm gonna set up the terminal."

"Just hurry before this thing explodes."

He popped the door open and descended the ladder with Hughey in tow, then removed the TAC terminal from the tiny hold.

— *Have you actually used one of these?*

— Once, a long time ago.

The terminal was little more than a small metal suitcase with a tachyon emitter, a folding receiver dish, and an old-school keyboard. He opened the buckles and removed the tachyon assembly, which resembled a telescope and had stubby, self-leveling legs. After unfolding them, he set it down and powered it up. The legs vibrated for several seconds to sink deeper into the ground for added stability. While they did that, he consulted the computer on his wrist.

— *You have the Stalwart's coordinates?*

— Yeah, but that may not mean a whole lot.

— *How come?*

— Because if there aren't enough working relays between here and there, it won't work.

He carefully entered the coordinates and double checked before he typed.

SOS. STRANDED ON E2. NADS ARE HERE.

— Well, here goes nothing.

He hit SEND on the keypad and waited as a meter clicked off the encrypted transponder codes of successfully pinged satellites with a few seconds in between. He figured it would take at least ten, maybe more to make it all the way to the fleet.

— Come on, baby ...

After hitting the fifth satellite, the meter paused and ROUTING ... appeared on the tiny display. It was taking too long. When the display read SENDING FAILED, he wasn't even surprised.

— *Well, shit.*

— Couldn't have said it better.

"Any luck?" Tati asked.

"You'll be the first to know."

— *What now?*

He only had the exact coordinates of one other TAC-capable satellite network in the entire cosmos. If it didn't work, all they could do was make a run for it to the salvage platform and hope to reach the fleet from there. But doing so risked the lives of the two young technicians inside if they were followed, and he was loath to do that.

The terminal was well-built and suited for all kinds of conditions, so the small keyboard was covered in a rubber material that made typing difficult with the bulky gloves. He entered the new coordinates then typed his message.

GS NEEDS THAT FAVOR.

An agonizingly long time passed between satellites on the status bar, but after successfully hitting seven relays, it indicated that the message was received.

"Yes!" he exclaimed.

"It worked?" Tati asked hopefully. "The fleet's coming?"

"Just waiting on a reply," he said, being intentionally vague.

— *Are you calling who I think you're calling?*

— It's our only other option.

Several minutes later, a reply flashed on the screen.

WHERE?

The knot that had formed in his stomach eased a bit.

E2 GEO FACILITY. NADS HERE. CAN'T REACH FLEET.

Again, he waited for the reply.

DON'T

A tremor powerful enough to make him lose jolted the ground, instantly breaking the precise connection.

"Whoa," he said. "Tots, you okay?"

"I'm fine. Did they respond? Is help coming?"

"Umm …"

An aftershock hit, nearly as strong.

— *Don't what? Worry? Move? Do anything stupid?*

— *That last one is a good general rule for you.*

He was about to re-calibrate the terminal when Tati said into his ear, "Ged, something's moving on the scopes."

He dashed back to the ship, threw open the door, and practically leapt inside. The ship's scopes tracked a small but distinct signal headed their way from the direction of the Ice Castles. Too wide to be the *Armstrong*.

"Is it Morpho?"

Geddy raised the ladder and tugged the door closed, then powered up the old ship. "I don't think so."

Panic again widened her eyes. "Is the fleet coming?"

"Possibly."

Her expression slackened. "What's that mean?"

He shoved the VTO throttle forward, and they shot up out of the canyon. Tati jerked her head down and right. "You left the terminal?"

"We don't need it anymore."

The ships were closing fast. Too fast. They'd never make it into space, and he couldn't fight them. Fortunately, he'd anticipated this scenario.

Skimming right above the trees, Geddy accelerated toward the little-known west entrance to the geothermal tunnels. Its only purpose was to pull air inside via a bank of industrial fans. It came into view as he banked hard left, away from the rapidly approaching ships.

"Wait ... what are you doing?"

"I know these tunnels. They don't."

"But—"

"We can't outrun them, Tots. This is our only play."

He flicked the switch to activate the ship's weapons systems, and a reticle appeared on the front shield. Once it locked onto the huge array of fans, he armed the missiles and hovered his thumb over the launch button.

"You're not gonna bill me for this, are you?"

"I've already written it off."

"Good."

He hit the button, and four of the ship's eight BD-4 Mosquito missiles streaked toward the opening. Only three detonated, but it was enough. They tore a hole in the upper left part of the metal vents, and he zoomed toward it.

Meanwhile, the Zelnad fighters were close on their heels — enough that Geddy half-expected a flurry of terrible purple bolts to hit at any moment. But not until the Bayonet darted through the smoking hole in the wall of fans did the shots slam into the metalwork with a force that shook the whole ship. Tati jumped and pinched her eyes closed, waiting for it to be over.

The tunnel began with a long straightaway. The ship's old NIDA-based scopes basically didn't work here, only showing the occasional blip as he urged her faster. Shot after shot exploded around them, showering the ship with bits of rock as he veered randomly from one side to the other.

The first junction was marked by a large ventilation unit on the roof. He ducked under it and immediately spun her around backwards. The barrage of bolts he unleashed into the metal box ripped it from the ceiling and it fell, hanging by a cluster of cables like muscle to a broken bone. He pivoted ninety degrees left and jetted down the next section as an explosion thundered behind them. Whether it was a ship crashing or another wayward shot, he couldn't tell, but with all the debris, maybe they wouldn't see which way he'd gone.

This tunnel angled down, taking a long and lazy right turn toward the pumps. Here and there, the planet's unsettled bowels had caused visible buckling in the metal supports. It didn't exactly inspire confidence.

A shot slammed into the tunnel wall right next to the ship, peppering the fuselage with more exploding rock as the force knocked them sideways. The heads-up display went *whoop whoop* and one of the three engines flashed red, meaning it was out. The Bayonet could manage with two, but one would be a tall order. The extinguishers ran their cycle and put the fire out as he shut off the fuel line.

Again, he flipped the ship backwards and launched two more missiles at the roof of the tunnel. This time, they both detonated, collapsing the already buckled supports as dirt and rock rained down behind him. He pivoted back just as quickly and continued downward.

"Are they still coming?" Tati asked, glancing nervously at the rear camera with her hand clamped over her mouth. His fancy maneuvering had her looking green in the gills.

The scopes no longer worked at all, so he couldn't know for sure, but it seemed nothing was on their tail anymore. He felt certain the missiles had collapsed the tunnel completely.

"I don't think so."

Another flashing red light on the display caught his eye. Fuel was leaking from the tri-valve, and fast. Clearly residual damage from the near-miss that nicked the engine.

"Shit. I've got to put her down."

"What's wrong?"

"We're leaking fuel. Just as well ... the methane's off the charts down here. Not a great place for flames."

Geddy slowed the ship as they approached one of the

maintenance stations where the pump jockeys used to take their lunch breaks. It was flat to facilitate the repair of trains and included living and sleeping areas. An employee railcar was parked on a side track.

The landing skids extended, he settled down onto the platform and powered down. Environmental readings showed methane concentration at thirty-seven percent, hydrogen sulfide at twenty. Without the suits, they wouldn't make it three minutes in here.

"What do we do now?" Tati asked.

He nodded at the train. "We'll take that car through the pump level and out the other side. As long as the track's not fucked, we should make it. With any luck, they won't be looking for us there."

"Then what?"

"Am I the kind of guy who thinks that far ahead?" He opened the door and extended the ladder, then came around to help Tati down. Hughey hovered silently beside him.

"How do we use the train without power?" she asked, descending the ladder largely unassisted.

He looked at her askance. "Don't you own this facility?"

"Owned," she corrected as she reached the ground. "And it was a hand-me-down."

"Well, these batteries last decades. I used 'em for power in the city. Not this one, thankfully."

Any one of the four batteries connected in serial under each train car would run the lights and appliances at the penthouse for a solid month — longer if he didn't use the blender, which he did a bit too frequently.

Glancing back at the tunnel, he opened up the hold and went back into the crate that had housed the terminal. Two brand-new short rifles and a pair of blaster pistols were inside. He loaded them and both spare O2 canisters into the cargo basket, then gave the Bayonet a final sweep to make sure there was nothing else useful to bring.

Returning to the train car, he opened up the panel in the floor and discovered emergency supplies that included more O2, water, and energy bars. The battery meter still showed seventy-two percent full. More than enough to reach the east entrance.

After helping Tati inside, he manually threw the switch that would start the car back onto the main track, then got in and closed the door. Once they started moving, Tati looked a bit less worried, and her color returned to normal. Hughey parked in the back corner.

"I'm glad you're here," she said through a weak smile.

"I'm glad I'm here, too," he replied with a wink.

CHAPTER 28

IT'S NOT GONNA BLOW ITSELF

The train descended briefly before reaching the pump level, the lowest point in the geo tunnels. Without the surprisingly bright landing lights of the Bayonet to dispel the darkness, they only had their helmets and the light from the car by which to see. Back when he worked here, it was always well-lit and noisy. Gliding down the track in near silence, the only bubble of light in a river of darkness, felt as surreal as it was scary.

As they went, Geddy found himself waxing nostalgic about the steaming gash.

The planet's crust was relatively thin, but the geo tunnels weren't nearly deep enough to reach the mantle where the shinium was. That was why he'd piled up labrozite explosive at the end of the unfinished tunnel they were about to reach. The explosion was timed to coincide with the fireworks on Settlement Day when the whole city was celebrating and the plant was closed.

All the subsurface data that figured into the plant's construction was readily available to employees, which was why he knew where to set the charges. The reason the tunnel was unfinished was because it encroached upon an area where the mantle bulged outward, and that made the engineers nervous. But it also made it the perfect spot to open a breach between the tunnels and the molten environment below.

More than anything, he'd been worried about unwittingly triggering a volcano, though the area lacked the pressure for that to happen. Indeed, when he detonated the labrozite, it seemed he'd gotten away with it. A gash opened in the relatively thin walls of the tunnel, and it was big enough for bots to go through. There were no after-explosions, and no lava burst spewed forth.

What happened instead was a defining moment in his life. Opening that particular hole in the earth at that particular time was a catalyst that upset a delicate balance in the planet's churning, molten guts. Ancient and terrible gases bubbled up through the porous crust, forming tiny cracks through which thousands, later millions, now surely billions, of cubic meters of flammable gas flowed into the atmosphere.

Similar cracks quickly opened in the tunnels themselves, causing a collapse that cut Geddy off from the exit. That he was able to follow one of the larger cracks all the way to the back side of the mountain was pure luck. With only emergency supplies, he survived in the barren, rocky mountains for three weeks, during which time he was declared missing and presumed dead. Only after the planet was evacuated did he circle back to clear the debris and shore up the tunnel so he could finish building the *Penetrator*.

The next junction was where it all went down. Nearby was a garage-sized storage room that should still be half full of labrozite.

When the train began to slow, he initially thought it was a malfunction. Then he noticed his hand pulling back on the lever like it had a mind of its own.

— *Why do I get the feeling this isn't just for old time's sake?*

— We have to assume no one's coming. That leaves it up to us to ruin the Nads' day.

— *You can't be thinking what I think you're thinking.*

— The planet's already hosed. There's enough methane in the air to turn this godforsaken rock into a s'more. In theory. I think.

— *How would you control the timing?*

The question stopped him. Labrozite was for demolition. It used triggers, not timers. The whole system, from the brick of explosive to the switches and relays, was made to work in one specific way. A timer wasn't an option even if he'd known how to make it. Failing that, it would almost have to be detonated from space, but he could hardly do that either.

— *It could be detonated manually.*

— Yeah, right. And who's going to ...

Geddy's eyes slid to his right to find Hughey Twoey still hovering plaintively in the corner.

Hughey could ensure the bots made it as deep as possible into the gash. It could arrange itself across the bricks of explosive and create the spark that would set it all off. It could do this on whatever schedule Geddy specified.

But Hughey wasn't his bot. It belonged to Jel. It was her constant companion. He couldn't use it as a smart fuse in order to take out the mining operation, could he?

Then again, the hour was awfully late.

"I feel like I should be telling you to stop," Tati said as Geddy finished loading the labrozite bricks into the last three working salvage bots.

"But ..." he said expectantly.

"But at this point, I want to stick it to those fuckers more than I want to be rescued."

"Just so we're clear, those two things aren't mutually exclusive. Yet."

"You really think this'll go according to plan?" she asked drolly. "You and Hughey are oh-for-one today so far."

"He wants a shot at redemption, dontcha, pal?"

As though in reply, Hughey broke himself into three even clouds of nanos and entered the salvage bots through the gap above the tracks.

The boxy bots' batteries weren't in the same class as the trains, but they had more than enough charge to get deep. Geddy turned to Tati, who was staying in the train while he and Hughey completed their task.

"You're not gonna leave without me, are ya?"

She gave a hard roll of her eyes. "Like I know my way around here."

"Yeah, but they're tracks, so ..."

"Yes, I'll wait!"

It still pleased him to push her buttons.

"Remember to watch your O2. If you get too low, connect your auxiliary tank like I showed you."

"Okay, *Dad.*"

They shared a laugh at the irony. Ivan wouldn't have taken any responsibility for keeping her safe.

Geddy activated the lead bot and walked beside it down the tunnel, its gears whining against the weight of the labrozite. It was essentially a square steel bucket with tracks, a multi-functional arm, and some basic AI that he and Eli had reprogrammed to collect shinium instead of junk metal.

How many days had he made this exact same trip down to the gash? Sometimes, he wanted off The Deuce so badly that he would make four, even five trips in a day. Others, he would go for weeks at a stretch without so much as thinking about it. Ambition was a fickle companion back then.

What a difference a year made.

By the time he reached the gash, it was starting to get toasty inside the suit, which meant he was approaching its upper thermal limit. The *Armstrong's* suits were better by far than the old Semenov hotsuits he used back in the day, which suggested the magma had risen higher still. If that was the case, then at least the bots wouldn't have to travel too far. Hell, they might just throw themselves in.

He placed them into standby, and Hughey emerged in three silvery clouds that reformed into his usual cylinder at Geddy's eye level.

"All right, pal, here's the deal. I need these bad boys as deep as they'll go. The more methane, the better. Two hours from now, detonate the explosive."

Geddy set the timer on his wrist computer. Meanwhile, Hughey shaped himself into two finger-like appendages that almost touched, then set off a little spark between them. That alone wouldn't ignite the air, and five hundred kilograms of labrozite may not do it either, but if it had a fair chance of fucking up their mining operation, he had to take it.

In a way, it was also goodbye.

"I'm sorry it has to be you, Hughey. You've been as much of the team as anyone, and we wouldn't have gotten this far w–"

Before he could finish, Hughey split himself up again and slipped back inside the bots, ready as always to do his duty.

"Not the sentimental type, I guess."

He took the bots out of standby. Their tracks spun briefly in the loose, silica-rich sand before slipping into the steaming gash one last time in a whirring procession. The heat emanating from it was enough to bend the air, and the suit felt like he was a tater tot. He turned away and trudged back up the tunnel.

— *You okay?*

— Yeah. Just a little anticlimactic is all.

— *What did you expect from a bot? Tears?*
— It's gonna be hard to tell Jel. And Morph.
— *They will understand.*
— I hope you're right.
— *I usually am.*

CHAPTER 29
BACK FROM BLACK

Geddy and Tatiana spoke little as the train car continued up and out of the pump level into what they called the machine level where the flash tanks, turbines, and generator were housed.

The main track only ran past, not through the wide, flat room overflowing with pipes and gauges and colossal tanks that stretched upward through the top of the mountain. Even now, having seen it a thousand-plus times, it was unsettling to see it not humming with power.

The plant had taken nearly a decade to build at eye-watering expense but at least it was well-designed. Components came from all over the galaxy, and the constant influx of deliveries and installations helped give birth to the planet's tourism industry. That largely centered around the many novelties and quirks of humankind, especially its unique obsession with shopping, and of course the stunning Ice Castles.

In about an hour and forty minutes, it would all be gone.

They glided silently through the central rotunda where Tati used to imperiously address grunts like him about things she neither understood nor cared about. They passed the rows of offices where foremen and middle managers figured out ways to boost production and lower costs, generally at the expense of worker safety.

His plan ended at reaching the entrance, at which point they had to hope the cavalry arrived before the labrozite detonated. Rescue wasn't all that likely now. The labrozite would blow, and then either something cataclysmic would happen or it wouldn't. Tymeri would come running or she wouldn't.

The end of the line was a utilitarian welcome center carved out of the side of the mountain. It had a food court, some retail, and a lame "History of Human Power" display comprising a series of animated placards around the perimeter. Workers entered through the security gate where the main tunnel ended.

They exited the employee area through a set of turnstiles and entered the eerily silent welcome center. A soaring glass rotunda focused sunlight onto a miniature of the facility, which itself was surrounded by etched placards describing its construction in boring detail.

"Somebody tried super hard to make this place a tourist destination," he said, shaking his head.

Tati sniggered. "Right? Like we invented geothermal power or something."

He ventured into the light and squinted up through the clear dome. The clouds were higher here but still thick and gray and strangely shaped, like upside-down cobblestones.

"Anything?" Tati squinted up herself but saw the same nothing he did.

"Not yet, but it's barely been an hour. She'll be here."

"She?? Who the hell did you c–"

Another jolt from underfoot cut her off, and she clamped his forearm like a vise, revealing her level of fear. A piece of the scale model, specifically the cooling tower, toppled sideways into the sculpted mountain beside it with an anemic *tink*. At least two of the Human Power placards slipped off their wall mounts and cracked. Moments later, a punchy aftershock loosened one of the panels in the dome overhead. It whistled as it fell, shattering all over the floor beside them.

"Outside!" Geddy pushed her ahead of him as they ran.

They burst through the long row of doors onto the tiled drop-off area where the monorail used to deliver visitors and workers. Geddy spun to see if anything else fell or crumbled behind them, but the tremor had ended.

"We'd better find a spot to hide." When Tati didn't reply, he gave her uninjured shoulder a slap with the back of his hand. "Hey, you hear me?"

When she still didn't reply, he turned left to find her facing out at the razed city of Laguna well below. Her icy blue eyes were wide as plates, and her lips trembled.

Eight of the triangular Nad fighters crept toward them from a couple hundred meters away. Two four-fighter squadrons struck the same diamond formation as before, the spaces between them tightening as they glided closer. It was easier to discern their design now. The fins were arranged in a triangle around a glowing metal sphere perhaps a meter across. Only a purple field of energy bound them together, allowing them to move freely in any direction.

Even from a good distance away, the power inside the ships seemed ancient and withering.

Tati whispered, "What do we do?"

His gut said to make a break for the welcome center, but they'd be cut down instantly.

"I wish I knew."

Ordinarily, Geddy would've shot his way out of a situation like this. The PDQ might rattle their cages, but he could only hit one at a time. That would only expedite their death. He could scarcely believe it hadn't come already.

"Do we go down shootin' like you said?" Tati whispered, her hands tightening around the rifle she'd only just learned to fire. The ships made for very small targets.

"Not yet."

It was possible, even likely, that the ships weren't those that had chased them in the *Armstrong*. In any event, there was no reason for the Nads to think or even assume he was the pilot of that ship and Tati a passenger. To them, they were two dopey humans who wandered out of a hole in the mountain. Maybe they weren't sure what to do, either.

"What's flying them?" Tati asked.

To be sure, there were intelligent beings that could have fit inside the spheres, but none were spacefaring as far as he knew. They must be autonomous. That wasn't a big deal. Pilotless ships had been around since the early postwar days, but they mostly delivered goods. They didn't fight. These were something else entirely.

"I'm not sure. Some kind of advanced AI, probably."

— Whaddya think? Are they gonna kill us or make us hosts?

— *I would never let anyone else in here with us.*

— Except Morph. Well, and Rai.

— *Is this really the best time to split hairs?*

Tati wasn't especially hopeful, but she definitely had a strong mind and, it could fairly be said, a healthy self-image.

As the ships' slow advance continued, only the spheres brightened and two adjacent triangles squeezed together, forming little tunnels like sideshow electrodes that converged on them.

They were preparing to fire.

As Geddy's gloved hand crept toward the PDQ, he felt like an Old West dueler, searching the spaces in between heartbeats for the exact right moment to draw. Only now, he was going to die no matter what.

His fingers had curled around the handle of his pistol when eight gleaming streaks spat forth from the opaque clouds. *A meteor shower?* was his first thought. But as they exploded against the fighters, the realization that they were missiles hit about the same time as the shockwave that sent them both sailing backwards onto the tile.

The impact knocked the wind from him, and stars filled his vision. But before he could gather his wits, something seized him like a firm hand, and he accelerated skyward. The wind whipped as it bent around his helmet, flapping the folds of his suit. After a moment, his vision resolved into the jerky recovery maneuvers of the Zelnad fighters, now at eye level and passing him in a high-velocity blur. To his right, Tati screamed.

As they plunged into the cobblestone clouds, there came a moment when he was certain they would collide with something hard. Instead, they slowed quite suddenly and were yanked sideways into the hold of a well-armed starship.

CHAPTER 30
LONG LIVE THE QUEEN

The hold door slammed shut behind them, casting the space in pure darkness save for a couple status lights near the ceiling. A sudden acceleration sent the two of them rolling backwards across the floor like a bottle on a bus. He crashed into the door with his bad shoulder, wincing with pain, but caught Tati before she did the same.

"Are you okay?!" he asked.

"I think so, you?"

"I'll live," he said, though he couldn't be certain either of them would.

"Where the fuck are we? What just happened?"

By then, his mind could grasp the fact that it was Tymeri, his old frenemy, holding up her end of a very expensive bargain. She'd used her gravity beam to suck them up into the clouds like she'd done to Oz.

"Believe it or not, I think we're being rescued."

Geddy rose shakily, still pinned to the hold door. Tymeri was trying to get into space and jump away as fast as possible, though she couldn't possibly know what she was up against. There wasn't time to explain all that over TAC.

He'd barely helped Tati to her feet when the first blasts from the fighters hammered the back of the ship, the impact sending them sprawling headfirst across the floor. This time, they caught themselves against the forward bulkhead, thankfully feet first.

"Enough with all the shooting!" Tati cried.

Before anything else could happen, Geddy sidestepped to the airlock door, then smashed the button that opened it with his palm. To his surprise, it wasn't locked. He was looking down a dimly lit corridor, at the end of which was the bridge.

He spun back to Tati, who had already crawled most of the way to him. Hauling her to her feet, he said, "C'mon, let's move."

Once she'd scrambled through the door after him, he immediately closed it behind her. "Okay, look ... I couldn't reach the fleet, so I contacted the only other person I could."

"Well, well," came a voice from the shadows of the corridor. Horschus, Queen Tymeri's Screvari lieutenant, emerged into a thin shaft of bluish light with a blaster leveled at them. "If it isn't Geddy Starheart."

"Tati, Horschus. Horschus, Tatiana Semenov."

"Semenov?" he asked with abiding interest. "Now that's the kind of gift that keeps on giving."

"No, that's herpes," Geddy said.

Tati spun her gaze accusingly toward him. "Why is this Screvari talking to me?"

"He's lickspittle to a pirate named Queen Tymeri. We go way back."

Horschus frowned and complained, "Hey, I'm right here!"

"Your phone-a-friend is a *pirate*?"

"Technically, she's Alliance-adjacent now, but yeah."

Another volley slammed into them, and the banked hard left. Geddy caught himself against the wall, and Tati fell into him. He caught a too-big whiff of her hair conditioner, the scent of which used to turn him into a slobbering dog.

"Starheart, get the fuck up here!" shouted Tymeri from the bridge. "Horschus, let them through!"

Geddy put a hard shoulder into Horschus and glared as he passed. He didn't have much time for lieutenants, consiglieres, or right-hand men of any stripe. He'd served as one to Tretiak for all those years, and he wasn't proud of it. Tymeri had a certain honor-among-thieves bearing that struck him as trustworthy even when she was trying to shoot him with his own gun back on Ceonus a decade earlier. Sometimes, bad people could still be counted upon.

"Shields, Nauthi?" She pronounced her Nichuan pilot's name *naughty*.

"Twenty-eight percent!"

Tymeri seemed to sense when Geddy entered the bridge. She spun around in a leather captain's chair not unlike the one in the *Fizmo*. Her beady arthropodic eyes bored a hole into him.

"What the actual fuck did you get me into?!" she demanded.

"I told you there were Nads here," he replied innocently.

"Nads are fucking *everywhere*, Starheart! You didn't say their whole fleet was here! What's chasing us??"

"Autonomous fighter, I think. Their weapons are badass."

"Yeah, no shit. Siddown and strap in."

She spun around to face forward as Geddy and Tati grabbed jump seats along the side. He signaled it was okay to remove her envirosuit helmet, but she shook her head. That was probably the smart play, but he couldn't breathe recycled air any longer.

"Hauthi, we're almost clear. Buy us five more seconds." She pronounced the twin's name *haughty*.

"You got it, boss." The Nichuan's spindly fingers flew over

the conventional controls of the old ship. No holoscreens here, which meant it was even older than the *Fiz*. Pirates preferred old ships because their obsolete communication protocols were difficult to track. "Shove some sticky balls in their faces."

Geddy and Tati both barked a laugh, earning a brief look of confusion from Hauthi as he struck a button. A long stream of staccato *doonk doonk* sounds came from above and behind them. In the screen's rear view, a cloud of metallic marbles flowed from the rear of the ship. It was only a moment before the Nad fighters struck it, but instead of tumbling off the side, the tiny spheres stuck like blobs of gum, clinging to the ships' fins and each other like scabs.

"Hooray for sticky balls!" Geddy said, earning a sly grin from Tymeri.

"Thank Lestiko," she said.

Geddy felt a pang of guilt about Hughey, which spurred him to check the timer. Fifty-four minutes remained.

The way the Nad fighters moved could only mean they were very light. Whatever metal was in the viscous marbles was heavy as hell, because before long, they began to fall behind, their sizzling purple bolts missing wildly.

It was a thrill to see, but the celebratory feeling was immediately erased when dozens more ships rocketed past the flailing ships firing all at once.

"Shit, there's more?! Hang on!" Tymeri screamed.

Shot after shot rocked the ship, and alarms sounded.

"Everything you've got to the rear shields!"

"Already there, T!" cried Nauthi. "Six percent left!"

"Everything we're got! Fire! Fire! Fire!"

Hauthi practically mashed the weapons console with his hands, and everything from missiles to what sounded like an antimatter cannon fired at the swarm of Nad fighters. Several shots hit the mark, but the fighters' shields shrugged them off like birds off a windshield.

"Where are we jumping to?" Geddy shouted above the din of alarms.

"Somewhere behind the line!" Tymeri replied.

"What line?"

Tymeri's ship fully cleared the atmosphere as the curtain of explosions from her hail-Mary barrage were swallowed by the near-vacuum. So many ships barreled through and lined up to fire that it seemed they hadn't stopped a single one.

She pointed at the screen. "That line."

As though materializing from stardust, a massive formation of ships jumped into space right in front of them. Hundreds of Berzerkers, Chimeras, a small fleet of rickety pirate vessels, and two enormous battle cruisers with the Alliance insignia proudly emblazoned on the side.

"Holy shit, you called in the cavalry!" Geddy exclaimed.

"Jump now, Nauthi!"

The Nichuan smashed a button on the console, and the front and rear images on the screen swapped places. The New Alliance fleet that had been in front of them now faced the other way toward The Deuce.

The cluster of Nad fighters was met by a cloud of disruptor bolts that sent them tumbling briefly backwards before they blinked away.

"Woo hoo! Yeah, baby!" Geddy shouted. Tati was across from him, laughing with relief and pumping her fist.

As the fleet continued toward The Deuce, Tymeri flipped them around to face the same direction. Every brick in the wall of ships was much larger than the Nad fighters. It almost seemed like an unfair fight, but he knew better. They were only regrouping.

The *Stalwart's* hangar doors stood open, and Chimera fighters were pouring out along with more pirate ships. Screvati Scythes spat from the back of the *Gallant*. The clones were about to be put to the test, and Geddy found himself nervous for them. Would all the simulations and exercises help them survive such a fearsome enemy?

Geddy was anxious to run to the bridge and help Verveik deliver the ass-kicking they all wanted. It seemed like weeks since he'd seen Oz and his crew. They were going to experience a real space battle together. That wasn't necessarily a good thing. If not for him, they'd still be snatching up scrap, destitute but relatively safe.

As they approached, the orange scrim of the force field appeared at the front of the now-empty hangar. He could just make out Oz and Doc waiting for him. On seeing Oz, his whole body relaxed. One way or another, everything would be okay if she was there.

Tymeri set the ship down, and they waited for the hangar to pressurize. A few minutes later, the field dissipated, and Geddy immediately lowered the ramp.

"Hey," Geddy said to Tymeri. Still rubbing her face, she turned the chair casually in his direction. "Thanks for keeping your word."

Her mouth parts formed an expression he could only assume was a demure half-smile. "Until you came along, it was about all I had. I should probably be thanking you."

"But you won't."

"I might, if you people repair my ship."

"I think we can make that happen."

CHAPTER 31

THE BATTLE OF THE DEUCE

Oz hurried up the stairs alongside Geddy as they ran from the hangar to the bridge. Without the clones and the constantly bickering pirates around, a foreboding quiet had enveloped the empty space. Doc had immediately escorted Tati to the infirmary, and Tymeri and her crew were appraising the significant damage to her ship.

"Hey, slow down," Oz complained. "What the hell happened down there? Are you okay?"

"I'm okay, but the Nads are mining shinium and we need to stop them. It's a big and well-protected operation. Their ships are small but powerful as hell. Like, blast through tukrium powerful."

They reached the bridge level and trotted down the hallway toward the doors. "The *Armstrong*?"

"The Nads shot it up. I had to put her down in an ice cave. Tati and I barely got out."

She grabbed a fistful of his jacket and stopped him in the corridor. "Wait — *Tatiana* was with you?"

"Oz, I love you, but now isn't the time for a recap. The

Armstrong wasn't flyable by me, so Morph used it as a decoy to help us escape."

"Oh, shit! Where is he now?"

He continued striding toward the bridge, but she didn't stop him. "I don't know. Tell me someone contacted the salvage platform," he said hopefully.

"Yeah, first thing. They've cleared out."

"Good. I need to talk to Verveik."

The bridge doors slid open, and they marched through. Voprot and Denk spun toward the sound.

"Cap! Boy are we glad to see you!" Denk said.

"I am happy!" declared the lizard.

"Me, too, guys. Mr. Junt, please hail the Gallant."

"On it!" Denk said.

Geddy marched over to the captain's chair and gratefully sank into the plush material. The battle group had formed into a concave shape like a bowl set on edge and was pointed at the cloudy north pole.

A few seconds later, Verveik's stoic face appeared on the screen. "Welcome back, Captain. So, what are we up against here?" Verveik asked.

"The Nads are mining shinium in the North and releasing even more methane into the atmosphere. That's what those clouds are. The planet's not happy about it, either."

"How many fighters?"

"Couldn't say for sure. They're light, nimble, and have extremely powerful weapons. Four of them took out one of the *Armstrong's* rear stabilizers with just a few shots. Their shields seem impenetrable."

"Speaking of which, where's your ship?"

Geddy hesitated, and the others closed in to listen. "It got shot up while I was gathering intel. I put her down in an ice cave. She was too beat up to make it to space, so Morph lured the Nads away while we made a break for it. That's when I used the TAC terminal to contact Tymeri. I couldn't reach the fleet."

"Made a break how? On foot?" Oz asked.

"In my dad's PDF Bayonet."

Verveik's stoic expression gave way to confusion. "What?"

"Dr. Nilsson hid the bubble drive in the Ice Castles, like you said. But Pritchard figured out where it was somehow and sent my dad to get it. He and Mom found it being guarded by a strange synthetic organism. Dad called it into Pritchard. His men overpowered the organism, took the drive, and killed my parents."

"Synthetic organism?" Oz asked. Geddy stared back, letting her reach the answer she already knew. "Morpho."

"Before she died, Nilsson figured out a way to transfer her Sagacean into a new form."

"My stars ..." Verveik muttered.

"Also, half a metric ton of labrozite is on its way to the mantle."

"Do I even want to know?" he groaned.

"I had to do what I could to stop the Nads. It probably won't work, but I figured enough heat might ignite all that methane and ..."

"Boom," Oz finished.

His eyes grew moist. "I left Hughey to detonate it. There was no other way."

The crew seemed to exhale at once as he delivered the bad news. Hughey had been a fixture in many of their adventures.

"How long before detonation?" Verveik asked.

Geddy consulted the timer on his wrist. "Thirty-three minutes."

"Then I guess we'd better get on with it," said the Commander. He switched to the open channel that the whole fleet would hear. "All ships and crews, battle stations. Prepare for an assault on the Zelnad mining facility. This enemy is unlike anything we've seen."

Geddy had devoted precious little time to learning his way around the ship he captained, a perfect example of the seat-of-its-pants New Alliance. They were still more or less making it up as they went.

His dearth of combat experience had him on edge. Heading into what might be a very consequential battle, he knew little about maneuvers or strategy. He could fly, and he could shoot. That wasn't enough to earn the command of such a large and powerful ship, but he'd have to act like it was and take his cues from Verveik, who had war in his DNA.

The big ship shuddered as it led the way through the upper atmosphere, but her advanced dampeners cut the usual vibrations even more than the *Armstrong*.

Another pleasant surprise was the *Stalwart's* sensor profile, which bordered on ridiculous. The scopes covered every imaginable wavelength and energy signature, and the image quality was stunning. The Nads' mining operation might as well have been right in front of them even though they were still five thousand kilometers away and blocked by clouds of gas.

"Captain, there's a massive electromagnetic signature headed our way from the facility," Doc said.

"How many?" Geddy asked.

"Several hundred, at least."

"All right, here we go," he muttered.

"First wave, deploy," Verveik said from the upper right corner of the display. "Scatter those fighters from our line of fire. I want a clean shot at the facility."

The privateers formed most of Verveik's initial wave. They peeled off from the outside of this cone-shaped formation around the two battle cruises and accelerated toward the target, an attack group maybe seventy strong.

Peering deep through the clouds, the scopes picked up the initial wave of purple streaks blasting out of the Nad fighters. What the hell would they do to those old-ass pirate ships? He already knew, but it was too late to do anything about it.

As soon as the shots flew, the first wave did as instructed, briefly exchanging fire before angling radially away from the facility and leading the fighters. Like Verveik wanted, they had an open, if long-range shot at the mining operation.

"*Stalwart*, weapons free," Verveik said. "Take out that facility!"

From this far away, the line of machines resembled a segmented worm with its head buried in Earth 2's skin, sucking its blood.

"Oz, fire forward antimatter cannons at will!" Geddy ordered.

"Cannons, aye," said Oz.

Four big cannons in the shape of a smile were mounted under the ship's blunt nose. A soft vibration traveled up through his chair as they fired with a throaty *whoom whoom*, pearlescent streaks of devastating antimatter streaming toward the facility like white-hot daggers.

Before they could connect, however, the cannon bursts collided with a shield over the entire operation and splashed outward like raindrops on an umbrella. The soft purple light of the shield flickered, revealing its immense shape and size.

Again with that strange purple energy. What the hell kind of power was that?

"Negative impact," Oz said.

"Doc, find me those field generators."

"Overlaying the projection," Doc said, and a reproduction of the shield appeared onscreen over the facility.

Shield generators for something this colossal would be the size of a house and hard to miss, but the perimeter revealed no obvious source of power.

"Do you guys see anyth–" Geddy began to ask the others.

A jarring impact rocked the ship, and reflexively grabbed the arms of his chair.

"Where'd that come from??"

"A Zelnad destroyer just jumped in behind the *Gallant*!" Doc said.

"Evasive maneuvers!" Geddy yelled. "Oz, let's see what a torpedo does to that shield."

Oz launched the first torpedo at the base of the shield near the outer part of the wormlike mining structure. As Geddy feared, it exploded harmlessly off the Nads' seemingly impenetrable shield.

"Shit. Denk, turn us around and prepare to engage!"

"Aye aye, Cap!" said Denk.

"*Stalwart*, don't you dare," Verveik urged on the open channel. "Second wave, get down there and find those generators. Give them cover, captain. We'll handle the destroyer."

"Aye, Commander," Geddy said.

Another group of ships, mostly the clones and the Screvari loyal to Balzac, peeled off the formation and raced toward the facility, engines blazing. Behind them, the *Gallant's* shields repelled another blow from behind as it pivoted to face the enemy. The spiky half-pyramids never stopped looking like flying noses. But other than the time over Gundrun when ten of them assembled into a supership, no one had ever seen them in battle.

It killed Geddy not to help, but Verveik was right. Destroying the facility was the point.

"Ninety-Two, find me a generator to shoot and don't get dead!" Geddy ordered.

"We're trying, Captain!" came clone Ninety-Two's voice. "Those fighters are everywhere!"

Geddy's head spun to Oz. "See what you can do about that."

She nodded and tagged dozens of fighters, then unleashed a barrage of targeted disruptor fire. It didn't kill them, but it knocked them off-course, including a few into the sides of the mountain.

Geddy glanced at their six. The *Stalwart* had slipped through the dense clouds, and the Gallant was no longer visible. "Doc, let's keep a visual on the *Gallant*."

Doc switched wavelengths and enlarged the scopes' view of the battle going on behind them in space. Both ships kept jumping and firing, jumping and firing. So far, the *Gallant's* shields appeared to be holding. Far below, clusters of woefully outmatched pirate ships were already limping toward open space. Every last one had a squadron of fighters on its tail. The explosions resembled a fireworks display.

Again, Oz targeted as many pursuing ships as she could, the sky filling with green bolts, but like Ninety-Two said, there were too many and their shields were unaffected.

— This was never gonna work. They're slaughtering us.

— *Then get everyone out of here or the war ends today!*

With Verveik tied up, Geddy was the ranking officer. He was about to give the order to retreat when a massive blast caught one of the fleeing pirate ships square in the ass, penetrating right through its depleted shield and blowing it to pieces in front of them. Debris pinged off the *Stalwart's* starboard shields. As powerful as the triangle fighters were, this had come from something larger.

"What the hell did that?!" Geddy asked.

Before anyone could answer, three Zelnad destroyers

emerged from the towering clouds over the facility like cloaked heralds of death, firing from all its facets on both the *Stalwart* and the smaller ships. Then, a series of pulsing, supercharged sound waves smashed into them, overwhelming the ship's dampeners. It shook them so violently that Geddy imagined rivets popping loose, screws coming undone, and electrical connections frying. It felt like his spinal fluid was being carbonated.

This was the same technology they'd deployed over Gundrun to clean up the last of the asteroid. Some kind of ultrasonic weapon and yet another devastating arrow in their quiver. The Alliance had brought knives to a gunfight, and he knew it.

"Fire, fire, fire!!" he ordered.

Oz unleashed a barrage of cannon fire and missiles at the colossal ships, each of which dwarfed the Alliance cruisers. Nothing so much as scratched them.

They weren't making a dent. And they couldn't jump in atmosphere.

Geddy checked the timer on the explosive. Twenty-one agonizing minutes still remained. They'd be lucky to last two. This could be it.

Maybe there was a way to give the Nads a little parting shot.

"Screw it, we'll target the mountain!" Geddy said to Oz. "Bring it down on top of the bastards."

"That will release even more methane," Doc said, smiling. "Tell Eli that was good thinking."

"Eli? No, no, it was my idea."

"Really?" asked Oz.

"Just blow up the damn mountain!"

She gave a sinister grin. "Are you thinking what I'm thinking?"

"Asteroid buster," he said, returning her look. "Do it."

The warship had two bombs designed to embed themselves on opposite sides of an asteroid and explode simultaneously on the same plane, splitting it apart. Ostensibly, it was to save an Alliance world from an asteroid impact. They were powerful enough to cleave the mountain in half.

Oz released the weapons, and they left the underside of the ship in unison, leaving bright streaks as they rocketed toward the base of the mountain on either side of the facility. Miraculously, they weren't intercepted or deflected by the hornet's nest of fighters. The bombs embedded deep in the ground, kicking up clouds of gray dust. For a moment, Geddy worried they were duds.

They weren't.

The synchronized explosion sent a ring-shaped shockwave across the face of the mountain, triggering a massive landslide. It began along a surprisingly straight line, and millions of cubic feet of volcanic rock collapsed right on top of the mining facility. By the looks of it, much of it went under the shield.

That must've pissed off the Zelnad destroyers, because a fresh volley of blasts followed immediately, violently shaking the ship as the front shield plunged from seventy-eight percent to thirty-one in seconds.

Geddy saw it in slow motion as he fell from his plush captain's chair, the chair he didn't really earn. Against the might of the Zelnads, the *Stalwart* was a toy, and he was just a kid playing war. They lurched hard to the left, throwing him onto the cushioned floor.

— Guess I forgot to buckle up.

— *Get back in that chair, Captain!*

Geddy shook his head, clambered to his feet, and sat.

"Cap, look!" Denk exclaimed.

The front screen was flickering badly, but not so much that he couldn't make out six dark gray Gundrun battleships, wreathed in the flames of a rapid entry. They descended out of the clouds directly overhead like muscular horses out of a lowland fog.

As they plunged down in front of the *Stalwart*, their forward batteries rained hell down on the Zelnad destroyers. A moment later, hundreds of the burly fighters called Brigands poured out, dropped into formation around the battleships, and immediately fanned out to join the aerial battle.

Geddy screamed with joy.

CHAPTER 32

SUCK ON THIS

Whether Gundrun's timely arrival was part of Verveik's strategy or a response to an urgent mayday, Geddy couldn't know. The heavily armored battleships that had formed a wall between them and the schnozzes banked, climbed, and rolled as they fired in a practiced maneuver that made them hard targets. The Brigands, meanwhile, seemed to be holding their own against the fighters.

It was an awesome sight. Gundrun had been fighting wars for thousands of years, and they were damn good at it. The Zelnads' targeting systems had a hard time connecting, and their shields were holding better than the much older Alliance ships.

"*Stalwart*, our shields are almost gone!" came Verveik's plea over the comm.

"Denk, Gundrun can take it from here. Get us back up there!" Geddy barked immediately.

"Thought you'd never ask, Cap!"

"All Alliance ships, get your asses back into space and jump to the rendezvous!" Verveik ordered.

Denk pivoted the ship around and gunned it while automated close-engagement defense systems kept stray triangle fighters at bay. Behind them, the remaining Alliance ships from the first two waves accelerated past the slower *Stalwart*, striving for open space.

Shields had dropped to eighteen percent.

Two minutes later, they crossed into space where the *Gallant* was still engaged in its blink-in, blink-out battle with the destroyer. Verveik was getting his licks in, but to little effect. Meanwhile, every purple beam that blazed out from the destroyer opened a fresh wound in the *Gallant*. A gash a hundred meters long had been carved out of the port side, and dozens of bodies were floating through the void.

Their shields were already gone.

"Commander, get out of here!" Geddy barked. "We've got this!"

"We do?" Oz asked. Then recognition fell over her, and she smiled knowingly. "We do."

"Draw the ship's fire away from the *Gallant*. All extra power to front shields. Ready aft torpedo two and prepare to fire forward batteries."

Oz gulped. Before he left for The Deuce, he'd told her about Lestiko's parting gift. "Aft torpedo? She's right in front of us."

"Yeah, but they're gonna jump behind us. The moment she disappears, launch that sucker. Denk, get ready to burn ass out of here."

"Ready on the throttle, Cap," Denk said.

"What if you're wrong?" Oz asked.

"I'm not."

— *But you could be.*

— Thank you, Eli, for reminding me.

"Fire! All you've got!"

To see the *Stalwart's* entire forward battery unleashed at once was awe-inspiring. If they were about to die, at least they'd go out shooting. The destroyer's seemingly impenetrable shield rippled as it pivoted away from the badly damaged *Gallant* and squared up to them. Purple beams immediately began slamming into them, and the shield sank like a stone. Twelve percent. Seven.

"*Gallant*, jump away!" he barked, and the Commander's ship vanished.

"Cap, we're takin' it on the nose here!" Denk said.

"That's the idea. Oz, be ready with number two."

"Aye aye, Skipper," she said, her voice shaking with fear.

— C'mon, you bastards. Do it.

They had seconds before the beams started ripping them apart, and they were almost out of missiles. The destroyer closed fast like it planned to ram them. The front screen was solid purple.

It was almost on top of them before it finally jumped.

"Now!!" he screamed, and Oz launched the torpedo.

His eyes darted immediately to the rear view. A bright streak emerged from beneath the engines and rocketed toward what was, for a breathless moment, empty space. The destroyer blinked into view half a second before Lestiko's gravity torpedo struck.

"Denk, pedal to the metal!"

Instead of dissipating harmlessly as all their other shots had, the torpedo flashed brightly then sucked back into itself as it collapsed into a singularity. As the ship receded behind them, it fired, but even the energy bolts couldn't escape its awesome gravity. A moment later, the pointy nose of the schnozz narrowed like it was being poured into a funnel and disappeared inside the black hole just before it collapsed entirely.

"That's far enough, Denk," Geddy said. They'd been at a full burn for the better part of a minute, far enough to avoid the temporary black hole created by Lestiko's weapon. "Take us back."

"Back, Cap?" he asked nervously.

"Yes, Lieutenant." He turned to Doc. "Where's the rendezvous?"

"Eicreon's moon, Sivar."

Geddy checked his timer. Eight minutes and change remained.

"Ged, what're we doing?" Oz asked.

"Seeing this through. Doc, get me the Gundrun commander."

"One moment, Captain." Half a minute later, he said, "I have a Colonel Malken on the comm."

"Put him through."

The Gundrun colonel came on screen looking annoyed. His eyes narrowed. "Who are y–"

"No time to explain, Colonel. In six minutes, there could be a chain reaction that ignites the atmosphere."

The colonel blinked as though he hadn't quite heard correctly. "I don't understand."

"You need to get out of there right n–"

Geddy's eyes widened, adrenaline flooding his heart. The three Zelnad destroyers were changing position, aligning with each other's long sides. He'd seen this before over Gundrun, albeit with many more ships.

They were forming a single, ultra-powerful supership.

"Colonel, they're preparing to fire. Go! Get away and jump!"

A brief inner conflict played out on his face, but he nodded, and a few seconds later, the battleships turned away from the Nad destroyers and began to climb away. But the destroyers weren't targeting the Gundrun. They were aiming directly at the *Stalwart*.

Two minutes still remained.

"Uh, Cap, we might want to jump," Denk said.

"Not yet. I have to know if this works. We can't have lost Morpho and Hughey for nothing."

"One hit from that thing, and we're a grease spot," Oz said.

"As the song goes, Mr. Junt, get ready to jump around. We're under two minutes."

Meanwhile, swarms of triangle fighters gathered into formations and raced toward them.

"Captain ..." Doc cautioned.

The same white-purple column of energy began to gather in the space between the three ships. It would fire any second.

But just as Denk prepared to jump them randomly through space, a fierce explosion lit up the opening of the superships' barrel. It traveled down the length of the formation, splitting apart whatever energy had begun to gather between the destroyers. They didn't explode but tumbled apart unsteadily in the air as the blast forced them apart.

"What the hell was that?" Geddy asked rhetorically.

"Cap, I've got a Berzerker comin' up hot." He looked up at his screen and gasped. "It's the *Armstrong!*"

Indeed, the wobbly, smoking ship came rushing up toward them, its missile pods empty and all three phantoms gone. Dark scorches streaked the wings and nose. Half the port wing was gone. She was limping badly but still on her feet.

"Ho-ly shit," Geddy said, laughing with glee. "It's Morph! Doc, make sure he can get to the rendezvous. If not, let him in."

"Yes, Captain!"

A bright orange light from the right side of the screen flashed in his peripheral vision, and he spun toward it. For a moment, it seemed like a hallucination.

— The timer!

Geddy sucked in a breath and checked his wrist. It was already at zero. When his eyes returned to the screen, he watched the whole north slope of the geo plant's mountain buckle, then explode with the force of an angry volcano. Then came another flash to the west, and a lengthwise crack opened in the earth, spitting rock so high in the air that it seemed it might hit them. The crack only widened as the pressure in the mantle released through the thin crust in a spectacular spray of molten fury.

"There! Can we go now?" Oz yelled.

Part of him — the same part that couldn't look away from the asteroid's collision with Gundrun's moon — wanted to stay and watch the whole spectacle. But that wasn't an option this time.

"Denk, get us out of here and jump to the rendezvous!"

Denk gunned the engines, pinning everyone to their chairs, but Geddy's eyes never left the rear view. Every gulch and valley between the geo plant and the mining operation was a bright orange artery spewing the planet's blood into the methane-saturated atmosphere. That fire joined with more fire as it flowed and burgeoned like a flash flood in hell.

By the time the fires reached the Zelnad facility, filling the area under the shield like water in a blister, they'd gone far enough that the scopes had trouble seeing through the clouds. The destroyers and the fighters were giving chase, but they wouldn't catch the *Stalwart* before they jumped away.

In a matter of minutes, they would be back with the fleet. Then it would be time to face the terrible question of what had been gained and lost.

CHAPTER 33

NERD TONIC

Outside Eicreon, the remaining Alliance and pirate vessels loaded into the cruisers for the brief jump back to their hiding place in the ion storm. Oz said all the other ships fit comfortably inside the two cruisers, and that they were both packed to the gills when they left. Now, the *Stalwart's* hangar was barely half full. The vast majority of the ships that made it back were the Chimeras and Berzerkers flown by the clones in the second wave.

The privateer ships were devastated. They were older, made for long turns in space and the occasional raid. Geddy doubted they would have survived a single direct hit. Many got blown up in the battle's opening moments, and the ones that didn't could only flee pursuers and eventually retreat, which they had.

But hundreds more ships were waiting at the coordinates when they returned. Merchant vessels. Kit ships. A Stemiran hospital ship. Freighters. Even a couple salvage trawlers. All there to do what they could for the Alliance.

Balzac, a handful of clones, and a grizzled assortment of old or injured pirates had stayed back to deal with the ongoing influx of volunteers. Jeledine had yet to return from Stemir. She didn't know about Hughey yet, and Geddy didn't relish telling her. But that could wait.

The day after they jumped back from the rendezvous, Geddy and Verveik strolled around the *Stalwart's* hangar together appraising the damage. The privateers who made it back looked shell shocked and angry. Oz had set up a makeshift triage center in the repair bay so the worst injured among them could be brought to the Stemiran hospital ship, whose arrival was well-timed. The New Alliance fleet boasted two medical ships, both of which still sat empty for want of a crew.

Now, the two of them were alone together in the officer lounge with the door closed. Geddy was nursing a cup of coffee, wishing he had something stronger. Verveik opted for tea. He had a hard look in his eye, the deep lines at the corners wrinkling with wisdom as he leaned across the table. Geddy feared his wrath.

"You did well."

Geddy cocked his head and looked sideways at the Commander as though he'd misheard. "What are you talking about? We just got our asses kicked."

"For your first combat command, I thought you handled yourself admirably."

Sincere praise from his childhood idol should've made him flush with pride, but he only felt responsible for the deaths of the dozens, if not hundreds of people who were his responsibility. None of it would've happened if he hadn't insisted on investigating the Ice Castles.

"The first and second waves got pummeled. You've seen the number of casualties."

"Yes, we took some heavy losses, but we should've been decimated. Against that kind of firepower? That maneuverability? Say nothing of our complete lack of battle readiness ... I was impressed by their firepower but not their fighting."

He hadn't thought of it that way, especially in light of the fact that he'd basically been shot down. But once Verveik mentioned it, it made sense on multiple levels. They had nothing to gain from conventional warfare. Geddy brought the fight to them, and they were caught completely by surprise. With the exception of the ship that got the drop on the *Gallant* — the one spaghettified by the artificial singularity — they'd only reacted.

Weren't they supposed to know every move before they made it?

"I take your point, but superior tactics won't matter if our shields and weapons are useless against them. We need Lestiko."

"We can't force his cooperation." As the words *Well, technically ...* drifted through Geddy's head, Verveik's look sharpened. *"We can't force him, Captain."*

Geddy held up his hands in mock surrender. "I know, but I got up close and personal with those fighters. Whatever's under the hood is next-level. Something we can't even get our heads around."

"I trust your appraisal." Verveik picked absently at his fingernails, his brow knotted in thought. "If it's better heads we need, then maybe there's another option."

Oz's head lay on Geddy's chest, her soft exhalations tousling the fertile valley of hair between his flabby pecs. The fleshy tendrils of her vascular locks pulsed gently in time with her heart. Somehow, it felt right to be in her quarters even though his were larger. It made their lovemaking seem more illicit somehow. Finding excuses to break their ninety-day abstinence agreement had become a running joke between them. After what happened on The Deuce and his encounter with Lestiko, he realized it was ludicrous to wait for anything.

"How's Tatiana's shoulder?" Oz asked.

"Doc said she's almost back to normal. Her lackey from Earth 3's picking her up in the morning."

"And Tymeri?"

"Ninety-Two said she finished her repairs and left during the night. I'm not sure where."

"I may be an empath, but I was wrong about her. She's an opportunist, but she has some integrity. I'll give her that."

"And she makes me hungry for seafood." Oz's chuckle was only half hearted. Something else was on her mind that she was hesitant to bring up. "What's wrong?"

"You haven't talked more about your parents."

Indeed, his retelling of events on The Deuce was spare and rushed. From the moment he'd seen their dead and frozen bodies in the Bayonet, he'd detached completely from all emotion. Even now, barely two days later, it seemed like nothing more than a realistic nightmare.

His eyes drifted from her to the ceiling, his phony mirth melting away. The only sound was the soft hum of the engines, easily discernible in the heavy kind silence.

"There's not much to say. I've already dealt with the *what* of their deaths. The why and how don't even matter."

"It's okay if you're not ready to talk about it. But don't pretend it didn't hurt. It insults my intelligence."

He hadn't even let himself feel what he felt in that moment and couldn't put a name to it.

"Fine, then I won't pretend. But I don't want to do this now. Can we change the subject?"

"Sure," Oz said with finality. "So you were stranded in an ice cave with your ex, knowing there's a pretty good chance you won't make it out, and … nothing happened?"

"Did I somehow characterize our predicament as sexy?" Geddy asked, irritated by the question.

"You know what I mean. If you really believed you might die? Hell, I might've gone for it."

"If you were me, or if you were you in the same situation?"

She shrugged. "Both."

Geddy pulled back wearing a bemused smile. "You would've switched sides?"

"I'm just saying, if anything happened, I wouldn't hold it against you ... for long."

"Only it didn't, therefore this conversation is just as pointless as the last."

Her sour reaction gave him a little stab of guilt. They'd made love minutes earlier. Why was he being so surly?

He let out a long, exasperated sigh. "I'm sorry. All this business has me missing our days on the *Fiz*."

Finally, she laid her head back down on his chest. It had begun to get cold.

"Yeah. Me, too."

As he relaxed, the moment felt right for the surprise he'd planned to spring.

"Verveik's formally inviting Ornea to join the Alliance."

She started to lift her head again, but he just pulled it gently back down on top of him. "For real?"

"If Lestiko won't help us understand this energy source of the Nads, Ornea's the next best thing."

"They don't have an army."

"No, but they have nerds with huge egos."

"Once again, it comes down to the nerds," she said.

CHAPTER 34
LATER, TOTS

Humans hadn't built ships since the days of the PDF, and the last of those ships not in a museum was still parked at the bottom of a canyon on The Deuce — if it hadn't been swallowed by the earth or buried in rubble. The ship that had come for Tati was, predictably, a Hovensby with its OEM version of the bubble drive. It was a status symbol, and that always mattered to Tati. But maybe that was changing.

The two young workers they'd left behind on the salvage platform responded immediately to Verveik's suggestion to leave. They took the small transport they'd come in and the other piloted Tati's ship — what she called her "errand" ship — back to Earth 3 without knowing her or Sworles' fate.

The hangar doors closed behind the Hovensby as it wound its way between the beat-up pirate ships that resembled rows of missing teeth. Those that were still flyable had been moved over to the heavy carrier, *Hardy*, deeper in the ion storm, which the Gundrun had taken over to help train officers.

It had only been three days since the battle, but the clones were already on the simulators learning tactics Denk programmed to combat the Zelnad fighters. By and large, their slobbering obsession with Tati and anything that looked, sounded, or smelled like her had diminished to a whisper. Now, they were no less distracted by her than any other man would be.

"So, did you ever fix those leaks in the Bubbles?" The underwater city on Earth 3 where most of humankind lived had been plagued by engineering issues.

She pursed her lips and nodded. "The new seals are holding so far."

"That's good news, right?"

"It is, but replacing every last one is gonna cost sixteen million, which means it'll be at least twenty in the end."

Earth 3 had no industry other than tourism, but that hadn't taken off yet. The dinosaur-like mogorodons that roamed the seas made people nervous, and rightly so. They'd also gobbled up most of the fish, which wasn't great news for the fledgling undersea colony.

The city was built upon the shallowest and sturdiest part of the seabed, so either they had to figure it out or contact a planet broker. As administrator of the colony, Tati was determined to make it work.

"Where's that gonna come from?" Geddy asked.

"I'm meeting with investors next week. And a few eggheads who think they know how to drive the mogorodons far away. We'll see."

The hangar pressure shield dissipated as the hangar pressurized. The ramp of Tati's Hovensby opened, and her personal security guy, Jeret, who had been on her father's detail, descended in his ill-fitting uniform. He stopped at the bottom, folded his hands in front of him, and waited like a good chauffeur.

"Jeret's lost a few kilos," Geddy said, smirking. "He must bend over a lot. To kiss your feet, I mean."

"He's obedient and loyal," Tati said. "That still matters."

"And all you have to do is feed and walk him every day," he offered with a smirk.

"What's your deal with him?"

"He's a douche hammer."

The click-clack of Tati's heels on the metal floor prompted Sixty-Three to flip up his simulator goggles and gaze longingly at her as she sashayed past. Geddy splayed two fingers out toward his eyes then jutted them back at the simulator. *Focus, man.* He reluctantly returned to his labors.

But the hardwiring the clones had received their whole lives to this point hadn't completely left them. A number of others also looked up as she passed, which she didn't fail to notice. Tati always knew when she was drawing attention even when it appeared she didn't.

He noticed her shoulder sling was gone. "How's it feeling today?"

"Still a little sore, but whatever Dr. Tardigan did worked wonders. I've got pretty good range of motion back already."

Geddy paused as he passed the final row of simulators, taking note that basically all the clones had stopped what they were doing to stare at Tati. It was hard to blame them, but still. They might as well have been teenagers.

"Listen, I'm really sorry about everything that went down on The Deuce. You were only in that situation because of me."

She gave him a sympathetic look. "No, it's my fault. You had better things to do than say goodbye to that dump."

"I wouldn't have missed it for all the methane in the world." He looked past her at the gawking clones and scowled.

— *So rude!*

— I'll never know where they got that from.

When she glanced over her shoulder at them, they didn't

even pretend to not be looking. She turned back to him wearing a sly smile. "It's not their fault, y'know."

"I know, but they've got a job to do."

She cocked her head, narrowing her big blue eyes. "How much of their time is spent on those simulators?"

"Five, six hours a day probably."

Surprise registered on her face. "And when they're not in here?"

"P.T. or classes with Doc, mostly. Why?"

"Do they even know what they're fighting for? And don't say the Alliance."

Geddy hadn't really thought of it that way. He and the crew all had myriad reasons to risk everything against the Zelnads. Family. Friends. Each other. What did the clones have?

Even though they were physically in their mid twenties, Doc figured their mental age was eighteen at best. He was teaching them about society and how things worked, and they'd made great progress. But suddenly, he found himself wondering if he actually knew the answer to her question.

"They know what's at stake."

She stopped and squared up to him. "That's not what I asked. Their first experience in the real world was a *battle*. To them, the world is a terrible and scary place."

"It is!"

Her acid stare leveled at him. "You know what I mean."

"What do you suggest? Field trips? Nature documentaries?"

Tati huffed and shook her head. "For fuck's sake, Geddy, do I have to spell it out for you?" She then turned on her heels and faced the clones who were all now staring at her. Without hesitation, she whistled, grabbed the bottom of her shirt, and lifted it up to her neck.

— *Well, that was unexpected.*

— Though not unwelcome.

"Take a good look, boys. These are what you're fighting for. Not the Alliance, not Captain Starheart. The galaxy's full of wonders. If we're all dead, you don't get to see any of 'em. Understand?"

Mouths hanging open, the clones nodded dumbly, and she tugged her shirt back down. Fluffing her silken hair over her shoulders, she turned back to Geddy and nodded with finality.

"There. That should boost morale."

Geddy flared his eyebrows. "The USO would've been proud."

"Thanks for the laughs, Geddy." She gave him a chaste kiss on the cheek, then gave it a quick couple pats. "I've got wet tunnels."

CHAPTER 35
HELLO FODDER

In the end, the Battle of the Deuce claimed sixty-two ships and a hundred three lives. Forty-one were pirate vessels, fourteen Screvari, and seven Alliance — all Chimeras piloted by clones. No Berzerkers were lost, a testament to the platform's sturdiness. The *Gallant* suffered major hull damage, particularly on the port side, and the repairs would be extensive. The *Stalwart* mercifully took no direct hits.

Of all the Berzerkers that made it back, none was more shot up than the poor *Armstrong*, which looked more like a possessed child's drawing than a warship. One of the underwing missile pods had been blown off. Two of the four engines were mangled beyond recognition. The only functioning weapon system was the plasma cannon under the nose. How Morph managed to hold his own against the Nads and still limp back was a question that might never be answered, even by him.

But in spite of all they'd lost and the chaotic execution of the battle, the mood in the senior officer briefing room was buoyant. Arbizander of Gundrun, the renegade Screvari Balzac, and Aezog the pirate, commanders of the armies that had joined the Alliance, had joined Verveik and Geddy to discuss the plan moving forward.

"Precisely what kind of weapon do you think the Zelnads are building with all this … shinium?" asked Arbizander, who shared their grave concerns about the Alliance's technological disadvantage.

"We don't know for sure," Geddy said. "It would help to know more about its intended target."

"That's this … Sagacea?" Aezog asked.

"Supposedly, it has a barrier around it that only shinium can penetrate. But I don't have to tell you gentlemen, it's not the size of the weapon but how you use it."

Balzac coughed to cover a laugh. Verveik remained stoic as ever as he spoke to their guests. "… Which is why we need to bring the fight to them."

"But even if we knew exactly where they were, our tech is inferior," Geddy reminded them. "We think we have a plan to fix that."

"A time machine?" Balzac asked.

"A Basoan named Lestiko managed to take back control from a Zelnad. He understands their tech. The gravity weapon we used on that destroyer was his design."

Arbizander flared his eyebrows. "Can he help us match their weaponry?"

"I believe he could. Unfortunately, he's too obsessed with figuring out how to separate hosts from Zelnads without killing both of them."

"What are you talking about?" asked Aezog.

Geddy described what they'd seen in the Empty and that Lestiko had run out of volunteers desperate enough to risk death in one of his separation experiments. How separating Nads from their hosts resulted in a cataclysm.

"We need him on our side, but we can't wait for him to come around," he explained.

"Short of kidnapping him, what do you propose?" Arbizander said.

"I'm inviting Ornea to join the Alliance," Verveik replied. "If they can help us understand this 'original energy,' maybe Lestiko will help us."

In fact, Lestiko made no such promise, but Geddy understood Verveik couldn't afford to be ambivalent.

Arbizander guffawed. "Ornea has no army." Oz, naturally, had said the same thing.

"Yours is the most powerful military in the galaxy," Verveik reminded him. "How many Zelnad ships did you destroy? We need better weaponry, and fast. This is our best shot at getting it."

Geddy cleared his throat and leaned into the pregnant silence that followed. "This isn't only about Lestiko. Millions of people have been taken over by these assholes. If there's a way to help them, we have to do it. It might be how we win."

Balzac sank back in his chair, his lips pursed doubtfully. Arbizander wore a similar expression, but both men seemed to know the score. No level of strategy, tactics, or training could overcome the Nads' technological advantage.

"Perhaps, but none of this matters unless your *Ornean* scientist, Parmhar Tardigan, can point us toward the enemy," Arbizander said.

"All the more reason to pursue other avenues," Verveik asserted.

Arbizander covered his doubtful look with deference. "Do what you think is best. But if there's nothing else, Commander, I have many ships to repair."

Verveik rose, followed by Geddy and Balzac. "As do we all."

Aezog remained seated, his eyes locked on Geddy's. He'd been silent the entire meeting. "A word in private, Captain?"

Geddy nodded okay, wondering what this might be about.

The others filed out, and he was alone with the pirate whom he barely knew. He folded his hands and looked expectantly at him.

"What can I do for you, Captain Aezog?"

"I lost seventy-eight people in your so-called attack."

"I know, and I–"

"We were fodder. Nothing more."

Geddy's chest reflexively tightened. He'd had the exact same thought. Indeed, the first wave was mostly privateers. Was that Verveik's intention? To throw them to the wolves?

"Verveik couldn't have known what he was dealing with. I barely got an SOS to the fleet as it was."

"Oh, I know. And what better way to test their defenses than with a bunch of pirates, eh? None of my people were trained for that kind of fighting, yet the Alliance-trained pilots in their shiny new ships had the good fortune of being the rearguard. Despite the fact that they were well-trained. Training seemingly reserved for men who happen to look exactly ... like ... you."

He emphasized this last word with an accusatory jut of his thick finger into Geddy's chest. Geddy slapped his hand away, and they both bolted to their feet, their faces centimeters apart.

"There wasn't time to get you trained up on Alliance ships, and you know it. In case you haven't noticed, we're making this up as we go."

The heavily muscled Gethenian leaned back with a smirk. "You don't remember me, do you, *Starheart?*"

Geddy had encountered so many pirates, mercs, and smugglers back in the day, they blurred together. "I wouldn't take it personally. I barely remember what happened yesterday."

"It was on Kigantu. You and a man with a nose like a limp dick were drinking at the Thirsty Thief."

Kriggy. He'd been taking Geddy for drinks at the Thief since his first facial hair. "I'm gonna need more."

"You were soused. Hell, we all were. Your friend was holding court. Man could tell a story, too."

That rang true. Kriggy liked to talk anyway, but after several mugs of ale, he became a wellspring of riveting tales. "Yes, he could."

"On this particular night, he favored us with a tale about the legendary ranse. The kind few men have lived to tell."

Geddy remembered the story well. It was one of Krigor's greatest hits. "The one where he knew he was gonna die."

Aezog snapped his fingers and smacked his palm on the table, smiling. "That's the one! A ranse took out his entire camp save for him. He froze in place for two full days afterward. Watched it all happen."

"Yeah, I've heard it a million times. What's your point?"

"Remember he said it changed him?"

"He realized he was powerless, and that realization made him free."

Aezog opened his palms and sat back again as though his point had been made. If so, Geddy had missed it.

"I'm not following."

"I was down there. I saw what we're up against." He shook his head. "I don't know what this is, but it isn't war. After this, I'm not even sure it's our fight."

Aezog had every right to be pissed, but he knew the score. This wasn't an elite fighting force yet, and it might never be. They came here out of desperation. Verveik sent them ahead because they were the worst pilots with the oldest ships and the least loyalty. If that made them fodder, so be it.

Geddy nodded over his shoulder. "Then there's the door. I'll make sure you get paid."

The pirate seemed taken aback by this. "Excuse me?"

"You want to run out the clock shaking down family starships on their way to grandma's house, I won't stop you. The rest of us are in the fight of our lives."

"But it's a losing battle. Choosing to let this ... Sagacea die is an honorable choice. A logical choice." Aezog sounded like he was convincing himself.

Geddy rose casually and pushed in his chair. "Then go with your honor intact. I'm deeply sorry for your losses."

CHAPTER 36
WHO CAN IT BE NOW?

Aezog was still rightly pissed about his losses, but he hadn't left either. The truth was, anyone in that first wave would've been decimated. That it turned out to be mostly untrained pirates in older ships was a result of the cold calculus of war.

Doc Tardigan had taken three assistants from among the remaining privateers and Screvari dissidents, each of whom had varying levels of medical skill. The ship's two autodoc bays were more or less the same as current models, and the diagnostic gear was more than adequate. Even so, Doc seemed glad for the help and relished the opportunity to talk and teach.

While his assistants attended to the wounded, he and Geddy sat on stools in the small lab beside the infirmary. Verveik's plan to recruit Ornea into the Alliance struck Doc as wise, though Geddy could tell he was conflicted about it. His home world didn't exactly hold him in high esteem.

"The technical hurdles to replicating Zelnad technology are considerable," he admitted. "Though if anyone could help besides Lestiko, it is Ornea."

"You think they'll be interested in a military problem?" Geddy asked

"We face extinction," Doc said. "That ought to be motivation enough."

"I'd like you to meet with Verveik before he goes to Tathe and makes his pitch. You know what they'll respond to."

"And what they won't." He gave a sheepish grin. "Of course, Captain, I will avail myself to the Commander." After a pause, he leaned in conspiratorially. "May I ask a personal question?"

"That's my favorite kind."

"Are you ... okay?"

Geddy blinked at him. "Do ... I not seem okay?"

"You destroyed a significant portion of your home world."

He raised two fingers and smiled. "Twice!"

"You jest, but it must be a lot to bear."

The Deuce was his home world, but it never felt like it. In his heart, he was an Old Earth kid born in the wrong century. If he could, he'd build a time machine to find out where humanity jumped the shark. Then maybe they never would've come to this galaxy where they clearly didn't belong.

Geddy couldn't change the past, but maybe he could change the future, distant though it was.

"Y'know, I have a purpose, and friends, and a woman who loves me. On top of that, I'm helping my childhood hero put the band back together to fight evil aliens. Twelve-year-old me would be like, 'Hell yeah, bro.'"

Doc beamed as broadly as Geddy had ever seen and nodded appreciatively. "Then, as they might have said on Old Earth, keep on keepin' on.'"

Jeledine's ship, *Bogart*, would've been awesome at Ponley Point. Like the late Tev Joclen's *Allegro*, it was built for speed but not so overpowered. She'd owned it as long as he'd known her. Sometimes pet owners started to look like their pets, and he felt the same about her and *Bogie*. Face-on, the wide-set wing-mounted engines resembled her eyes. Its landing skids, her skinny legs. Well-equipped though it was, speed was its strongest defense. She was always trying to make it run more smoothly or to coax a little more thrust out of its sleek, custom-built engines.

She'd returned from taking Ori back to Stemir while everyone was asleep. Geddy didn't even know she was back until Denk mentioned it at breakfast. Her ship was parked in the executive hangar, and the cameras indicated she was still there working on it.

After eating, Geddy descended the elevator with Morph on his shoulder to find her standing under the port engine of the Bogart with her comically large goggles on, applying a delicate weld to something overhead. A white-hot light popped from her torch, and shielded his eyes as the hangar doors parted.

"Looks hot," he offered from behind her.

She glanced casually at him over her shoulder, lifting off the goggles just long enough to make eye contact before returning to her work. "It should. It's synthetic yastrine."

He nodded knowingly and leaned against the wing, keeping a safe distance from the torch. "Yastrine. You don't mess around. How was your trip?"

Jel didn't look up. "Let's just say my family's preference for Ori has only grown with time. Especially now that she and Ahne ..."

"What?"

I don't know what happened with her on Basoa, okay? Whether it was Lestiko, or seeing her again, or what, but she's ... different."

"Different how?" he asked.

Jel's small face pinched as though struggling to understand and she took a small file from a pouch around her waist. As she buffed off some jagged bits, she said, "Like, motivated and happy and just ... better. In fact, she kinda talks about Ahne now like you talk about Eli."

— *Which is to say, mostly nicely?*

— When you're not nagging me.

— *I don't nag! I merely offer unsolicited feedback.*

— Seriously, we could be on to something here.

Jel continued, "It's like that Zelnad of hers is ... lifting her up. Does that make sense?"

Geddy's eyes popped as wide as they got. "You have no idea. Jel, do you know what this means? Ori didn't 'break through.' I think she and Ahne just realized the only way they win is by by not playing the game."

— *That's very insightful, Geddy.*

— Hey, I think about stuff sometimes!

Jel did her best to mirror his excitement, but an added dose of confusion made it seem all the more phony. "All civilizations collapse for the same basic reason — a failure to cooperate. A constant battle for control. Don't you see? Ori fought Ahne long enough that they both realized it couldn't go on like that. That they needed to unite behind a common purpose."

"What purpose?" she asked.

Geddy shrugged. "One that requires cooperation. For me and Eli, it was building the *Penetrator*. We both wanted off that stupid planet and out of each other's consciousness. At first. But then I was like, 'hell, who else have I got to talk to?' After seventeen million years adrift, I guess Eli thought the same thing."

"That's nice and all, Ged, but look at what she endured to get there. How hard she fought and for how long. Most people who join the Zelnads aren't that strong."

His grin broadened further. "I know, which is why we can't help them."

Exasperated, Jel dropped the file on the floor with a jarring *clank* and squared up to him with her hands on her hips. "Then just who exactly do we ..." Her eyes slid askance. "Wait — you can't mean what I think you mean."

"I do."

"You think we need to help ... the *Zelnads*. As in the ancient aliens that want to kill the universe?"

"They're doing the same exact thing they want to wipe us out for. Overpowering people and seizing control to their own ends. They're no better than us."

Her face relaxed as though she understood, but in reality she couldn't connect to his excitement. She didn't know how in love Sagaceans were with their own logic. Proving their hypocrisy could be a weapon in itself.

She forced an awkward smile. "That's great, Ged. I'm excited for her, and I guess for you, too. Look, ah, not to change the subject and all, but ..." Jel began, brightening despite her lingering confusion. "Where's Hughey?"

That's what he'd come to talk about. Bots were her constant companions and had been since she was a kid. Both Hugheys were nonverbal, hyper-competent, highly advanced shifter bots. Hughey Twoey was a replacement for Original Hughey, whom she'd loved more than any flesh-and-blood person as long as he'd known her. He didn't relish breaking the news.

In anticipation of her grief, he'd stuffed a few tissues in the pocket of his coveralls, ready to offer one depending on her reaction. He'd never pegged her as sensitive, but women had a maddening way of hiding their true selves.

"He, ah ... didn't make it out."

Before she could say anything, he stumbled over the explanation. First, his failed attempt to extend the *Armstrong's* antenna, then about the labrozite and the creaky old salvage bots that Hughey shepherded into the mantle. The whole time, Jel kept working like he wasn't there.

"As always, he did what needed to be done. Abruptly and without a tearful farewell, but still." But her labors still didn't abate. "That's it. That's what happened."

"Okay. Thanks for telling me."

Her non-reaction puzzled him. Was she numb? Had Tati already told her? "Whaddya mean, 'thanks?' I sent your bot to its death."

"I had a bad feeling about your trip," she admitted, flicking off the torch and raising the goggles. "I'm glad he was of use. Hughey was not alive, therefore he can't be dead. And thanks to our friend, Lestiko, I can just replace him like a bad part."

"But he was your friend." All he wanted was a reaction equal to the guilt he felt, but he wasn't going to get one. Not from Jel Berwynd. He'd known her long enough to know that.

She gave him a crooked smile, looking for all the world like his mother whenever he said something adorably naïve. "No, he was a companion. You're my friend. Oz and Denk and Doc are my friends." Morpho slung himself over to Jel's shoulder and nuzzled into her neck, and her upturned lips blossomed into a laugh. "And this guy, of course, and Eli, and Voprot."

"Voprot?" Geddy said, smirking back.

The corners of her pale blue eyes crinkled at him. "What? Did you think I was going to be torn up over a *bot*?"

"Well ... I mean ..." he stammered, "... you two seemed pretty tight is all."

Her eyes softened, and she gave them a bemused roll. "Look at you, ya softie! Twenty credits says you brought tissues."

"What?? Heh, yeah, right ..."

— *Geddy* ...

Now it was his turn to roll his eyes. He pulled the tissues

out of his pocket, crumpled them up and threw them at her. "Add it to my tab."

"Your credit's only good to a point, buddy boy. You should know never to bet me."

He exhaled and looked at her sideways. "You're sure?"

"I'm sure I'll never finish this mod unless you leave me be," she teased.

Geddy raised his hands in surrender and strolled away. After a few steps, he paused and turned back. "I'm really sorry."

"Forget it." She gave a dismissive wave of her left hand. "See you at lunch."

"Yeah, see you."

He continued across the deck to the door and exited. When the elevator opened, though, he sent it up empty and pressed himself to the wall beside the huge window that overlooked the hangar. Jel kept welding for a minute or two, then paused, raised her helmet, and leaned on her hands. After a quick check to ensure she was alone, she knelt and picked up one of the balled-up tissues. While she was still on one knee, her head lowered, and she sobbed uncontrollably.

— I knew it.

— *Aren't you going to comfort her?*

— Nope. That'd only make things worse.

"Captain Starheart, please come to the bridge," came Denk's voice over the ship-wide loudspeaker. "Code ... uh ... red-ish?"

Calling the elevator back would catch her eye, so Geddy turned and took the stairs. It was only three flights, but bounding up winded him a bit. He paused outside the bridge entrance to catch his breath. The crew didn't need to see how out of shape he'd gotten.

— *You should take the stairs all the time.*

— Fighting evil aliens counts as cardio.

— *Then you're not doing enough of that, either.*

Once his breath normalized, he drew himself taller and stepped forward. The bridge door slid open as he approached.

"Lemme guess. More volunteers?"

Doc and Oz stood behind Denk's pilot chair with their arms crossed. The three of them spun around nearly in unison.

"Not exactly," Oz said. "Come look."

Geddy joined her in front of the screen. The lone ship hovering in front of them was instantly recognizable, but his brain tried to convince him it was a mirage.

"You gotta be shittin' me," Geddy muttered.

It was the *Red Raven*.

CHAPTER 37
FULL OF SHIP

Safely behind the pressure shield, Geddy watched the approaching salvage vessel with his chest defiantly puffed out. The last time he'd seen Beebit Tompanov and the *Fizmo's* rival trawler, *Red Raven,* was over Gundrun during their desperate and ultimately fruitless effort to shore up the khetaka. They'd made a bet over who could deploy the asteroid-pulverizing satellites faster, and Tompanov won. Ever since they parked the *Fiz* in the corner of the *Stalwart's* hangar, he hadn't intruded in their lives.

Ninety-Two stood to his right, and Oz and Doc to his left. As the ship entered through the doors, they began to close behind it.

Geddy sniffed at the air and turned to Ninety-Two. "Smell that?"

"Smell what?"

"The galaxy's asshole."

"Who is this person, exactly?" asked Ninety-Two.

"A Kailorian trawler captain. We have a history."

"What's he doing here?"

"He claims to have something we want. It's probably a

prank. If he hands you something that looks like a can of peanuts, don't open it because it'll be a snake. Like him."

The hangar doors slammed home, and air rushed in through hundreds of overhead vents. The speed with which the hangar re-pressurized never failed to amaze him.

Tompanov's ship was half again as big as the *Fiz* and much newer, with a dull red coating befitting its name. It eased its way toward them and settled onto the landing pad as the pressure shield dissipated.

"My guess is, he heard the Alliance was paying and came running," Oz said.

The ship's ramp lowered with a faint hum.

"It seems you don't like him very much," Ninety-Two offered.

"Glad you picked up on that," Geddy said. "But that's all in the past."

Tompanov's skinny legs appeared first as he descended the ramp. He had to duck pretty low on account of his high-crested blue head. His XO, a Zihnian improbably named Steve, followed closely at his heels. His head easily fit under the fuselage, though he was still a good bit taller than Denk. For reasons no one could guess, Tompanov dressed like some kind of self-styled priest, with a high-collared maroon cloak connected at the neck by a silver chain.

Oz looked up at him with her lips pressed tightly together like she was trying to stifle a laugh. Geddy smiled back and shook his head as Tompanov and Steve approached them with his irritating smirk.

"Hey, dickface. I decided to set a good example and not turn your ship to dust," Geddy said in greeting. Ninety-Two's head jerked confusedly in his direction.

— *Yes, I can see how you've let bygones be bygones.*

— Baby steps.

"I'm not sure even the *Raven* is a big enough target for the likes of you," Tompanov sneered. His eyes settled on Ninety-Two and his brow furrowed. "I quit drinking years ago. Why am I seeing two of you?"

"This is Ninety-T–"

"Ogos," Ninety-Two interjected, drawing himself taller. "My name is Ogos. I am the captain's genetic twin, but we are not the same."

— *He chose a name?*

— *So it seems. I like it.*

"Indeed you are not. You haven't let yourself go," Tompanov chided, oddly appreciative of Ogos' fit, youthful, hopeful appearance. His eyes slid back to Geddy. "You literally had to make a friend? Being you must be even worse than I thought."

"What do you want, Tompanov? Directions to the cosplay convention?"

"In fact, Captain, I come bearing gifts. Gifts I believe your New Alliance will pay handsomely for."

"I'm not sure you know what a gift is."

"Follow me." He turned with a flourish so his cloak floated up behind him.

As they walked, Steve raised his right arm and triggered the hold doors to open and the back ramp to lower.

"My scopes picked up a series of large energy discharges from Earth 2," Tompanov said. "Typically, that means a battle, and battles create salvage. I was curious enough that I burned two novaspheres getting there. During a very successful run, I encountered a rather unique item."

They came around to the back of the ship and climbed the ramp to the hold. When they reached the top, Geddy froze in his tracks and his jaw hit the floor.

He recognized chunks of the *Gallant* that had been blown off along with two badly damaged pirate ships. But at the center, locked in place by a system of metal mesh, was a perfectly intact Zelnad fighter.

"Holy shit," Geddy reflexively took a step back from the deadly craft.

The obtuse triangles that formed the wings were maybe four meters on a side and made of some otherworldly material he didn't recognize. A composite, perhaps, or some kind of smooth crystal. Each smaller triangle was sandwiched atop another with a uniform gap in between as though they repelled each other. In the center sat the meter-wide metal sphere, which was also suspended in an invisible field and polished to a mirror finish. If it had a seam, it wasn't obvious.

"I had a feeling this would interest you." Tompanov was a bit too pleased with himself, probably relishing the big payday he clearly came to get.

"Has it powered up?" Geddy asked, venturing closer. "Have you seen any purple light around it?"

He shook his elongated blue head. "It hasn't done anything. In fact, it has no energy signature at all."

"How could that be?" Geddy asked.

"Is it autonomous?" Oz asked, crouching a bit too closely for his taste.

"That is our working theory." Doc stood over Oz's shoulder, his eyes sparkling with curiosity. "How remarkable! I'll need extensive testing."

"How do we know it's not gonna come to life and kill us?" Oz asked. "It doesn't even look damaged."

"We don't," said Geddy. "For all we know, it's some kind of Trojan horse."

"Then how the hell do we study it without putting the ship at risk?" she asked.

"Captain, the battery room in engineering was designed to contain an explosion. If any place on the ship could withstand an energy discharge from a ship this size, it's there," Doc said.

"Tompanov knows all about unplanned discharges, don't you Beebs?" Geddy asked, glancing sidelong at their guest.

The Kailorian's self-satisfied look knotted into a scowl.

— What do you think, E?
— *That it is not autonomous.*
— Then what's flying it?
— *I am not sure, but I sense the harmonic. It is faint but unmistakable.*
— Is that good or bad for us?
— *I do not think the vessel intends to harm us.*
— Why not?
— *Call it a gut feeling.*
— You don't have a gut. I do.
— *Oh, I know. You follow it without a spare thought.*

Geddy pointed to where the mesh over the ship was anchored to the floor. "This mesh ... Gundrun steel?"

"As is every bolt and rivet on the *Raven*," boasted Tompanov.

Even that wouldn't last long under the withering power of these ships, but if Doc was right, they only needed to get it onto the service elevator and down to engineering. It was a calculated risk, but if there was a faint chance of reverse-engineering the weaponry or figuring out an effective defense, they had to take it. As much as he hated to admit it, it *was* a gift.

"Shall we discuss terms, then?" Tompanov asked.

Geddy turned to Oz and Doc. "Give the grown-ups a moment, won't you?"

They both eyed Tompanov warily as they left the hold and descended the ramp. Tompanov gave a tiny nod to Steve, who dutifully about-faced and disappeared through the airlock that presumably led to the bridge.

Tompanov's shit-eating grin spread across his entire punch-worthy face. "As lucrative as my exploits have been to this point, this should enable a very comfortable retirement on *Pretensia*."

"I can't imagine a better place for you. And as much as it galls me, yes, we'll talk terms. But first, I have one question, and I need you to answer honestly."

His gaze narrowed, and he turned his head slightly to the side as though it was some sort of ruse, but Geddy remained stone-faced. "One question?"

"One."

He paused a moment before squaring up to him and folding his hands behind his back.

"Okay, Starheart. How may I illuminate you?"

"The Zelnad research ship you were hauling in ..."

Tompanov bristled at its very mention. "The one you *stole* from me? What about it?"

"Tell me what you know about it. And don't leave out any details."

An inner conflict briefly played out in his beady orange eyes, but they didn't look away. "It's some kind of research ship. I was hired to find and retrieve it."

"By who?"

"That's two questions," he sneered.

Geddy closed the distance between them, making himself as big as he could. Tompanov sucked in a breath but didn't flinch. "How about not being an insufferable prick for thirty seconds? And don't say that's three questions or I'll drop you right here."

He huffed, expelling breath that smelled of mothballs. "I don't know. It came directly to me through the band of thieves and they paid in advance."

"Where were you gonna bring it?" Geddy demanded. "And don't lie."

Again, he hesitated. "Aku."

"Aku? Why?"

"I haven't the faintest. You now know everything I do about it. And that's five ... no, *six* questions for the price of one. Speaking of price ..."

After they snatched the research ship from Tompanov and accidentally jumped the *Fiz* into Kigantu's atmosphere, they effectively stole it a second time from Voprot, who stumbled across it on his trek through the desert. It was completely empty. They hauled it into one of Tretiak's hangars where Geddy realized only he could open it again. It was supposed to be collateral to buy back the *Penetrator*, but he never saw the money or learned what happened to it after it was sold at auction to a Screvari accompanied by the late Sammo Yann.

Eli believed the mysterious ship was sent to find Sagacea, and that its crew was vaporized when it attempted to cross the barrier. Of course, there was no way to be sure. But if it had in fact been there and back, then the Nads would do anything to get the data off it. The problem was, he didn't know what happened to it after it sold at the Double A auction.

But he sure as hell knew who would.

CHAPTER 38

SITTING ON YOUR ASSET

Tretiak Bouche, Geddy's old boss, had always been enigmatic. In private, he could be fatherly and almost, but not quite, kind. When he was alone, which was most of the time, he pored over ancient texts and listened to chatter on the band of thieves, forever searching for the next priceless artifact or constructing an elaborate myth to help sell an ordinary one.

The Double A was where he really came alive, transforming himself from the Tretiak Geddy knew into the Auctioneer with effortless panache. His showmanship and flair for the dramatic was as big a draw as the auction itself. When he was working the door, Geddy saw many of the same faces over and over — people with the means to submit a winning bid who were only there for the spectacle of it.

Like Geddy, he'd left Earth 2 at a young age. He hated everything about the planet, from its barren landscape to the study in excess that Laguna became. In that day, the Double A was little more than a glorified bazaar at the back of a cave where a few dicey items were worthy of bidding.

But Tretiak was savvy and smart. He somehow knew that

even Aquebba, dirty and dangerous as it was, could become a refuge for a more subversive slice of society. A place where the dregs and cast-outs could toast their awfulness, cast off the shackles of decorum, and be who they really were. Such a concentration of thugs and thieves kept the IJC and law abiders far away, which made it the perfect place to auction off ill-gotten goods.

For most of Geddy's life, he lumped Tretiak in with the wretched and villainous like he was their king. But as the Auctioneer, he was equally at home hobnobbing with the cabal of rich, unprincipled avatars who ran the galaxy. The day Geddy realized he was becoming equally comfortable around the same people was the day he made plans to leave.

But now that Tretiak was the head of the Committee, Geddy had started to see him differently. Such a powerful group needed someone to pull the strings, grease the skids, and marshal resources. All he'd ever done, really, was the thing he was best at — being Tretiak Bouche. It was a bit ironic that he was helping reform the Alliance, because historically, Tretiak's only allegiance was to himself. Running the Committee wasn't an act of selflessness and it didn't reflect a change of heart. It served his interests to maintain the galaxy's status quo.

Since the *Armstrong* was still being repaired, Geddy and Morpho took one of the other Berzerkers to Nirnaya Station where Tretiak was still holed up. The justice ship's comms array was powerful enough to reach every corner of the galaxy, it was well-protected, and the IJC fully supported the Alliance. Still, it was curious he hadn't been back to Kigantu to check in. Geddy didn't even know if the auction was still going in Tretiak's absence. It was hard to imagine.

After docking, one of the android workers led him back to the room where Zereth-Tinn shot and killed his half brother,

Sammo-Yann. His eyes lingered on the spot where it happened and the shock of the moment returned anew.

Tretiak was seated in the middle of the long table behind a battlement of holoscreens, each of which was cluttered with various feeds from around the galaxy.

"What a welcome surprise," Tretiak said, forcing a faint smile. "Have a seat."

He rose from the table and met Geddy with a handshake, then gestured at the two end chairs, well away from the screens. They sat.

"I understand you had quite the adventure on the ol' Deuce."

"You don't know the half of it," Geddy said.

He related the finer details of what happened with him and Morph, omitting the bit about his parents. Just because he and Tretiak were on the same side didn't mean they were pals. He ended with the story of Tompanov's unexpected delivery of the fighter.

"Do I even want to know what an intact Zelnad ship cost us?" Tretiak asked.

"Forty-five million."

He gave an indifferent shrug. "Meh. Eilgars probably made that in the time it took you to say it."

Geddy's old Ceonian friend owned the galaxy's largest fortune and was still bankrolling the Alliance while it got its shit together. He could only assume Gundrun's recent commitment came with a substantial investment that would ease that burden.

"Nad ships are actually why I'm here."

He cocked his head curiously. "All right …"

"The research vessel we brought to Aquebba … What happened to it?"

He shrugged. "It sold at auction. You were there, as I recall."

"I mean where did it wind up?"

At this, Tretiak leaned back in his chair and let out a long sigh, rubbing his eyes. "I figured we'd come around to this eventually."

Geddy's heart picked up a few beats. "Come around to what?"

"Geddy, no one besides me knows what I'm about to tell you."

"Okay ..."

"A Screvari named Kanitil submitted the winning bid. Fourteen point seven. But as you know, I'm very careful about where my money comes from."

That much was true. During the early days of the Double A, Tretiak sold a crate of Gundrun rifles to a guy who claimed to be running them to a warlord on Zihnia. It turned out he was actually paid by the Gundrun military to deliver the weapons, all of which had hidden tracking devices. The warlord and all his people were slaughtered.

Ever since, Tretiak personally vetted every winning bid to ensure it was clean and that the bidder was who they claimed to be. That meant no government money and nothing that could ever be traced back to the Double A. Hundreds of top bidders had been rejected over the years and the money, which was held in escrow, was returned. Rejected bidders were permanently and unceremoniously banished.

"Why? What happened?"

"Something about him rubbed me wrong. Maybe because he was with Sammo Yann. Anyway, while you were cooling your heels in one of my cells, I did some digging. He hid his tracks well, but I eventually traced that money back to the Screvari Circle."

The Circle was the cruel and deeply corrupt government of Aku. It was formed when a cluster of industrialists who had profited immeasurably from the Ring War staged a coup.

They'd been trotted out with the rest of the Coalition during the big announcement on Xellara. That they were in league with the Nads was never in question.

"What did you do?"

"Same thing I do to anyone. I rejected the bid and showed him the door."

A broad grin split Geddy's face. "That was ballsy. What about the ship?"

Tretiak, however, was not smiling. "Well, now that's where the story takes a bit of a turn. The next afternoon, while they were repairing the hole you made in my warehouse, I had the ship moved into the deep vault."

Geddy shot up from his chair and grabbed handfuls of Tretiak's lapels in his fists, their faces so close, he could smell his aftershave. "You've had it this entire time?!"

He didn't even blink. It wasn't exactly the first time Geddy was so incensed at him. "An intelligence asset isn't much good if you can't understand it. From what I recall, you didn't even know how to open the door."

As much as he hated it, and boy did he ever, Tretiak was right. Other than the Zelnads themselves, he only knew one person who could possibly extract the data from that ship, and he wasn't cooperating — yet.

He released Tretiak's sport coat with a frustrated grunt and plunked back down in his chair, fuming.

Tretiak smoothed his jacket and calmly asked, "Would you care to know what happened after it went into the vault?"

"You know I do."

"That same day, I received a message from the Screvari Grand Chancellor that I was to release the ship to his emissary or else. I knew it was no idle threat, so I shut down the auction and left."

He could hardly believe his ears. Tretiak didn't scare easily. "Left? How?"

Only then did Tretiak allow a tiny grin. "In the cargo hold of a merchant vessel bound for Zorr."

Geddy barked a laugh. The irony was delicious. He'd stowed away himself on a similar ship when he was a kid, which was how he wound up on Kigantu. Picturing Tretiak, who was somewhere in his mid-sixties, doing the same thing was too perfect.

"Lemme guess ... where you connected with Zirhof."

Zirhof of Zorr was a mutual friend who dealt often with the Double A, though never in person. He was one of a handful of collectors who Tretiak trusted enough to submit secret bids remotely.

Tretiak nodded. "He showed me what was on those quantum cubes you recovered from Old Earth and told me everything. Between that and what happened with the ship, we knew we had to act fast. We met with Eilgars and Hau to secure financing, then started pulling in the other Committee members."

"What about the Double A?"

"Still dark. Maybe forever, who knows?"

"Kriggy?" Geddy asked, curious as to the fate of his duplicitous old friend.

"I can't reach him."

A cocktail of conflicting emotions ran through him. Mostly, though, he felt hopeful. In snatching the Zelnad research ship out of Tompanov's greedy hands, he'd inadvertently scored the Alliance an asset that could point the way to Sagacea. An asset the Nads would do anything to find.

That was the good news. The bad news was that it was still on fucking Kigantu.

CHAPTER 39
GUMSHOE

The battery room was a smallish warehouse designed to house the ship's backup power system. The fusion core couldn't explode, but the batteries absolutely could, so its walls were thickly shielded with layers of tukrium and fire foam. Geddy had only been down to engineering once, but there wasn't much to see. It was fully automated and only needed staff in case of a problem, which fusion cores rarely had. Ordinarily, the core drove power to the engines and all the ship's systems. In an emergency, the batteries could power the ship for up to a week.

For obvious reasons, the containment area didn't have windows, so Geddy, Oz, and Doc had gathered around a camera feed next door in engineering control, a surprisingly small room considering its importance.

Doc had begun his analysis of the fighter by removing the Gundrun steel mesh around it, which was a tense moment for everyone. But it didn't activate, and in fact, very little had happened at all since then. Geddy had never seen Doc so frustrated, but he was simply out of his depth. Once again, he found himself wishing they had Lestiko.

The triangular fins, which weren't physically attached to each other or the central sphere, were held in place by a force Doc couldn't identify or quantify, somehow repelling while also holding it tightly together at a precise distance. His instruments didn't detect a flicker of power coming from any part of it, suggesting it was dead or deactivated despite being otherwise intact. All told, it was an anticlimactic experience for everyone, and they still hadn't learned anything useful about the damn thing.

It was starting to seem like they'd handed Tompanov an early retirement and gotten nothing in return.

Today, however, they were gathered to observe the results of an intriguing theory of Doc's. Back on Kigantu, the research ship with its strange organic skin would only respond to Geddy's touch. That suggested Zelnad technology could only be accessed by those with the harmonic. The ship's central sphere appeared seamless, which meant it either didn't open at all or that only a Zelnad or Sagacean could open it.

The logical choice to test this theory was Morpho.

Despite the ship's unique properties, it sat inert on the room's floor, leaning on one edge like a kid had left it in the driveway. Morpho closed the vault-like door behind him and slinked toward the sphere one tenuous tendril at a time. As seemingly impervious to injury as Morph had been, the kind of energy they were dealing with had no analog in their world. An abundance of caution made sense.

"What if this doesn't work?" Oz asked, her eyes searching Geddy's.

"Then we do as my people have done for millennia and bang on it with a hammer. Or I could shoot it with the PDQ."

"The latter would not be advised, Captain. If the blast were to ricochet, you might–"

"I was joking, Doc. Mostly."

Morph's black, sticky form slung himself up to one of the

fins then made a slow circle around the mirrored tukrium sphere. Doc had already been over it several times but couldn't even tell for certain if it was solid or hollow.

After circling the ship, Morph hopped across the curved inside edge of a fin onto the sphere. Oz gave a little gasp, but nothing happened. Morph sat atop it a moment, looking for all the world like he'd laid a giant chrome egg, then slowly made his way around it in a descending spiral, working toward its equator.

The moment Morph reached the sphere's midline, he abruptly stopped.

"What's happening?" Geddy asked rhetorically. "Why's he stopping?"

Morpho shot out one cluster that latched to the top of the sphere and a second group to the bottom. The moment he did, the ship jolted upright, balancing perfectly on the sphere.

Oz's hand shot out and grabbed Geddy's forearm. Something had happened.

— *It's like battery terminals! He connected them!*

"What'd Eli just say?"

"That it must work like a battery. Morph connected the two poles."

At any moment, the ship could swell with the purple energy and blow Morph to bits. But it didn't. He shot more tendrils out above the midline, reaching halfway around this time, then did the same to the lower half in the opposite direction. As soon as he did, the gummy muscles of his little body began to contract.

"Holy shit, he's unscrewing it," Geddy muttered.

Indeed, a narrow gap appeared as though something had come unlatched. Morpho gathered into himself and began pushing the two halves apart.

He'd only widened the gap to a couple centimeters, three at most, when the top half rocketed to the ceiling, clanging off it like a bell. A shapeless gray mass shot out, expanded into a hood, then fell atop Morpho, enveloping him completely. The thing immediately contracted to the size of a basketball and began to fling itself back and forth across the room like a coked-up superball.

"Shit!!" Geddy angrily slapped the table and unholstered the PDQ as he burst through the door. "It's a damn trap!"

"Geddy, wait!" Oz cried after him.

The room was only a few meters away, but unlike the other doors on the *Stalwart*, it didn't simply open because he got close. The lock was controlled by an old-school keypad, but his shaking fingers only managed to tap one digit before Oz's powerful hand clamped on his right shoulder and yanked him away.

"I said wait, you idiot!"

"Morpho's being attacked!"

"Were you not listening to Doc? You can't fire that thing in there!" she protested.

"Watch me."

Again, he took a step forward to enter the rest of the code. This time, she stepped in front of him and shoved him back. "Geddy, stop it!"

Geddy jabbed his finger at the door. "What's wrong with you?! We have to help him!"

"Actually, Captain, I do not think he is in danger," Doc said behind them, leaning out of the control room. Oz spun to face him. "See for yourself."

The two of them rushed back to the control room behind Doc and leaned in around the video feed. The pale gray ball of goo was still bouncing around the room, but was now swirled with black.

Geddy and Oz exchanged a look of abject confusion.

— *Are they fighting or are they …*

— Rounding second base? I'm not sure.

Oz had been right, of course. Whatever was happening here exceeded their understanding, and the time-tested method of hitting or shooting wouldn't help. The thing inside the sphere was twice as big as Morph, a lighter color, and didn't have the same shiny, wet appearance. But other than that, they were clearly made of similar stuff.

If they were witnessing a fight, it wasn't much of one. If it was an embrace, it teetered on violence. If it was an intimate encounter, it was more spirited than most.

"Fascinating," Doc said, enthralled by the display.

"What should we do?" Oz asked.

"Let them finish?" Geddy suggested.

Doing nothing proved to be the right instinct because a minute later, the volleyball-sized form slowed and stopped a couple meters in front of the door. Then, like separating two half-chewed pieces of gum, the two entities peeled themselves apart. Morpho seemed perfectly fine.

Still stunned by what had transpired, the three of them could only watch as Morpho let himself out of the room.

Geddy dashed back out to meet him, wide-eyed and confused as hell. Morph closed the door behind him as casually as if he'd checked the status of a casserole, seemingly unconcerned about the Zelnad synthetic still inside.

"Well?" he asked. "What the hell just happened?"

Morph hopped up to his shoulder and snaked a tiny thread of himself into Geddy's ear. The familiar painful pop made him wince as always, and then there were two entities in his head instead of the usual one.

— What the actual fuck, Morph?

— **Calm down.**

— I'll calm down when you tell me what the hell I just saw.

— **We were communicating.**

— That ain't what it looked like, pal.

— **Enthusiastically communicating. The entity was …**

— Was what?

— I suppose you might say it was happy to see me.

— *Is that a Zelnad in your pocket, or …?*

— Happy? It's a damn Zelnad!

— Yes, but it no longer wishes to be.

He thought back to Durandia, where the Zelnads trying to steal the crypsid queen basically chose death over imprisonment. He thought of the desperate hosts who volunteered for Lestiko's experiments. They were different forms of Zelnad from this one, but they all seemingly wanted the same thing — to find equilibrium with their hosts like him and Eli, to get rid of them altogether, or to perish.

If what Morpho said was true, then this wasn't an enemy pilot anymore. It was a damned deserter.

CHAPTER 40
BIG O ENERGY

Geddy popped a couple painkillers in advance and laid down in his quarters with the lights off. That always seemed to help. With the Zelnad synthetic still down in the containment room, Morpho plugged into his ear and downloaded all that he had learned while they were entwined.

Like two computers talking to each other, Morpho and the other synthetic had exchanged a great deal of information in a very short time — much less than it took Geddy to comprehend it. He could only handle Morph being inside his skull for ten or fifteen minutes at a stretch before he developed a splitting headache. Some days, it seemed he couldn't even make sense of his own thoughts, let alone those of his Sagacean companions.

The Zelnad blob called itself Eveth. Like all Sagaceans, it was ejected like a dandelion seed, and after millions of years adrift, it landed on a distant world. There, it was transferred into a synthetic organism. It never knew how it got there, but it learned how to pilot one of the triangle ships, and now that was its only purpose.

After the Battle of The Deuce, the other Nad ships returned to space and jumped away, but something stopped Eveth from doing likewise. It found itself alone. Unsure what to do or where to go, it powered down. Shortly thereafter, Tompanov came along in the *Raven* and picked it up for salvage.

Since then, it had essentially been playing dead.

Eveth didn't know where the ship was built. Few Zelnads did, it guessed, probably as a hedge in case of capture or, in his case, desertion. Jumps between HQ and other places like Earth 2 were not under the control of individual pilots.

It claimed to know nothing about the mining operation. Only that its job was to guard it. It had been doing that for months while Tatiana's platform did its thing, oblivious to what was happening in the North.

Any number of Zelnads could have developed a similar durable form to Morpho, who Dr. Nilsson brought to life. Synthetics had been around a long time, and the two of them were likely different versions of the same basic premise — a lifeform that could be manufactured and didn't have anything so messy as mortality or will. A synthetic slave completely under Zelnad control.

But something in Eveth made it question its purpose, and that decision indirectly landed it here aboard the *Stalwart*.

During their entwinement, Morpho also questioned Eveth about the ship's power source. It explained that the ship ran on a charge stored inside the sphere's shell.

— Okay, but what's charging it?
— **Original energy.**
— *I didn't know it could be harnessed.*
— **That makes two of us.**
— Original energy? Sounds like a sports drink.
— **It may be the most powerful force in the universe.**
— Then why am I just hearing about this for the first time?
— *Because even we don't entirely understand it.*

— Dr. Nilsson called it dark energy. It is a repellent force that accelerates the universe's expansion.

— Is it more repellent than Tompanov?

— **Yes, though not by much.**

His mind reeled. Was original energy related somehow to the experiments Lestiko was doing in the desert? How did the Nads produce and capture it? Was that the key?

— Did it say anything about their base? Like maybe where it is?

— **It doesn't know the location, however it does exist.**

— Is it on an exoplanet? A moon? What?

— **It is a refinement and manufacturing operation in open space. One is for isolating shinium and the other is to build ships and weapons.**

— How many ships?

— **Millions.**

Geddy's heart sank, because this confirmed his fears. The Nads had been propagating for eons, all building up to the destruction of their home world and themselves. Even if they were matched technologically, their sheer numbers might make beating them impossible.

— Is that where all the hosts are?

— **That is not clear.**

— Whaddya mean? They're either there or they're not.

— **Eveth has only seen other synthetics.**

— What do they need millions of ships for?

— **To protect their weapon.**

Now they were coming to it. Back on Aku, the Metallurgist said they needed his ship's shinium to build their weapon. That made sense, since only shinium could pass through Sagacea's protective barrier. But he never knew what sort of weapon or if that story was even true.

— What kind of weapon?

— **Eveth does not know. Only that it is very large and still**

under construction.

The obvious guess was some kind of mega-missile, but that seemed conventional and even crude for them.

— When Lestiko separates a Zelnad from its host, there's a massive explosion. Is that original energy?

— **I believe so.**

The realization hit all three of them at once. Geddy actually felt it happen, like a circuit had just been completed.

— Holy shit, guys.

— *You don't think ...*

— **Hosts are the explosive!**

They couldn't know this for certain, and if they ever did, it might be too late. But damned if it didn't fit. Millions of hosts had been lured away never to be seen again. Oraisa's story had added crucial detail. The Zelnads convinced people that they were part of a bigger plan that ended with a glorious journey to Sagacea. There, all their troubles would disappear, and they would join an ancient continuum of peace and serenity. All they had to do was board a transport to Aku.

But it was only a beautiful lie. From Aku, they were spirited away to the base to become part of a colossal bomb. All they needed was a shinium-clad ship packed with hosts and a trigger to separate them all at once when it breached Sagacea's barrier. It had to be absolutely colossal.

Not only would they doom civilization to snuff itself out — they would take out every last living host in the process.

Assuming this theory was true, it still left one big question unanswered. Where did this original energy come from? Did they rip Zelnads from their hosts and cast them aside like spent cartridges? Or was it harvested like exotic matter was for novaspheres? If it could be harnessed some other way, they needed to find it and fast.

That meant that Lestiko's problem was almost certainly connected to the one the Orneans would try to solve once they officially joined the Alliance. Thanks to Verveik's shrewd politicking, that was now a foregone conclusion.

— We need Lestiko.

— *Send Doc. Stay focused on Kigantu.*

Eli was right. Lestiko and Doc were kindred spirits of a sort. They could relate on another level, and maybe Doc could get Lestiko excited about the opportunity to work with the Orneans. Hell, he could even take Eveth along for added incentive. Geddy would feel more comfortable with it off the ship anyway even though Morph seemed to consider it trustworthy.

Retrieving the data from the research vessel would be dicey. The place had to be crawling with Nads looking for it. It would call for a small team that knew Aquebba. People he could count on to get the job done and get out alive. Who would laugh at his crude jokes when he really needed them to.

Fortunately, he had just the people for the job.

CHAPTER 41
COME BACK, SHAME!

The fighter still hovered one meter above the floor, the soft purple of its original energy power casting the attached tangle of sensors in the same subtle hue. Doc had been studying the ship for days, taking readings and forming hypotheses about what this "original energy" was and how to harness it.

Eveth did not intervene. It sat on the back of Doc's chair, just watching, for hours. As far as Geddy knew, it hadn't attempted to plug into Doc's brain like Morph did with him. Whether that was because it didn't know how or that Doc hadn't invited it to, he couldn't have said. For his part, Morph seemed satisfied that Eveth was on the level. Satisfied enough, at least, that he was comfortable taking him to Basoa in a few days' time.

It was oddly soothing to watch Doc work from the safety of engineering control. He bristled with curiosity, eyes burning as brightly as the glow coming off the ship. Day and night, he labored to understand. To answer the questions he was smart enough to ask. It was every bit as impressive as watching a top athlete or an exceptionally flexible Stemiran dancer.

Geddy felt the same way. He was in his element, too, only now he had some authority. Some real agency over his own destiny.

The work was critically important, which Doc also relished. The power of the Nads' weapons was only half the problem. It was the effectiveness of their shields that really messed shit up. After a while, you got a sense for how your enemy's defenses were holding up. Disruptor blasts had a different look when they impacted weak shields. That's how you knew you had them on the ropes.

In this case, nothing, from plasma and antimatter cannons to missiles to torpedoes, made a dent. It was like those movies where the hero lands the first punch on the massive bad guy with his full weight behind it and his chin barely moves. How do you fight an enemy you can't harm? That doesn't care about self-preservation?

— Maybe we need to lob some really sick burns at them.

— *Or slash their credit rating.*

— That's actually not a terrible idea.

A retinue of Ornean leaders and scientists was on its way to the *Stalwart*, which was cleared of ships other than the clones' Chimeras. They'd already received highly detailed briefs so they could choose the best people for the challenge.

There was just one problem. The author of those briefs was Doc.

To put it charitably, he was *persona non grata* on Ornea. He had been cast quite literally as a permanent stain on his family's otherwise sterling reputation. A dour relief of his face was chiseled into the University of Tathe's wall of shame, a sneering paean to other offenders of Ornea's draconian academic laws. Roughly a year earlier, he'd been summarily banished never to return.

Now, Ornea was coming to him. But no one from the delegation knew he was a senior officer in the New Alliance.

No way around it. It was going to be awkward.

"Cap, Doc — the Orneans are here," came Denk's voice over the comm.

Doc paused his labors at the holoscreen he hadn't looked away from for hours and sat back in his chair, pausing momentarily before looking up through the window at Geddy.

Showtime.

Parmhar Tardigan had come to the *Stalwart's* hangar to support his brother and brief the Ornean delegation on his activities. He seemed buoyantly optimistic that they would find the Zelnad base soon. He was held in higher esteem than Doc but had been on his way to a life of academic irrelevance. That would've forced him into commercial work — another badge of failure for the proud Tardigan clan.

"You okay?" Geddy asked Doc, who was as animated as a statue.

"I am fine, Captain, thank you."

Doc and Parmhar stood to his right and Verveik to his left, hulking over him like the giant he was. They'd both donned their Alliance dress uniforms for the occasion. Though they were stiffer and more uncomfortable than the day-to-day coveralls, they looked sharp and official. Geddy thought back to what Ninety-Two — now Ogos — had said about pride.

"Let's go," Verveik said.

He began toward the approaching retinue, which was led by a handful of male senators. Ornea had no president or other supreme leader, which contrasted with the military's obsession with hierarchy.

Geddy had gotten so accustomed to seeing Doc dressed like one of the crew that it was jarring to see other Orneans in their full academic regalia.

— *A little over the top, if you ask me.*

— All that's missing are the wands and pointy hats.

"Are we supposed to genuflect?" Geddy murmured, earning a slight upturn of Verveik's mouth.

They met halfway between the handling platform and the Ornean transport, which appeared out of place in the vacant flight deck. The clones were lined up in two long rows to either side, also in dress uniforms. The Orneans studied them with great interest until they spotted Doc and Parmhar.

"Greetings, honored guests," Verveik said. "Welcome to the *Stalwart*. I'm Commander Verveik."

"I am Lorin Altam," said the shortest of them, an old but feisty man with a perfectly trimmed white beard. "I've been authorized to speak on behalf of the senate regarding this matter. My colleagues here asked to bear witness to these proceedings."

Verveik gave a respectful bow. "It's a pleasure to meet you, senators. This is Captain Starheart, Chief Science Officer–"

"Krons Tardigan." His lips formed a line as he spoke Doc's name like he'd tasted poison. He locked eyes with Verveik. "What's the meaning of this, Commander?"

"Dr. Tardigan wrote the brief you all read," Verveik replied. "Your scientists will be working with him."

The four senators behind him fell into an anxious huddle which Altam silenced with a pointed stare. His eyes crawled over Doc as though Verveik's statement couldn't be true.

Doc drew himself taller and cleared his throat. "The senator is correct. I did write the brief. But there is much more to impart and to learn."

"Hmph." Now Altam looked accusingly at Verveik like Doc wasn't there. "This man is a disgrace, banned from Ornea. A totem of shame to his entire–"

"You're not on Ornea," Geddy interrupted. He didn't need to look up to feel Verveik's eyes burning a hole through him.

"Dr. Tardigan has more than earned his place as a senior officer in the Alliance."

The senators exchanged dubious looks. "I am a man of science myself," Altam said, finally looking Doc in the eye. "I must admit ... the work you've done is exceptional, Dr. Tardigan."

Doc's face flushed, and he gave a gracious nod. "Thank you, sir."

At least temporarily assuaged, Altam turned his attention to Parmhar. "The same could be said for your work. Perhaps we can help accelerate the discovery of the Zelnad base."

Parmhar cleared his throat. "Actually, Senator, I believe we have."

Verveik's, Geddy's, and Doc's head snapped to him in unison. He was bursting at the seams with excitement.

"Parmhar?" Doc asked. "What are you talking about?"

"Late last night, one of my assistants informed me of a massive spike in the tukrium readings. Bigger by far than anything we've seen. It simply has to be the Zelnad base."

"We found them?" Geddy said dumbly, turning to Verveik with a broadening smile. "We fucking found them!"

"Oh, Parmhar!" Doc wrapped his brother in a joyous hug. "All those years ... all your work!"

"A little luck was all we needed, Krons. We caught a break," Parmhar said, grinning from ear to ear.

As Parmhar was speaking, distant murmurs came from the direction of the Ornean ship. The academics who'd accompanied the senators descended the wide ramp as their eyes swept the hangar like tourists. Altam noticed Geddy's attention shift and turned casually.

"As promised, we have brought volunteers from our most esteemed institutions," Altam explained. "Your work thus far on this novel energy source sparked great interest among our academic community."

He'd barely finished speaking before he heard Doc give a little gasp, his hand flying to his brother's shoulder. "Parmhar."

At the back of the gaggle of academics loomed a figure in cream and gold robes, elegantly folded and wrapped about his proud shoulders. A buffer had formed around him as though the others afforded him a wide berth. Geddy recognized the getup immediately.

It was Pyrus Tardigan, Doc and Parmhar's disapproving father.

— *Oh, shit.*

— *If it isn't Ornea's Father of the Year.*

Noticing the brothers' troubled expressions, Altam frowned. "Is ... there a problem?"

Of course, Verveik had no idea what was going on. All he knew was that the formal agreement with Ornea wasn't official until he and Altam both signed it. There was still every chance this could fall through.

"What is he doing here?" Doc mumbled.

Neither Altam nor Verveik understood the source of the tension that had fallen over the scene and looked expectantly at Geddy.

"It's complicated," Geddy offered. "Family drama."

The academics had spotted Doc and were already having hushed exchanges as they glanced nervously back at Pyrus. He finally caught up, and his disapproving gaze set upon his two sons. Silence fell over the group as his peers parted to allow the old man through. Whether that was out of fear or loathing, Geddy couldn't tell.

The expression on his stoic face was somewhere in between disgust and confusion, like realizing last night's takeout had already gone bad. He took a few hesitant steps closer until he was shoulder-to-shoulder with Altam. A painful silence ensued while the others waited for their revered elder statesman to speak.

It was Doc who broke the silence. "Hello, father."

In lieu of replying to his son, Pyrus first regarded Parmhar, then Geddy with faint recognition. "You."

"Thanks for coming, Pyrus, but we already know the secrets of the universe."

Verveik leaned over, his giant head looming over Geddy. "Care to fill me in here?"

"It seems my father has once again bullied his way into something that doesn't concern him," Doc said.

Pyrus, who had obviously never been spoken to with such disrespect, was too shocked to reply. One of the other academics leveled an accusing finger at Doc.

"That's Krons Tardigan. An exile!"

"Yes," Doc said stiffly. "And the author of the research brief you all have certainly pored over. Except, perhaps, my father, who never had a mind for science."

The gaggle exchanged looks of shock, both at the insult and the fact that his tireless work had lured them there.

"Your hypotheses are certainly intriguing," noted the oldest of the three female academics.

"And your methodology sound," added another. "Whatever misgivings we may have about him, the work he's done on this strange energy is extraordinary and I'm eager to explore it."

Everyone nodded in agreement except for Pyrus, whose face reddened with rage.

He held up his palm, and the academics quieted. "There are ethical questions to consider. I was the obvious choice."

Doc took two quick steps forward until he was almost chest to chest with Pyrus, who flinched at the sudden advance.

"Screw your ethics, father. We face extinction! Unless we prevent the destruction of Sagacea, the river of civilization will flow inexorably toward ignorance and excess until only primordial life remains. The candle of knowledge drowned in its own wax!"

Parmhar joined Doc as though forming a wall between Pyrus and the others.

"He is right. Our work here demands the rigors of science. Not the vagaries and vicissitudes of philosophy."

Pyrus' left eye twitched at the insult. He was about to speak when Altam stopped him short.

"I agree with the Doctors Tardigan. This process needs catalysts, not inhibitors."

— *Wow, they really do all talk like Doc.*

— *I recognized a few of those words.*

"You'd do well to mind your tone, Senator," Pyrus hissed.

"And you yours. Wait for us in the transport, won't you?"

"How dare you!"

"Remind me, Pyrus — how long has it been since you published?" Pyrus' face reddened with embarrassment as Altam continued. "Perhaps a tenure review is overdue."

Pyrus looked pleadingly at his fellow academics, all men and women of science, who clearly agreed. The other four senators stood in solidarity with Altam, who did not seem the least bit intimidated.

With a contemptuous sneer, Pyrus took one last look at his defiant progeny. "I have no sons."

With that, he turned on his heels and strode angrily toward the ship, his exaggerated footfalls echoing across the hangar. Each one allowed a bit more oxygen back into the proceedings.

Doc's lower lip trembled a moment, then he returned to where he'd been standing beside Geddy.

"Let's crack on, shall we?" Altam asked brightly.

Verveik let out the long breath he'd been holding and produced the small tablet on which the agreement was drawn. Altam applied his signature to it as the other senators looked on. Then Verveik applied his own signature and tucked it back into his jacket. In his hands, it looked like a toy.

He held out his giant hand toward Altam. "Welcome to the Alliance, Senators of Ornea."

Altam grinned and took his hand. "Our best and brightest are at your disposal, Commander." He nodded over his left shoulder at the eager academics. "In the meantime, we've got a long trip back."

"Actually ..." Geddy began, retrieving the bubble drive terminal from the table behind him. He handed it to Altam. "This'll make your return trip a lot shorter."

Altam took it with great interest. "What is it?"

"A bubble drive terminal. You'll be back in Ornea before Pyrus can finish his first complaint."

He gave his head a doubtful shake. "That is a remarkable gift, Captain, but we don't know how to use it."

Geddy smirked and gave a shrug. "You guys are smart. You'll figure it out."

CHAPTER 42

THE MORE THE MAYO-IER

Voprot sat on his haunches in the officer's mess eating the same sandwich as the rest of the crew, a turkey on rye that the recombinator did surprisingly well. That was how it went sometimes. The coffee was rough, like English translated into Xellaran and back again, but the hot chocolate was on point. It took a lot of trial and error to see what worked and what didn't, which he supposed was part of the fun.

Since the Orneans' arrival three weeks earlier, the crew had been working their way through each other's native cuisine in a rotation. Today was Geddy's turn, and a turkey sandwich on rye had come to mind. He must've seen it in a movie or something because it wasn't a thing anywhere in this galaxy. Come to think of it, poultry in general didn't have many analogs here. Another piece of history that died when Old Earth did.

"Whaddya think, V?" asked Denk. His jaw moved a lot when he chewed, like a ruminant animal. It gave the impression he relished whatever he was eating, which he generally did.

"I like it," said the lizard.

Everyone's head swiveled toward him, their jaws hanging

open. Voprot's sandwich was about the size of a man's thigh. He didn't even look up until he'd bitten another hunk out of it.

"Say that again," Geddy said.

"I ... like it." He hadn't finished chewing so bits of sandwich popped out from between his sharp teeth.

"That's a complete sentence."

"I know."

A delighted smile split Geddy's face. "That's a complete sentence, too!"

"I have been working on it," Voprot said.

"Since when?"

"Here and there," Jel said. "We've all been helping him."

A pang of guilt rippled through Geddy. Ever since becoming a captain in the Alliance, he'd been busy supporting Verveik. Oz was there for some of it, but his whole ordeal on The Deuce didn't involve the crew at all. It was tough to realize things were different now.

Voprot was still very young, but he was maturing, and Iondra, the female Kigantean from the Myadan Xoo, was always on his mind. They talked all the time, and he wanted to be smarter for her. Girls did that to you.

"I think it's good, too, Cap." Denk couldn't tune into awkward silences. "What do you call the goopy white stuff again?"

"Are we still talking about the sandwich?" Geddy asked, smirking at Oz.

"Mayo," she replied for him. "They call it mayo."

"Mayo. Well, I think it's the best part. I ate a corner that didn't have any on it, and it wasn't as good."

"It makes stuff taste better," Geddy said.

"Why they not just make things taste good without it?" Voprot asked.

Geddy frowned and studied the sandwich briefly. "That's a really great question."

"We sure coulda used it on Durandia growin' up, I'll tell ya that," Denk said. "In fact, we shoulda put it on the esnip bake last night."

"Can't argue with that," Oz agreed, and nods traveled around the table.

"It's weird without Doc here," Jel said.

"I know," Geddy agreed. "But he's our best shot at convincing Lestiko to help us."

Doc had spent about two weeks bringing the Orneans up to speed on his research and helping them set up their own scientific instruments in the containment room. Once they'd gotten to work, he'd taken Eveth with him to Basoa.

"Listen … there's something I need to tell you guys."

They listened closely as Geddy detailed his conversation with Tretiak about the saga of the Zelnad research ship. He hadn't even told Oz yet.

"The ship I claimed for Kigantu?" Voprot asked.

Another pang of guilt. "Yeah, that's the one."

"It's really still there?" Denk asked.

"As far as Tretiak knows, it's still locked up tight. He can't reach any of his people in Aquebba."

"Lost contact with a distant and largely uninhabited planet crawling with evil aliens?" Oz asked with a roll of her eyes. "That always ends well."

"I take your point, but that's a risk we have to take."

"So what's our play?" Jel asked.

"We put together a small team led by someone who knows their way around. A team with a wide range of skills who can blend in anywhere and has luck on their side."

He gave Jel a sly wink and stuffed in the last bite of his dry, artificial-tasting sandwich, dabbing at his chin with a napkin as he finished chewing. Jel looked at Oz, who looked at Denk, who looked at Voprot. Geddy glanced down at Morpho on his shoulder.

Jel's glossy lips curled into a grin. "Hypothetically, when would this team you speak of need to be ready?"

"Two days. Hypothetically."

Oz's alarmed look panned across the table. "But Doc ...?"

He gave her a grim look. "Probably won't make this trip."

She paused a moment to digest the fact that they wouldn't all be together for this trip, then her face brightened. "Ideally, I'd imagine this team would be tired of being in space and spoiling for a fight," Oz added with a smirk.

"And wanting to see home again," Voprot added.

Denk continued his exaggerated chewing with his eyebrows raised, following the conversation but not the innuendo.

"Well, I say better them than me!" he said. "Those suckers can have Kigantu. I'm gonna stay right here on the *Stalwart* with you guys."

Oz shared an affectionate laugh with Geddy and Jel. "He means us, Denk."

His apple-cheeked face reddened even further. "Oh. Well ... heck yeah, then." He jabbed his thumb into his solar plexus. "But I'm drivin'!"

They fell into fits of laughter, then Geddy realized there was an aspect he hadn't considered until then. "Y'know ... we can't exactly show up on Kigantu in the *Stalwart* or even the *Armstrong*, can we?"

They all sat up. "Are you saying ...?" Oz asked, her eyes twinkling.

He shrugged. "Can you think of a more discreet option?"

"The *Fizmo*?" Jel asked. "Can that thing handle another entry?"

"Of course she can," Geddy said. "Probably."

"I have kinda missed it," admitted Oz.

"The ship?" Voprot asked.

Her big eyes grew glassy. "That, too."

The young woman from the IJC's intergalactic registry office was Zorran, professionally dressed, and cute as a button. As the line of clones inched along, it was sometimes hard to tell who was flirting with whom.

They barely ever saw the Orneans, who had turned the containment room into a full-on laboratory dedicated to the study of original energy. Geddy had poked his head down there a couple times to ask how the work was going, but they only gave him a condescending look like he couldn't possibly fathom the answer. It was hard to know whether they were making progress or not.

"Okay," the girl said brightly to One-Eleven. "You are officially registered with the IJC as Brill Tomlind. Congratulations."

— *You'll never remember these names.*

— Yeah, I'll probably stick with the numbers.

One-Eleven left, and One-Twelve came up to the table.

They'd all taken their own path to choosing names. Some studied history, others searched popular baby names, and others simply rearranged letters until they stumbled on something they liked.

"Hi there," she said, looking up at him. "You must be One-Twelve. What would you like your name to be?"

For whatever reason, One-Twelve was obsessed with Old Earth. The contents of the quantum cubes had long since been loaded into the Alliance database so it could be accessed at any time, though some of it was classified.

"Juan Rodriguez," he said.

For an exact genetic copy of Geddy who had literally never been outside, it seemed an odd choice. But most ethnic names had died with Old Earth, too, meaning he'd quite likely be the only Juan Rodriguez in the entire galaxy.

"Pleased to meet you, Mr. Rodriguez," she said, typing the information into her holoscreen. "Does Juan start with a W or an O?"

"Actually, it's a J," he said, and proceeded to spell it for her.

"You might say he's Juan in a million," Geddy quipped. When they only stared back, he thumbed over his shoulder. "I'll, ah … check on you guys later."

Ninety-Two, now Ogos Garurian, had gone first so he could get back to work. Geddy and Verveik picked him to captain another battle cruiser, the *Dauntless*, and he had already selected his command crew from among the other clones. They were on the near side of the Karrea Ion Storm getting a feel for the big ship. Meanwhile, the *Resolute*, one of two colossal troop transports, was the new processing center for the continued influx of volunteers. Repairs had finally been completed on the *Gallant*, which was finally ready to fly again.

Because of the storm, which made deep scans impossible, they needed ships on all sides to watch for unfriendlies. They could no longer afford surprises.

For its part, the Gundrun second fleet was parked over the nearby gas giant, Sulrinda, retrofitting its ships with the bubble drive. It was reassuring to have them close, although even mighty Gundrun had been humbled by the power of the Nads.

Which was why, when the alarm sounded and Oz's voice came over the loudspeakers, Geddy's neck hair stood on end. "General alert! Battle stations! This is not a drill!"

— *Oh, no! Did they find us?*

— *I sure hope not.*

He bounded up the steps two at a time to the command level, making yet another mental note to do more cardio. Meanwhile, the clones sprinted to their fighters. Geddy burst breathlessly through the door of the bridge.

"Somebody talk … to me!" he said, panting.

Oz leapt from her weapons station to meet him. "There's a whole goddamned armada headed straight for us. Thousands of ships. Tens of thousands, maybe."

"Zelnad?" he asked anxiously. If so, they'd made a woeful miscalculation.

"I don't think so," Denk said over his shoulder. "Unless our scanners are on the fritz, they look like Triad ships!"

"Contact Verveik and Arbizander," Geddy said, taking his seat in the captain's chair.

"Already done," Denk said.

The huge front screen glittered with hundreds, perhaps thousands of signals. Smaller boxes along the left and right border showed rotating schematics of individual ships based on their transponders. The formation resembled a flying mountain, higher in the middle than on the ends. Ghruk was on the left, Kailoria on the right. Eighty years earlier, there would've been three times as many. The center of the formation was mostly Screvari.

It didn't make any sense. The Triad planets had fought more wars than almost anyone. You didn't just form a line like redcoats and show up on someone's front door.

"This is no attack," Geddy said. "I'm not sure what this is."

The green ring around the screen lit up, and Denk spun back. "We're being hailed by the Screvari command ship."

Geddy slid forward in his chair. "Put it through."

The face that came on screen was unfamiliar to him, another ghoulish, pale-gray Screvari face with expressionless black eyes like the holes in a bowling ball.

"I am General Grozuc of the High Command," he growled. "Who am I speaking with?"

"Captain Starheart of the Alliance ship *Stalwart*," Geddy replied, trying to sound unintimidated. "You guys are a long way from h–"

"*Captain?*" His wrinkled lips curled derisively around the title. "I seek an audience with Commander Verveik."

It was hard not to be mildly insulted, but at least in this instance, Geddy knew better than to argue. "Denk?"

"I've got him now."

A moment later, the screen split, and Verveik's graven face appeared. His eyes narrowed suspiciously at the Screvari.

"This is the commander," he said.

"Commander, I am General Grozuc of the High Command. I've been authorized to speak with you on behalf of the Triad."

The last time the Alliance squared off against the Triad, it walked away victorious. But it was the very definition of a Pyrrhic victory, costing both forces so dearly that they fell apart. The galaxy hadn't been the same since. But this time, the Triad had a massive advantage. More ships, better trained soldiers, and a united front. The New Alliance barely had its feet under it, and the vast majority of their fleet was still unused and hidden deep inside the storm.

Verveik's voice was calm and sure. "State your business."

As though on cue, the entire Gundrun fleet blipped into view around the *Stalwart*. It was like being cornered in an alley by a bunch of thugs only to have the football team roll up behind you. A moment later, the two other Alliance battle cruisers above them and to the sides. Arbizander's face joined the others, filling all four corners of the screen.

"Your show of strength isn't necessary, Commandant Arbizander," Grozuc said. "We're not here to start a fight."

"Then speak plainly, General," Verveik growled.

Grozuc's face pinched as though he was taking a rough shit, and he let out a pained breath before responding as though the words burned coming out. "The combined armies of the Triad wish to pledge their support … to the Alliance."

Everyone's jaw hit the floor.

"You do?" Verveik and Arbizander asked nearly in unison. Geddy figured he'd best keep his trap shut for once.

"The Coalition is no more," Grozuc said. "We can no longer ignore the threat the Zelnads pose to the intergalactic order."

— *Holy shit!*

— As always, you captured my thoughts perfectly.

Verveik formed the closest thing to a full smile Geddy had ever seen. "In that case, General, you are most welcome."

CHAPTER 43
SADDLING UP

The *Penetrator*, the one-seater Geddy and Eli built together, was in the same place it had been since they recovered it from the secret lab on Aku — the starboard side of the *For Sale Make Offer's* capacious hold, right in front of a stack of perpetually empty storage crates. On account of its short wings, it was angled slightly so the straps could secure it tightly to the wall. In the months that followed its recovery, it had become more of a fixture than anything — a ship-shaped piece of cargo that did nothing but take up space and remind Geddy of his past.

He'd unfastened one of the crates and placed it in front of the craft so he could sit. Sleep came fitfully these days, if at all. During the weeks that followed the Triad's arrival, he tossed and turned so much that Oz generally opted to return to her own quarters down the hall once she got tired. So it had gone that night.

Being wide awake, he'd sought the bottle of Kailorian gin from his closet. When he took it out, he noticed the single thin piece of shinium that remained from the *Penetrator*, the one the Metallurgist had taunted him with.

He turned it over in his hands as he sat in the *Fizmo's* silent hold with only Eli for company. These days, he was almost never alone with his thoughts, which was probably for the best. The resilient metal didn't look all that different from aluminum or the other alloys that formed the outer skin of ships like it. But it was nearly as malleable as gold once you got it hot enough. The trapezoidal piece was no more than forty centimeters on the longest side, and it weighed next to nothing. It was faintly concave on account of where it fit on the ship. Empty holes ran along each edge where the rivets had been removed. Those were shinium, too.

He took a pull straight from the bottle and winced. It made your throat raw after a while. Could it be that you were only supposed to drink a small amount at a time?

Nah, that couldn't be right.

"You remember making this piece?"

— *Can't say I do.*

In all, one hundred thirty-two individual pieces comprised the *Penetrator's* outer skin. Each took him about a week to make. The salvage bots would bring out the ore, which on a good day had tiny silver veins running through it. The tunneling equipment in the geothermal plant included a rock crusher, which turned the ore into a gravelly material before it went into the smelter. Thus began the slow and laborious process of refining the remarkable metal and shaping it into sheets.

Looking back, he could scarcely believe he'd done it. That night before her maiden voyage, getting sotted on the last bottle of Old Earth whisky, had been so cathartic. The final chapter in a long slog that was supposed to end with a test flight the next morning. A couple quick laps around the planet to make sure everything was working as expected, then he'd top off her fuel and take Eli back to Sagacea.

"Hey, how were we supposed to reach Sagacea if you don't know where it is?"

— *I thought you'd never ask.*

"Guess I'm thinking more clearly than usual."

— *It was never about Sagacea. It was about you.*

"But ... the whole point was to get you home."

— *You didn't want me in your head. You needed to believe you could get me out of it. Otherwise, you wouldn't have kept going. You would've become as hopeless as Lestiko's volunteers.*

He was about to reject this claim, but Eli was right. It wasn't until well after the planet evacuated that Geddy fully accepted the alien voice in his head. By then, they were already deep in the process of building the *Penetrator*. It gave shape to the long, lonely days and gave him a purpose. What would he have done without that? What would he have poured his guilt into otherwise?

Even then, Eli knew him better than he knew himself.

"If we'd actually taken her off-world, where would we have gone?"

— *To get novaspheres I suppose.*

"But I didn't have any money."

— *No, but you knew people who did. Tatiana, for one.*

"She thought I was dead."

— *You could've made up any story you wanted.*

"Okay, but then what?"

— *Then I would have said the same thing I did after your first visit with Tev on Pretensia.*

"That we're bound together."

— *Yes.*

"That my end is your end."

— *Yes.*

"Do you have any idea how pissed off I would've been that we couldn't reach Sagacea?"

— *Yes. But you would have understood.*

A warm glow spread through his limbs, and not only from the gin. "Because building this ship together kept us alive?"

— *No, Geddy.*

This all started with him wanting Eli out of his head. But by the end, his only motivation was to help his friend return home. Even if it cost him their companionship. Only Sagacea wasn't his home. Geddy was.

Tears welled in his eyes, then began to stream down his cheeks in rivulets.

"Because I ... love you."

— *Yes, Geddy. And I love you.*

"Would it work if I thought about a hug right now?"

— *It will have to do.*

Denk grunted as he dragged the massive hose across the floor of the *Fizmo's* hold. He'd slung it over his right shoulder, the business end bouncing up and down like a half chub as pale green liquid dripped grotesquely from the coupling.

"What the hell is that?" Geddy asked.

"Nutrimush," Denk replied with misplaced enthusiasm. "Well, the closest the kitchen could manage, anyway."

"You remember it's not a long trip anymore, right? We've got a bubble drive terminal. Right Jel?"

Jeledine was across from him in the maintenance area performing checks on their suits, which he hoped to hell they wouldn't need.

"Plus a backup!" she called over her shoulder returning as always to her labors.

"Well, Cap, you can never be too prepared," Denk said, unmoved by the argument.

It seemed Denk's hose was getting harder to drag the closer he got to the coupling, which was near the workbench. Geddy cast a glance back toward the open hold door, noting that it had hung up on the bottom. Denk was straining so hard that half its length had lifted clear of the floor.

Geddy was about to intervene when Voprot appeared in the opening carrying a small crate. On noticing the stuck hose, he set the crate down and casually freed it from where it had caught. When it immediately went slack, Denk did a hard face plant on the metal grate three meters shy of the tank.

"I fixed the hose, Denk!" Voprot said, quite pleased with himself.

"Thanks, V."

Denk grimaced as he got back on his feet, then dutifully took up the hose again. He secured it to the coupling and opened the valve, and it stiffened as the viscous goo pumped in.

"Denk, you flushed all the old stuff out of the tank first, right?" Geddy asked.

"Uhh …" Denk said.

"Where this go?" Voprot asked Geddy before his stomach could finish turning.

"Where *does* this go," he corrected.

"I am asking you."

Geddy took a cleansing breath and smiled pleasantly. "What is it?"

"I not know."

— *Well, he learned 'I.' At least it won't be Voprot this and Voprot that anymore.*

— Imagine how Iondra will swoon.

Voprot had fatefully met another Kigantean, a female, on Myadan. He'd been on his self-improvement kick ever since. He set the crate down and Geddy knelt to remove the lid. The whole thing was dense foam except for a single unopened bottle of Old Earth. A broad smile split his face. A small note attached to the front label read, *Something to fight for.*

A parting gift from Tati. He should've known she'd have another bottle somewhere. Hell, she probably had a vault full of them. But she gave one to him and the crew, and it was thoughtful.

"My quarters," he said, replacing and securing the lid.

"Okay." He picked up the crate and ambled away.

While the thought of returning to Kigantu filled Geddy with dread, Voprot was as happy as he'd seen him in weeks. He was out of his element aboard the *Stalwart* and eager to be somewhere familiar. The rest of the crew seemed to feel the same way, and for them, the *Fiz* was that place.

Oz ambled through the door next carrying her giant duffle. Everyone had ditched their Alliance uniforms, including her. She was back in her classic dark gray outfit, the skin-tight pants showing off her toned legs.

"How we looking?" she asked as she approached.

He grinned lasciviously. "Better than ever."

She rolled her eyes. "So predictable."

Nodding at the duffle, he asked, "What the hell are you bringing? This is an in and out operation. And not the fun kind."

"Yeah, well, you never know what'll happen in these kinds of places."

She unzipped the bag halfway and pulled out a tiny corner of a shiny red material from between the handles of her blades. The moment he saw it, his loins stirred.

He raised his eyes to her. "No way."

It was the outfit she'd donned for their fight over the Hell Well back on Caloth. The Crimson Queen, a handle earned fighting for cash during her days with the Xellaran resistance. It was the only way to earn their respect. Until Caloth, she hadn't worn it in a decade, and he hadn't even seen it since.

She smirked and tucked the stretchy material back inside. "Just in case."

"In case of a prize fight or in case we do some role-playing in my quarters?"

"Just ... in case," she coyly returned, and continued toward the open airlock door.

— *Well that's certainly tantalizing.*

— *You don't gotta tell me, pal.*

As the crew of the *Fizmo* completed their preparations, they meandered back into the hold. Voprot helped Denk drag the limp hose back outside. They gathered in a small circle at the center where Doc had led them in so many sesehlu sessions on their long journeys together. It had taken on a certain significance for them, a gathering place outside the bridge or the galley.

"All right, listen up," Geddy said, rubbing his hands together. "This is a dangerous trip. We don't know what to expect. Chances are, Kigantu is crawling with Nads. Ranses might've breached the city. It could be even more of a hellscape than usual. Finding and retrieving the research ship is gonna take some special skills." He gestured toward Voprot. "Like strength. Maybe the occasional helper verb."

"I am make ready," said the lizard.

He heaved a sigh and turned to Denk. "And a great attitude."

Denk snapped his heels together like a legionnaire and drew himself to full height as he saluted. "All day long, Cap!"

Smiling at Oz, he said, "And smoking hotness." When she scowled, he added, "But mostly resilience."

She gave a demure grin. "That's a little better."

Jel stood with her arms folded and her left hip thrust outward, her lips swishing back and forth.

"And ingenuity."

"If I didn't keep you people out of trouble, you'd never leave," she joked.

Geddy turned his head and glanced down at Morpho. "And determination."

Morpho gave his own crisp salute.

"All right, let's saddle up," Geddy said.

"Hold up. I think you missed a few," Oz reminded him with a smirk. "Like loyalty."

"Leadership," added Jel.

"Faith," Denk said.

"Patience," said Voprot.

— *Don't forget love.*

"What did Eli say?" Denk asked.

Geddy struggled to respond. It was all too much. Oz let him off the hook.

"Love," she said, smiling warmly. "He said love." Seeing him about to lose it completely, she jutted her chin toward the bridge. "C'mon, guys. There's plenty of time for mush later. Let's see if this thing turns over."

"I'll be right there," he called after them as they left. "Just need a moment."

Oz and the others proceeded through the airlock, and she gratefully closed it behind her with a warm smile back toward him. As soon as it sealed, the floodgates opened. Geddy hadn't shed real tears since learning his parents died. Everything he should've grieved or rejoiced about ever since burst forth, shapeless and ugly. He sank to the floor with his head between his knees and let it come.

— Good grief, E. I'm a mess.

— *Now you all know what you're fighting for.*

— I preferred Tati's approach.

— *Are you about done?*

— I think so.

— *Then get your ass up. You're Geddy Muthafuckin' Starheart.*

Geddy wiped his face on his sleeves, sucked a schlogg of snot deeper into his sinuses, and got to his feet. He smoothed his beard, tugged down his old NASA jacket, and took a deep breath.

— Thanks for snapping me out of that.
— *Anytime.*
— Off we go into the wild black yonder.
— *Yes!*
— But first, a tissue.
— *Also yes.*

NEXT IN THE REASSEMBLY SERIES

Vinci-books.com/dark-dodgers

Ancient prophecies, unstoppable foes, and a fractured alliance. Can Geddy unite the galaxy before it's too late? Find out in *Dark Dodgers*!

Turn the page for a free preview…

DARK DODGERS: CHAPTER 1
SLOW GIN FIZMO

Voprot, the colossal Kigantean who resembled an irradiated iguana, lifted the dice cup from the Fizmo's galley table and grinned. The moment he did, Geddy Starheart's stomach flooded with bile.

"Uguinok!" exclaimed the lizard, clearly having expected everyone to be happy for him.

"What the shit?!" Oz slurred, her nose wrinkling distastefully.

Denk gathered his scoring sticks in disgust and re-sorted them in the tray, shaking his head. "V, I love ya like a brother, but that ain't right."

"That not uguinok?" Voprot asked, genuinely confused.

"I mean that you keep winnin'."

Geddy slid another fifty-credit square into the kitty and rubbed his face, noting that his drink was empty. "Anyone else's glass have a hole in it?"

"On it." Oz teetered as she rose from the galley table.

— *She's hitting it harder than usual tonight.*
— You noticed that, too?
— *I wonder why.*

— You and me both.

They'd been at it for hours, yet Voprot's winning streak had only extended. He barely even knew how to play. Wasn't that always how it went?

Voprot's lucky streak contrasted starkly with their own. Since jumping into space over the reviled desert world Kigantu — the planetary equivalent of dry anal — the crew of the *For Sale Make Offer* had been killing time waiting for a massive sandstorm to clear. It followed a northeastern track, suggesting it originated in the south. It had engulfed Aquebba entirely, and Jel figured it would be at least another sixteen hours before they could even think about an entry. Everyone was getting on each other's nerves.

Oz returned with a fresh bottle of Kailorian gin and refilled everyone's cup as Voprot's claw swept the little pile of credit squares at the center into the growing mountain in front of him.

Denk also got up. "I'm starvin'. Who's up for nutrimush? Cap? Oz? Nutrimush? Jel?"

"I thought you said, 'food.'" Realizing his sour stomach had no buffer against the harsh liquor, Geddy added, "Yeah, okay."

"Nutrimushes all around." He gleefully removed a stack of bowls from the cupboard.

"I wish Doc was here," Jel mumbled. She rarely imbibed, but when she did, she often became sullen.

Doc Tardigan had taken Eveth, the Zelnad deserter, with him to Basoa to convince the reclusive genius Lestiko to help the Alliance. Lestiko was host to a Zelnad but had figured out how to regain control. In so doing, he had gained deep insights into their tech and the so-called original energy that powered it. That made him invaluable to Doc and the Ornean scientists who were studying it.

All Lestiko cared about was learning how to separate

himself from his nasty entity, Rai, without killing them both. He believed that the massive energy it released was being exploited by the Nads in order to create a weapon capable of destroying Sagacea. A weapon made of hosts.

Geddy's eyes slid from Jel over to the nutrimush spigot, where the greenish-brown paste had begun to emerge. It coiled lazily in the bowl before softening into it like an incel into a lounge chair. Its distinct smell, an earthy tang that stuck to your clothes, drifted through the galley.

"It's extra thick today, guys," Denk said, moving on to the next bowl. "We must be near the bottom."

"Please don't say bottom." Geddy turned away from Denk's labors and tried not to gag.

— *How is he always in such good spirits?*

— You saw Durandia. Anywhere else would seem like nirvana.

Having filled everyone's glass, Oz returned to her seat at the hexagonal metal table and took a swig directly from the bottle. The others exchanged concerned looks.

"Everything okay?" Geddy asked her.

"Don't I seem okay?"

"Just ... sad, I guess."

"Fuck sadness." Jel raised her glass to Oz.

Oz gave her a crooked nod and did likewise. "And fuck the damn Dans — er, Nads. Ha!" She took another guzzle and smacked her lips. "Ahhh."

Geddy felt a presence over his shoulder. Jel raised her eyes to the door and squinted. "Oh, hey."

Tretiak Bouche had entered the *Fizmo's* galley, joining Voprot as the only sober ones left. He'd been sitting at the comm station for hours trying to reach Krigor, his and Geddy's mutual friend, in Aquebba. Jel said the storm's iron-rich sand created too much interference, but he kept at it anyway. As hard as it was to believe that he actually cared about Kriggy, people could still surprise you sometimes.

Denk returned to the table with two full bowls, which he gave to the ladies. "Pretty girls first. Hey, Mr. Bouche. You want some nutrimush? It's only slightly fermented."

Oz made a show of scooping the stuff onto her spoon and slipping it into her mouth. "Mmm ... you can really taste the cricket meal today."

"A tempting offer, but no thank you. I came to say goodnight."

"Still no luck reaching Krig?" Geddy asked.

For three long weeks, the storm had raged, and they were no closer to Aquebba. But the moment it broke, they had to be ready. The Zelnad research ship they'd yanked out of Beebit Tompanov's greedy hands hadn't been sold after all. Tretiak had hidden it in the Double A's so-called Tomb, the location of which he alone knew. They'd come to Kigantu hoping that the mysterious empty ship had actually discovered Sagacea's position. If that was true, then the Zelnads would be equally desperate to find it.

Tretiak shook his head. "I'll try again in the morning. Let me know if the storm breaks." He disappeared down the hall.

Having distributed all the bowls to the crew, Denk returned with one of his own, bigger than even Voprot's portion, and settled onto the seat. "Well, everyone, better dig in before the skin forms!"

By the time the bleary-eyed crew stumbled into the bridge the next morning, the storm appeared to be dissipating. Still no luck reaching Krig, but Geddy had lived through enough sandstorms in Aquebba to know that the comm array on the mountain could become encrusted with sand. If that was the case, they might have to wait until it was safe for Krig to venture outside and clean the housing.

If the bars and brothels on Turduranto Street were lucky, a resupply ship had arrived shortly before the storm. Running out of booze with the galaxy's dregs cooped up inside would've created an entirely different set of problems.

Having just refilled his mug of coffee, Geddy returned to the bridge and stared down at the fading spiral of sand from the captain's chair. Oz's eyes were closed, her crimson tendrils spilling over the back of her seat by the weapons console as she loudly snored.

Jel sat next to Tretiak with her headset on, busily scanning recorded and current chatter on the Band of Thieves and emergency channels in hopes of learning what happened down there.

The last crew member plopped down onto Geddy's left shoulder, giving him a start.

"Dammit, Morph, how many times have we talked about sneaking up on me?"

— *Maybe you should tie a bell to him.*

Geddy laughed out loud, and so did Oz.

"Ha! Good one, E."

She'd begun picking up much of what Eli said, asserting that it was just her keen Temerurian empathy. It was getting to where his and Eli's conversation was no longer private when she was around. He wasn't sure how he felt about that.

Morpho seemed to give a shrug, then relaxed into his shoulder.

— *Perhaps the day will come when you can tune with Morpho without the ...*

— Aural sex? That would be nice.

Lestiko had taught Geddy how to tune, or psychically connect, to other hosts. He'd been practicing with Morpho here and there but hadn't made much progress. He needed more coaching.

"Hey." Oz opened one eye but didn't raise her head. "You sure you're feeling all right?"

"You of all people should know a hangover when you see it."

"That's fair."

She gave an impassive shrug. "Besides, what the hell else are we supposed to do?" He'd barely opened his mouth to reply when she added, "Actually, don't answer that."

"Ged, I might have something here," Jel said to his right. "Fair warning, it ain't much."

He swiveled the chair toward her. "Expectations set to low."

"It's a snippet of a conversation between a Zorran transport and a private Zihnian ship." She threw the recorded audio to the front screen.

"… just glad I got out of Aquebba when I did," said a gruff male voice.

Another male with a thick accent asked, "You mean the storm?"

"Well, yeah, there was that, but I mean the firefight."

"I heard it was a bar brawl that spilled onto the damn street."

"I dunno, man. I was already halfway up the spaceport steps when I heard the blaster fire. It sounded pretty heavy to me."

The recording stopped, and Geddy turned expectantly to Jel.

"Told you," she said.

Indeed, it wasn't much to go on. Bar fights were a daily occurrence in Aquebba. Sometimes, blasters were drawn, but only rarely fired. As rough as it could be, the city was surprisingly self-policing. Most altercations got shut down by owners before bolts began to fly. That an apparent gunfight broke out the same time as the storm rolled in made him suspect a correlation.

But this wasn't getting them anywhere. They had to see for themselves.

"How are winds in the lower atmosphere? Above the storm, I mean," Geddy asked Jel.

She switched screens and consulted her atmospheric data. "It'd be risky. High winds, particulates ... it's your call."

Geddy activated the speaker in the hold. "Denk, Voprot ... return to the bridge. We're going down."

**Grab your copy...
Vinci-books.com/dark-dodgers**

DARK DODGERS: CHAPTER 2
RAW-DOGGING THE ENTRY

Denk punched the *Fizmo* through the upper atmosphere at a shallower angle than Geddy would've, and he feared it would kick them back into space if it didn't tear the ship in half. But the kid had spent a good chunk of his young life at the controls of the old trawler. He knew what he was doing, so Geddy kept his mouth shut.

Of course, the big, boxy ship had the aerodynamics of a barn. As it screamed toward Aquebba, yellow flames licked the edge of the badly flickering front screen, the vibration threatening to liquefy their insides. Even so, in his blurry peripheral vision, Oz was still half asleep.

Tretiak, cinched tightly into the jump seat, wore an expression somewhere between disgust and terror. He surely wondered why they couldn't have taken literally any other ship to Kigantu. But he also must have understood that the *Fiz* wouldn't attract attention like an Alliance ship. That was valuable, especially if the place was crawling with Nads as they suspected.

Jel and Voprot sat opposite each other at the rear of the bridge. As usual, Voprot looked like a kid on a rollercoaster, his tongue half hanging out over jagged rows of teeth. For Jel, this was just another day at the office.

The violent shudder tapered off as they dipped below the clouds and the city in the desert appeared. Denk eased back on the throttle, and the engines that operated at a faint hum in space settled into a throaty rumble.

Tretiak was the first to unbuckle and return to the communications console. His desperation to reach Kriggy surprised Geddy. The man was as inscrutable as they came. But the further away he got from his persona, the Auctioneer, the more humanity percolated through his cold manner.

For the millionth time, he donned the headset and said, "Merchant Niner, this is Sales Manager. Do you read?"

Tretiak didn't like anyone to know when he was coming or going, so employees referred to him in conversation as Sales Manager.

Still no reply.

The swirling storm, less opaque than it appeared from space, had largely moved past Aquebba and was on a northeastern track toward the mountains. Sand had piled up in massive drifts along the ranse wall, particularly at the southwest edge. When that happened, the dreaded ranses could, in theory, climb over the top. In such cases, drones would drop weights on a path leading away from the city so the infernal creatures would follow the vibrations.

Soon, everyone from barkeeps to madams would emerge with shovels and blowers to clear away drifting sand. By nightfall, it would be piled in the streets and bulldozers would return it to the desert through the main gate. Then the party would begin anew with the hope that the next storm was way off. Usually, it was. Sometimes only a week would pass. Such was life in a desert hellhole.

Denk dropped lower as he made a slow circle around the city. Zooming in revealed signs of a fight, with fresh blast marks on buildings and dozens of sand-covered bodies in the streets. That wasn't entirely unusual for Aquebba. A pissing contest between a couple of pirates sometimes descended into a full-scale riot. Any unclaimed dead were launched far over the wall to be ranse food, and the city went about its business. Thinking about it now, it was pretty fucked up.

— *Where is everyone?*
— *I'm wondering the same thing.*

The look on Tretiak's face suggested he did, too.

"Sales to Merchant Niner. Come in, Merchant Niner, over," he repeated, again to no effect.

They were close enough to the comm array, perched atop the hill behind the Double A, that it was plainly visible. The housing appeared intact and clear of sand.

"Aquebba Station, requesting clearance to land," Denk squeaked.

No response. Denk quartered back toward Geddy with a bewildered look.

Even through the beige veil, he noted that maybe half of the oval spaceport's entrances were closed. Normally, they would've been sealed against the storm. The attack must've come before.

— *What do you make of this?*
— *I dunno, but I don't like it.*

"Jel, how are the winds at the surface now?"

She consulted her readout. "Gusting to thirty knots."

With a small ship, that was too much wind to land safely. Not as big a deal for the *Fiz*, though its flat sides would make her tricky to fly.

"Think you can bring her in?"

Ordinarily, landing at an intergalactic spaceport without clearance could get you shot down. But it was clear that no one was manning the cannons today.

Denk didn't hesitate. "No problem, boss."

"Are you sure about this?" Jel cautioned. "We might not be able to reach the fleet from down there."

Geddy shared her concern, but they'd already waited this long, and there was no guarantee their window wouldn't close again. "I hear you, but we need to know what happened here." He turned to Oz, who looked like death warmed over. "Weapons and suits. Take Voprot."

She saluted sarcastically and unfastened her restraints. "Aye aye, sir."

— *She's not okay.*

— No. Once she sobers up, I'm gonna find out why.

Denk brought them down, holding the big ship against the wind as sand buffeted the fuselage.

Fortunately, the large entrances were on the leeward side of the spaceport. Once Denk got low enough and squared her up, the wind became less of a factor. Drifts of reddish sand stretched across the open door. The interior was dark.

Geddy activated the landing lights to reveal an empty bay. Various pieces of equipment and loaders were intact but scattered as though hastily abandoned. No security force was there to greet them. In fact, there were no signs of life at all.

Once they were through, Denk extended the skids, eased the big ship onto the floor, and powered down. Oz returned from the hold with a thick scarf wrapped about her head and a pair of goggles, her energy blades strapped across her back. She handed Geddy a scarf and goggles of his own.

"Thanks." Geddy got up and tugged it on. "Oz and I'll do a sweep. Keep the ramp closed until we get back." His trusty PDQ blaster was strapped as always to his thigh.

"Be careful," Jel warned. "Whatever happened here might not be over."

"Can I come?" Voprot appeared through the airlock wearing a hopeful look. He'd grown up here and didn't need a suit. "I am eager to breathe the Kigantu air."

It was still weird to hear the lizard use complete sentences.

"Like an alpine meadow, I'm sure. C'mon, then."

He excitedly fastened his electric whip to his belt and was the first to stand beside the exit. Once Geddy and Oz joined him, he activated the ramp. As it lowered, a puff of sand blew up through the gap. Voprot's clawed foot hit the floor the same time as the ramp stopped, and he marched confidently forward with Geddy and Oz in tow. The ramp closed behind them.

He placed a hand on Oz's shoulder. When she raised her eyes to him, he mouthed, *Are you okay?*

Please stop asking, she mouthed in return.

Their view of the hangar's yawning expanse was obscured only by the wide central support column. Still, it appeared completely empty. Not once in his eighteen years here had Geddy ever seen that.

"This place must've cleared out in a hurry," Oz noted.

If so, it suggested the attack came from the other end of the city, giving the spaceport time to clear out.

Voprot knelt to take a handful of sand from a sinuous pile on the floor and sniffed at it, letting it fall through his reptilian fingers. "It is good to be home."

"I couldn't agree less," Geddy said. "Let's check out the portmaster's office. The exterior cameras feed into there."

Geddy drew the PDQ as he brushed past Voprot and made a beeline toward the office at the back. Oz readied her blades, which hummed with power and cast the dust-littered concrete floor in a faint red glow. Voprot followed at a distance.

The remnants of the storm whistled through the open bay doors. A distant, rhythmic squeak of metal on metal. No signs of life. And yet, it didn't feel entirely empty.

Stacks of shipping crates and abandoned loading equipment made ample hiding places. Even with the wind, anyone still in the city would know they were there. Their footfalls echoed too loudly in the cavernous space. Geddy signaled to Oz that he'd take the left side of the column and that she and Voprot take the right.

Halfway around the column, a faint shuffle from overhead stopped him. Before he could raise his eyes, a shadow fell over him, and the PDQ was yanked away by a large, rough hand. Half a second later, his legs were swept out, and he hit the concrete so hard that stars filled his vision. A nearby commotion suggested the same had happened to Oz. His eyes cleared just enough to see a hulking figure growl and raise its foot to cave in his face.

As the muscles in its sinewy leg tensed, a sizzling blue cord coiled around it and yanked taut. Geddy barely rolled clear before its owner landed beside him with a bone-jarring thud. A moment later, Voprot drove his knee into the fallen assassin's chest, his full weight sinking into it.

"Do not move," he growled.

Looking down at his fallen foe, Voprot bent low and tilted his head curiously, blinking as though in abject disbelief.

"Father??"

DARK DODGERS: CHAPTER 3

— *Wait ... father?* Eli asked.
— I mean, I figured he had one, but I thought maybe, y'know, eggs ...?
— *He'd still have a father. Unless Kiganteans reproduce asexually.*
— Uf. That'd be a drag.

Voprot promptly removed his foot from his father's chest and extended a claw to him, ignoring Geddy as he rolled painfully onto his side. His powerful arm hauled the even larger Kigantean to his feet.

"Oz ..." Geddy wheezed as he scanned the floor for the PDQ.

"Be with you in a moment," she said.

"Voprot, it really you?" asked the burly Kigantean in a deep voice.

Geddy spotted his blaster a couple meters away and was about to retrieve it when a second Kigantean's hand picked it up. At the same time, Oz appeared from the other side of the column, her blades in the hands of yet another Kigantean pushing her ahead of him. Or maybe ahead of *her?* With the codpieces, it was impossible to know.

"It long time," Voprot said.

"Don't worry, I'm fine." Geddy slowly got to his feet but was instantly surrounded. Oz's captor shoved her inside the corral of giant, scowling reptiles with him.

"Who they?" demanded Voprot's father.

"That Geddy and Oz. My friends. Guys, this is my–"

"Father. We sorta pieced that together," Geddy finished.

"And my cousins! And two I not know."

More light had filtered into the hangar, making their captors easier to see. Unlike Voprot, who had recently completed another molt, the Kiganteans were more brown than green, bits of sand pinched beneath their scales. Their ranse armor bore the scars of numerous run-ins with the foul creatures. All carried the same whips as Voprot, but his father also had a tall metal staff wrapped in leather. Each end flattened to a double-edged blade that looked like it could slice through anything.

Voprot's father advanced on Geddy, his chest puffed out as the vertical slits of his orange-yellow eyes narrowed imperiously.

"*Friends?*" he sneered. "Kiganteans have no friends. Not even on Kigantu."

That was a hard point to argue. According to Kriggy, Aquebba was built atop an ancient Kigantean city. Its life began as a prison colony several hundred years ago, and now it was a haven for thieves and vice. Most visitors to Aquebba didn't even realize Kigantu had natives other than ranses. Vanishingly few had ever seen one.

"I get it, big guy, believe me. But Voprot actually has many fr–"

A blaster bolt cut him off, tearing a divot from the column

above their heads with a powerful sizzle. All seven Kiganteans whirled toward it, whips unfurled.

Tretiak, flanked by Jel and Denk, emerged from behind a set of crates, blasters leveled at the wall of lizards.

"I'd let them go if I were you," Tretiak warned.

Geddy raised both hands. "Guys, it's cool. This is a misunderstanding."

Voprot pushed his way through to stand in front of him and Oz. "Geddy is right. It cool."

Tretiak's eyes narrowed suspiciously. The rest of the crew tentatively lowered their weapons, but he only tightened his grip. "What happened here? Did you people do this?"

"You dare accuse Dheson of Kigantu of mass murder?" Voprot's old man hissed.

"They not enemies," Voprot asserted. "Only wonder what happen."

A tense moment followed, during which it seemed as though Dheson might lash out with his whip and relieve Tretiak of his arm.

"Before storm, strange ships fill the sky," he explained, sweeping his big hand overhead for emphasis. "Looking for what? We not know. Men ask us about some ship. We have no ships. Foolish young scout attack, and men destroy camp. Many dead. We come under cover of storm seeking revenge but everyone dead here, too."

Tretiak lowered his blaster and muttered, "Damnit."

Geddy frowned. "You know what they're talking about?"

He stroked his long, pointy beard and shook his head. "Those men weren't from Aquebba, Dheson. They were Zelnads. My guess is, they asked around here first and didn't like the answer."

Dheson seemed highly doubtful of this reasoning. "Zelnads? I not understand."

Voprot jumped in to reply. "People with other people inside." He tapped his head. "Like puppets but bad."

— *That's actually a very succinct explanation.*

— Is there such a thing as a good puppet, though?

"What ship they want so bad?" asked Dheson.

"The same one we're looking for," Geddy said. "And the only reason this place isn't a smoking crater is because they didn't find it."

"Yet," Oz pointed out. "Did the strange ships leave?"

Dheson blinked as he looked at her. "Woman ... allowed to speak?"

"She talk all the time," Voprot replied. "Never punished once."

"Okay, two things ..." Oz began through clenched teeth. Geddy touched her forearm and shook his head. *Not now.* Her face reddened with anger, but she settled for deep breaths.

"Osmiya's right," Tretiak said. "They know it's here. Once the storm breaks, they'll be back. That means we've got a few hours at most."

"Then let's get moving." Geddy turned to Tretiak. "And hope that Kriggy's still alive."

Jel decided to stay with the *Fiz* out of her growing concern that they wouldn't be able to call for backup. Meanwhile, Geddy, Oz, and Tretiak decided to see about Kriggy and any other survivors before making for the Tomb.

Before they even stepped through the threshold of the open bay door, Geddy realized he had under-appreciated the protection the hangar offered. He had to lean into the wind to stay upright, and visibility at ground level was ten meters at best. Morpho tightened his grip on his shoulder.

The Kiganteans' leathery multiple eyelids were perfect for

this harsh environment. And their hooded, deeply recessed nostrils acted as natural filters. They struck a streamlined shape on all fours that allowed the sand to sweep over them like a river over stones. At times, Geddy lost sight of them.

The suit's filtration system suddenly required greater effort to breathe. A flutter of panic quickened his heart.

— I love Krig like family, but if we don't find him in the next five minutes, I'm gonna have a full-on freakout.

— *Slow and steady. I'm right here with you.*

— Which makes it that much more cramped.

The wide-open gate in the ranse wall might've been a parting gift from the Nads. Fortunately, the whole city sat on a concrete slab, so even if they got in, they couldn't sneak up on you. The wall's chief purpose, then, was to take the sting out of the incessant winds and provide a sense of safety. Not that anything about Aquebba was safe.

Most of that concrete was coated in ripples of sand, giving the impression the desert was eager to claim it. As they'd seen on their approach, half-buried corpses dotted the streets. Mostly business owners, Geddy supposed, who didn't look kindly upon the Zelnads' interrogation.

Kriggy would have defended the tattoo shop and the Double A to his dying breath. Only if he was the last man standing would he ever dream of leaving. For reasons only he understood, Krig loved this place.

But his was among the very last shops on Turduranto, which dead-ended at the Double A on the opposite end of town. If the Nads went in through the front door, they would've had to go through Kriggy. But he likely didn't know where the Tomb was any more than Geddy did. He always figured it was somewhere beneath the auction room, but even that was a guess. The most valuable items sometimes wound up there. If nobody with the auction had ever seen an item before it went on the block, then it likely came from the Tomb.

A body lay in the middle of the street, its face half-covered by sand. Geddy and Tretiak exchanged a grim look. It was the owner and namesake of the bar on the left, Doo Doo's. He was a jolly, but rough character who never liked Geddy. The feeling was mutual.

He pointed down at the corpse and said, "That's Doo Doo."

Denk said, "Geez, Cap, have some respect for the dead."

"No, that's his name." He indicated the bar's sign behind where Denk stood. "Kinda fitting he wound up lying in the street, though."

Oz's exasperated sigh rang inside his helmet. "Let's keep moving."

With the Kiganteans still on point, they continued until they reached Kriggy's place. The tattoo parlor's lone window, bulletproof alycite like all the rest, was intact. Sand had piled knee-high in front of the door.

Geddy turned to the others. "Wait here for us."

They needed Voprot's help to get it open wide enough for Geddy and Tretiak to slip through. The moment it snapped shut behind them, he threw off his mask and panted, his face slick with sweat. He withdrew the PDQ and inspected it for accumulated sand. Outside, the others lined up against the wall of the bar across the street and out of the wind.

"Krig!" he shouted. "It's Geddy and Tretiak!"

Silence.

— *Does he have a place to hide? Like a safe room or something?*

— Not that I know of. He'd probably go to the Double A.

— *What if he couldn't?*

There wasn't much to the parlor — only a short counter, the chair, the cabinet that held his inks and needles, and the curtained door to the back room where he lived. Not exactly secure. However, a faint funk hit Geddy's uncovered nostrils that seemed out of place.

Everything was in its usual spot. With the gun leveled at

the curtain, he swept it aside and cleared the room. No signs of a struggle or anything amiss. Just the weird smell.

"Krig, if you can hear me, we have food and water. Remember that big, ugly trawler? We've got a lot to talk ab–"

A faint sound cut him off. Something between a whimper and a sob from the direction of the couch.

"Did you hear that?" Geddy whispered.

Tretiak nodded, wrinkling his nose at the room's sour smell.

Geddy tiptoed over and ripped off the cushions, which he never would've dared to do otherwise out of fear for what he might find. But it was only crumbs and candy wrappers.

The sound came again, louder.

"Krig? Is that you?"

"Lever ..." returned a muffled, raspy voice.

"Kriggy! Where are you? What lever?" Geddy's eyes darted frantically around the couch in search of a lever or the source of the sound — whichever came first.

"The bandit," he croaked.

The whole time he worked at the Double A, Geddy only bid and won one thing — a working replica of an Old Earth slot machine. He paid three grand for it. Zirhof, who loved such artifacts, let him win the bid.

But despite hanging out with Kriggy often in this room, he'd never given it a pull until now. When he finally did, electric motors engaged with a springy sound, and the entire couch hinged open from the back. As it did, Kriggy rasped, "Oh, thank the stars!"

Geddy holstered the pistol and joined Tretiak before the opening. Kriggy lay at the bottom of a cramped crawlspace in his usual clothes, albeit stained with sweat and piss. His head lolled back and forth as though delirious, his phallic nose flopping grotesquely from side to side.

"Are you okay? What the hell happened?" Geddy asked.

"The latch ... wouldn't open ... from the inside," he croaked. "Water."

Morpho slung himself over to the little sink in half a second, filling the tallest glass he could find and returning to them without spilling a drop.

Meanwhile, he smiled at Tretiak. "Hey, Boss."

Tretiak allowed a relieved grin. "Good to see you, Krig."

Krig noticed Morph on Geddy's shoulder and squinted. "What the hell is that?"

"That's Morpho. He specializes in sticky situations."

Geddy climbed down the little steps and knelt beside his old friend. He shoved a cushion under his head and lifted the glass to his lips. Half of it spilled sideways as he drank. The smell was overpowering.

"We thought you were dead," Tretiak said.

"So did I," he sputtered, his voice already much clearer. "I knew the storm was coming. My left knee told me. So I closed up and crawled down here to wait it out."

"Without food and water?" Geddy asked.

"I didn't exactly figure on bein' here so long." He blinked, shaking his head, and tilted the glass once again to his friend's grateful, cracked lips.

"So you've been in here for like thirty-seven days?"

He stared up at Geddy, momentarily disbelieving. "If you say so. Is the storm gone?"

"Almost, but ... there was an attack."

"Attack?" Kriggy asked. Geddy nodded. "Who the hell would attack Aquebba?"

Grab your copy...
Vinci-books.com/dark-dodgers

ABOUT THE AUTHOR

C.P. James writes cinematic sci-fi with humor and heart. He lives in the magical country of Ecuador. His first novel, *The Perfect Generation*, was published in February 2018. A dystopian trilogy, The Cytocorp Saga, was released in 2020. Reassembly, a humorous space opera, was launched in April 2021.